TAMPA TWO

Books by David Chill

Post Pattern

Fade Route

Bubble Screen

Safety Valve

Corner Blitz

Nickel Package

Double Pass

Tampa Two

Flea Flicker

Curse Of The Afflicted

TAMPA TWO

A Novel By

DAVID CHILL

For Lynn Balsamo

One

There are certain people who are always in trouble. And no matter how hard you try to avoid them, their troubles often extend to you.

When I first met Judy Atkin, she was young and very pretty, but also frightened and damaged. As far as I could tell, almost ten years later, she was still frightened and damaged. But she was no longer so young and no longer so pretty. Her most striking feature continued to be that pair of big, blue eyes, although back then, they seemed to radiate innocence. Today they struck me as weathered and bloodshot, and her eye makeup was stained with tears.

"I am really, really sorry for what happened," she said, as more pools of liquid formed in those expressive eyes. She wore a tight-fitting tank top and tight-fitting jeans. Both were blue and they accentuated the blue in her eyes.

"I'm sorry, too," I said dryly.

Judy and I first became acquainted when I was working vice out of North Hollywood, and I arrested her for prostitution. There had been an uptick in streetwalkers along Lankershim Boulevard in Sun Valley, and the Chief of Police wanted to show a strong presence. It was a demonstration mostly designed to quiet community outrage, but it was largely whack-a-mole and would have no long-term impact. The hookers simply moved elsewhere to ply their trade, and they would ultimately return to Lankershim when the LAPD focused resources on a different problem.

My arrest of Judy was a run-of-the mill collar. She offered me sex for money, and in turn, I offered her a pair of handcuffs and a reading of her Miranda rights. That she was young and innocent was obvious. She didn't even ask if I was a cop, one of the standard questions that working girls put to johns before steering the conversation toward fornication. I briefly considered letting her go with a warning, but knew that would not sit well with my partners.

As it turned out, Judy was a minor, just seventeen, a runaway from the Midwest. Hers was a sad tale that I saw repeated again and again. Girl is abused, girl leaves abusive situation, girl falls into a nightmarish trap that becomes worse than the one she left. In most instances, I simply processed them through the system. Judy was the one exception, and I made her the exception because we shared something in common, an unfortunate congruence in our backgrounds.

"I heard you got fired by the LAPD."

"Yes," I said. "A long time ago."

It was, in fact, eight years ago that Internal Affairs asked for my badge and gun, the final chapter of my checkered police career. Judy's betrayal had been the tipping point, separating a by-the-book cop into an angry, rogue officer who meted out justice whenever he saw fit. The LAPD was like any other large organization, which is to say, aberrant behavior would not be tolerated. The police could not allow officers to continually go against policy. Judy's actions ultimately led to my dismissal, her accusations against me triggering the chaos that forever changed my world. It was a world that would never change back.

"I made a very big mistake," she said, looking down at the floor.

"You did."

She hesitated. "But I need your help. I've got a big problem."

"Why me?" I asked. "And why now?"

"I don't have anywhere else to turn."

I looked Judy over, and as much as I despised her behavior, I had trouble despising her as a person. I saw her as the equivalent of a wounded animal that snapped at you, even though you were just trying to help it. The animal was engaging in self-preservation; it did not know any better. Maybe it had never experienced someone in the world who tried to be good to it.

Now I was faced with a quandary, that of whether I should try and help Judy once more, and risk being bitten again. I had paid an enormous price for my mistake, and it had taken years to navigate my way to another path. I had become deliriously happy with my beautiful wife, my wonderful son, and the life I had rebuilt. I did not want to step backward.

But being a former cop and a current private

investigator, I am guilty of having a fatal flaw. I have a curious nature. I wonder about things and take pride in being a student of human behavior. I am full of questions about people, and why they do what they do. I poke and I prod until I have an answer. That the infamous Judy Atkin was now sitting in front of me, poisonous as she had been, a nasty toxin that had already left me scarred and altered should have propelled me to turn her away without a second thought. Just like I should have walked away from her many years ago. But we are who we are. And as Oscar Wilde once wrote, the only way to fully get rid of a temptation is to yield to it.

"Tell me about your problem," I said, finally giving in to that natural curiosity that was both a blessing and a curse.

Judy shivered. "First, thank you for agreeing to meet. I know it's a Saturday morning, and I know about our ... history. But I don't know where else to turn. And my problem can't wait."

"Why not?"

"I think someone is going to kill me," she managed, her eyes still cast downward.

"Have they tried to kill you yet?"

"No. But something's going down tonight. At my ... place of business."

"Have you considered not being there?" I asked politely.

"It's not an option," she said, her breathing escalating.

"Why not?" I asked, my curiosity again getting the better of common sense. "From the beginning. And don't leave anything out."

She nodded and tried to compose herself. "Okay. To start with, I'm back in the life."

"Were you ever out of the life?"

She shrugged. "On and off."

I looked past her and shook my head. That she was still turning tricks came as no shock. Judy had arrived in Los Angeles and was immediately scooped up by a pimp trolling the local Greyhound station. She didn't know he was a pimp, of course. He was friendly, giving, treated her nicely, and offered her a place to stay. Not unlike what I had done. The difference was the pimp put Judy out on the streets to earn; he treated her royally when she made good money, and then he beat her when she didn't make enough. She could have run from him, but there was no place for her to run to. She had no way out. That is, until I arrested her. And took her in. I wanted to give her another chance. But selling her body was easy money for an attractive 17 year-old, who had no other marketable assets besides her good looks and a surprisingly moral flexibility.

"Tough to get away from that life," I observed. "Go on."

"Yeah. Well I ran into this guy I knew, his name's Owen. He owns a condo in Santa Monica. A couple of us girls work out of there. He gets us clients, mostly through the internet. They show up, we do business and that's that."

"Except this time."

"Yeah. The other night I had a client. Really big guy. Turns out he was a football player or something. Everything went good, but I got a call this morning. Owen said he has a video of us together. Said he was going to post it online unless this football player paid him $20,000. He's supposed to drop the money off tonight."

"So Owen planted a video camera in your bedroom."

"Yeah."

"This football player must be pretty ticked at you."

"Yeah."

"Who is he?" I asked.

"Owen said his name was Walter Anawak. Name didn't mean anything, I don't follow football. But he's really big, said he came from Alaska originally. I think he's an Eskimo or something."

I frowned. The name Walter Anawak may have meant nothing to Judy, but it meant something to me. Anawak had been a starting left tackle in college for the Washington Huskies, and he was a good one. During my recent, three-year tenure coaching at USC, our defensive coordinator tried various ways to neutralize him. But he was too big, too quick, and too smart. The best thing to happen to Washington's opponents came when Anawak left school early for the NFL this year. He was now in L.A., playing for the Rams.

"Okay," I said. "Do you happen to know if Walter Anawak was married?"

"No. At least I didn't see a ring on his finger."

"Then what leverage does this Owen have? " I asked. A sex video wasn't great publicity, but it wouldn't come as a big surprise. A football player getting it on with a girl isn't news. Even if he paid for it. In fact, some players preferred this type of arrangement. They got their physical needs taken care of, and they normally didn't have to worry about any entanglements with the girl afterward, and certainly no worries about a pregnancy or lifelong paternity obligations. The transaction was the equivalent of cash and carry.

"It's a little complicated," she started.

"It always is."

"This football player got a little rough with me."

"In what way?"

"Well," she said a little haltingly. "Some guys like it rough. They like slapping a girl around before they do it. It's sick, but I didn't really mind."

"Because you get paid extra," I surmised.

"That. And I don't care about a little pain. It's not a big deal to me."

I stared at her, but I knew this was not totally unusual. Girls who enter prostitution sometimes had been abused as children. The ones who had would often grow used to degradation. They may not have liked it, but it became familiar. And out of familiarity evolved a bizarre sense of comfort, even if it meant getting hurt. A girl who had a normal upbringing would recoil at being beaten. A girl in an abusive situation might become accustomed to it. But oddly enough, the more pliable a call girl was when it comes to violence, the less risk she would have of actually getting injured. By accepting violent behavior, rather than resisting it, her client would be less likely to go overboard and actually inflict a serious injury.

"And Walter Anawak naturally doesn't want a recording of him beating a girl to go public."

"He's pretty angry," she observed.

I could imagine. For a pro football player, this was a huge risk to his career. The NFL had taken a dim view of any sort of domestic battery, and even the hint of sexual assault could end a career. It was no surprise Anawak would be furious and want to confront Judy. But there was also a hole in her story. I didn't think this was really Walter Anawak, or, frankly, any other pro football player.

"I have no idea what to do," she said, and reached over to pick up one of my business cards. She fingered it carefully.

"And you obviously can't go to the police because your job is, ahem, illegal."

"Obviously," she said, looking back up at me.

"And this guy Owen wants to get the money but doesn't want a big guy to confront him. So he's sending you in. Brave fella."

"I know. Owen just wants the cash. He said I had to do it or I'm out on the street. If I get that far."

"Meaning?" I asked.

"Owen's unstable. He said he'd kill me if I didn't show."

"Nice friends you've got there."

Judy frowned. "I haven't always made the best decisions."

"Clearly."

"I'm supposed to collect tonight at the apartment. And I'm scared something bad is going to happen."

"Don't blame yourself. You might get killed if you don't show up. And if this Walter Anawak is really angry, you might get killed if you do."

"You see the problem," she said, and glanced back

down at my business card.

"Sure. And where do I fit in with all this?," I responded, asking the burning question for which I was quickly provided the likely answer. "You want me to come along and keep the peace?"

She nodded, but it was the nod of a young child. By my estimation, Judy was now 27, although she looked older. In her line of work, girls age fast. They see too much, and they absorb too much. The money is good, but it never lasts. And it wears a girl down, aging her well before her time.

I sat back and thought about her request, although mostly about how best to turn her down. There was no upside in this for me. The man might be armed. He might bring along a friend. And he was clearly angry. In blackmail cases like this, paying up is no guarantee the shakedown will end. Especially when there's a recording. In a digital world, evidence can take on a life of its own. And there was another oddity to this situation, but I decided to keep that tidbit to myself.

"I'm sorry," I told her. "No. Too many things could go south. I'd be walking into a landmine. As would you. Again, my best advice is to not show up. Maybe you should dump Owen, too. Or better yet, get out of town. Sometimes the only way to rid yourself of a problem is to leave it behind."

Judy shook her head emphatically. "No. I can't do that. Other girls will be in the unit."

"Tell them not to be there either."

"I don't know," she said, lowering her eyes. "This has

gotten really complicated. I don't know what to do."

"That's why you came to see me."

"Yeah."

"Why did you think I'd help you? After ten years. And after ... what happened between us."

"I don't know. And again, I'm, really, really, really ... "

I waved my hand for her to stop. With over twenty years in law enforcement, I had grown tired of apologies, the overused *mea culpas* designed to elicit an action. It was employed, not because the person had any regrets, but because they wanted something from you. And in the case of Judy Atkin, there was nothing she could ever say to undo the damage left in her wake. Departing L.A. had been the best action she could have possibly taken ten years ago. Returning now had no benefit. Not for me, anyway.

"If you're committed to going through with this thing, what you need is muscle," I told her. "A big guy, or even better, a couple of big guys. You want to make this Walter Anawak think twice before starting anything. Football players are tough, but they're also public figures. They don't want publicity for the wrong reasons. If this guy really is Walter Anawak."

"So you'll help me?"

"No. I told you that. That's not what I do. And I owe you nothing. In fact, you owe me."

"I can pay you. I make a lot of money. And if I keep this gig with Owen, I can pay you whatever you want. Anything you think is fair. A thousand dollars? It would be just for like, one hour of work."

"No."

"Two thousand?"

"Look. I'm not going there with you. It's not about money and it's not a negotiation. No discussion on that."

"Can you at least help me find someone who will?"

I rolled my eyes. I didn't know a lot of other private investigators, I didn't go to whatever conferences or meetings they attended. I knew a few ex-cops like me who were in this line of work, but I certainly wasn't going to put them at risk.

"You can go on the internet. I'm sure if you Google private investigators in Santa Monica, you'll get some names."

"How will I know if they're any good?"

"You won't," I said. "But for two thousand dollars an hour, somebody will be willing to show up. Interview them. Make sure they're big and bulky. And make sure you tell them exactly what's going to go down, so they can be prepared. That's the best I can do for you. All things considered."

"Are you sure there isn't anything I can do to change your mind?" she asked, leaning forward so I wouldn't miss any glimpse of cleavage.

"I'm sure," I said. Never was I more sure of anything in my life. And never would I believe I'd again get sucked into the drama that was Judy Atkin. But life takes you down strange paths.

Two

After Judy left, I spent a long time staring out of my office window. It faced west, and on a clear day I could see Santa Monica and a trace of the blue Pacific. Today was sunny, but there were some streaky clouds in the distance that were morphing into the shape of a quilt, a long series of puffy white patterns revealing only small patches of blue sky. These honeycombed clouds were a bellwether that rain was coming, probably soon, and probably within the next few days. October was often like this, the start of the rainy season. A meteorology professor once told me the honeycomb was caused by warm air rising at the same time cold air was falling. The result was an impending storm.

I took a sip from my cup of Starbucks, but it had grown cold, and I tossed it into the trash. My mood had grown dark. I did not want to see Judy Atkin again, and I knew the bitter memories would begin to simmer within me. Judy was trouble, she would always be trouble, and the best way to counteract people like that is to avoid them like the plague. But like many plagues, you can only do so much to stay out of their path. Sometimes they infect you, as much as you try and steer clear of them.

I checked my voice mail and heard the deep-throated message from a potential client, a referral from one of my favorite people, Honey Roper. This man had worked with Honey and had a problem he needed my help with. His name was Gary Wynn, and while he had a baritone voice, his tone sounded anguished. When I called him back, he asked if I could meet him for lunch tomorrow. He lived in the Valley, and the restaurant he selected was expensive. I joked that he would have to pick up the check. After a long, cool silence, he said, yes, of course.

No sooner had I hung up when my phone buzzed with a text from Gail. Her Mommy and Me class had ended, and she and Marcus were going to lunch with a new friend that Marcus had made today. The new friend and his mom liked ramen noodle soup, and they were all headed to a Japanese restaurant a few blocks from my office. Gail asked if I would like to join them.

Sawtelle Japantown is the Westside's version of Little Tokyo, a cluster of shops and food outlets that stretch three or four blocks. There are an inordinate hodgepodge of Asian restaurants that cover everything from sushi bars and yakitori places to Korean barbecues and Chinese dumpling houses. But the main theme remains Japanese, and there are at least half a dozen places that specialize in ramen noodles. They all vary in price but they are consistent in sporting menus and traditions I found a little baffling. Soba noodles or udon. Artisan noodles that you dipped in a thick broth before eating. Tonkatsu soup which called for boiling pork bones all day, and sometimes all night. Seasoned eggs with an exterior the color of warm cocoa, but with yolks that oozed a bright orange. These places were a segment within a segment, a representation of contemporary Los Angeles, a cornucopia of choices, something for everyone.

The restaurant was deceptively small, and it was hard to gauge size because the ceilings were very high. When the ceilings are high, it feels as if there is more room. There were only about six tables and two booths, in addition to a long counter that sat ten people. Most of the seats were filled, and mostly filled with Asian patrons, which was normally a good sign.

Gail and Marcus had corralled a high wooden booth, and were seated with another mom and a little boy about Marcus' age, almost four years old. The woman was blonde and peppy, attractive in that L.A. way, meaning ridiculously slender, with a face that was not exactly beautiful, but pretty in an unassuming way. She was on her phone, and looked up and smiled. Gail was sitting across from her, looking insanely gorgeous as always, but my bias of having fallen in love with her on our first date was always in evidence.

"Hi there," I said, slipping in next to Gail and giving her a kiss on the cheek, squeezing her hand slightly.

"Daddy!" yelled Marcus. "I made a new friend today! His name is Frankie!"

"Marcus," Gail interrupted. "Remember we use our inside voices?"

"Oh, yeah," he said, the volume turned down for a brief

moment. "Hey Frankie! Is your daddy coming, too?"

"I dunno," Frankie said, and he picked up a straw that was sitting on the table next to his water cup. He used his front teeth to rip the top of the paper off, then he spit it on the table and blew hard into the straw. The rest of the paper flew into my lap.

"Oh, Francis. You know better than that," his mother said in a distracted way, before finishing her call and turning to me. "Hello. I'm Brittany. Nice to meet you."

"Pleasure," I said, albeit with a bare minimum of conviction.

"Daddy!" Marcus exclaimed. "We did yogurt today!"

"Yoga," Gail corrected him.

"Aren't they a little young?" I asked, thinking back on my own poor attempts at yoga. I had come away not with increased spiritual revelations, but rather with a nagging ache in my thighs that needed over a week to fully heal.

"Oh, no," Brittany jumped in. "Yoga can be great for kids. Start them early. It's wonderful for stimulating creativity."

"Good to know," I smiled, hoping that Marcus would at least have a child's flexibility to get him through the yoga sessions in which I had failed so miserably.

The server came over to take our order. Both Gail and Brittany had a dozen questions for him, as they created custom orders for themselves and the kids, ensuring sufficient protein and an absence of spicy flavor for Marcus. Unlike Gail, our son's food choices tilted to the bland and familiar, much like mine. Finally the waiter turned to me. I hastily picked up a menu.

"I'll take the number one," I said, about two seconds after glancing at it. There's usually a good reason a particular dish is listed as number one. It is often the most popular item, if not with patrons, then with the chef. I didn't look too hard at what it came with, mostly because I sensed I wouldn't understand what it was. If I didn't like it, I simply wouldn't eat it.

"Let me ask you something," I started. "Have you enrolled Frankie in a yoga class before this?"

"Oh, he's been to a few. I want him to get a diverse sampling of what the world has to offer. In fact, we're taking him on a trip to Antarctica next month."

"Brrrr," I said. "Although in November, that would probably be getting closer to summertime in the South Pole."

"Daddy!" Marcus exclaimed. "Can we go with them? I want to see Ant... what was that again?"

"Antarctica," Brittany said. "And of course you're welcome to go. My husband Clark's directing a film, he has a few scenes to shoot there."

"Documentary?" Gail asked.

"Oh, no, it's a feature. Action adventure. Kind of like *Titanic* meets *Jeremiah Johnson*."

"Your husband works in Hollywood," I mused, knowing a lot of the people you run into in L.A. work in the industry, in some capacity or other. "Do you?"

"Oh, sort of. I started out as an actress. But I'm aging out. Once a woman gets past 30, the number of roles dries up."

"Is that how you and your husband met?" Gail asked.

"Oh, no. Well, not exactly. We met at Yale. I was a drama student, Clark was in law school. I think meeting me piqued his interest in entertainment. A lot of attorneys wind up doing something other than practicing law when they get out into the real world."

"No business like show business," I smiled.

"Well, the money can be quite good," she acknowledged. "It'll help pay for private school for Francis."

"Oh," said Gail. "Where are you applying?"

At that point I looked out the window at the traffic starting to deepen on Sawtelle. It was a Saturday, but it was also lunch hour, and the crowds were starting to gather. Looking away was also a convenient opportunity for me to avoid the gnarly discussion of schools, the one topic that nearly all L.A. parents eventually default to in conversations. Where are you thinking of applying, where do you think you'll get in, who do you know, what are the odds. In my mind, there was just one issue, paramount and prescient, that rose above all others. What will it cost.

"We're applying to Mirman," Brittany said, with no small measure of pride. "Francis has been tested at a 155 IQ. He more than meets their requirements."

"That's wonderful," Gail said.

"Where are you sending Marcus?" she asked.

"We're weighing our options," I smiled, breaking in, partly to make my presence felt and partly to prevent Gail from moving forward with an idea we had barely discussed. Marcus would not start kindergarten for two years. No sense in rushing things. We had had a difficult time simply deciding where we should send him to preschool. Gail wanted him to go to an exclusive, wildly expensive preschool in Santa Monica called Applewood, but I gently steered her toward a more affordable one closer to our house. I used traffic as an excuse. In L.A., traffic is always a good excuse for doing just about anything. Or sometimes doing nothing.

Brittany took a sip from what looked like an iced latte she had brought in with her from The Coffee Bean. "Well, you shouldn't wait too long. Applications are being taken now for Pre-K. It's an important step in their cognitive development. I can help you with Mirman; we know the director. Marcus seems super bright, I suspect he'll have no problems testing high on the IQ exam."

"IQ exam?" I peered at her.

"Yes, they have a minimum requirement of a 138 IQ."

"Ah," I said. "Keeps the riff raff out."

"Um, sweetie," Gail said. "Maybe we should discuss this later."

"Maybe indeed."

Brittany smiled at us. "I hear Gail works for the City Attorney's office. That's just wonderful. Are you an attorney as well?"

I smiled back at her. "I work in law enforcement," I said, neglecting to expand on the details. I'd been kicked off the police force ten years ago, and was now a private investigator who had just been approached by a prostitute, a former client who was fearful she might soon be murdered. Somehow I did not think this would fit in smoothly with the conversation surrounding expensive private schools and our children's bright futures.

"Oh, my," she exclaimed. "What a couple! You're both fighting injustice!"

"Yes," I said. "And I hope you don't have any weed on you."

"Um, now, sweetie" Gail interjected, her eyes shooting daggers at me. "You're no longer an officer of the law."

"Right. Very true," I responded, sensing we'd be having a further conversation about this tonight. I turned to Brittany. "I'm actually a private investigator."

"Ooooh. You mean like Magnum?"

"No."

"I don't understand."

"He's a TV character. I'm real."

"Oh," she responded, still looking a little confused. "That sounds like a fascinating line of work."

The waiter returned at that moment carrying five very large, steaming bowls of soup. He placed one down in front of each of us, issuing a broken-English warning that they were very hot. I looked down at the steam rising from my bowl of broth studded with sliced pork, chopped green onions, and that oddly discolored seasoned egg, that always seemed to be perfectly soft-boiled.

"My job has its moments," I said, picking up what passed for a spoon, something more akin to a small ceramic ladle, and letting some broth seep onto it. Blowing softly on the soup, I took a sip. It was indeed very hot, but it was also very good. I took a slurp this time, and was lucky enough to corral a piece of fatty pork, which surprisingly did not taste all that fatty.

"Um, sweetie, is everything okay?" Gail asked, looking over at me, her soft gray eyes oozing mostly concern, but a little annoyance as well.

I looked at her. "Judy Atkin showed up in my office today."

"Oh, my," she said with a frown.

"Friend of yours?" Brittany asked.

"Former client," I said, not wanting to get too into the details with a pair of kids nearby, although they were doing a good job of giggling and ignoring us completely. "Sad story. Not a good upbringing, compounded by some bad choices."

Brittany nodded. "You really can't overstate the importance of parenting."

"True," I concurred, still looking at Marcus and Frankie. "You certainly can't."

At that point, Frankie took a too-large sip of soup, and suddenly his eyes bulged and a look of horror came over his face. He spit the mouthful onto the table, grabbed a glass of ice water, and shoved his mouth down into it.

"Francis, that is really inappropriate!" his mother scolded him, reaching for a handful of napkins to wipe up the mess.

"It's crazy hot!" he yelled after pulling his head up. "You almost killed me!"

Brittany wiped the table furiously, and again admonished Frankie to use better manners, and to take small sips. He glared back at her.

"No," he declared. "I won't. You're not the boss of me."

Gail and I glanced at each other and then over at

Marcus. He was busy playing with the noodles, not eating, but mostly swirling them in the dish. We didn't know how carefully he was paying attention to what his new friend was doing. But I did know our child was like a sponge, absorbing almost everything that came his way, and could be counted on to squeeze it back out, often when it was least expected.

*

Even in a small coffee house like Priscilla's, Honey Roper was easy to find. She had dark blonde hair, china blue eyes, perfect skin, and a smile that could start a clock. I had met Honey a little over four years ago, when I was hired by her father to help disengage him from a murder charge. Her father was a wildly successful sports agent without a moral compass. Honey, on the other hand, was thoughtful, decent, and had seemingly inherited her father's brainpower, without his personal deficiencies. But few of us live charmed lives, and as lovely a person as Honey Roper was, she was also damaged. To her credit, she hid that side of her as best she could.

"Well, hello there," she said, and rose to give me a hug. "It's been a while."

"Too long," I smiled.

"I know. In fact, Gail and I have been planning lunch for months, but something always seems to come up. Usually work, and it's usually me."

"Glad to hear you're busy," I said, and excused myself to get a cup of coffee. It didn't have the jolt of a Starbucks

Grande, but on a Saturday afternoon, it would do.

"I was working this afternoon down in Anaheim," she said. "Your timing was perfect."

"And I hear congratulations are in order. Gail told me you were promoted. Director of Marketing at Disney. That's an achievement."

"I've worked hard. In fact, I beat out a colleague who had an Ivy League MBA. If I can't outsmart 'em, I'll outwork 'em."

"They teach you that saying at UNLV?"

"Nope. I came up with it myself."

"You're pretty wise," I noted, and needed to caution myself against being too flirtatious. If there was one woman who could make me forget I was married, it was Honey Roper.

"Well, thank you, sir," she smiled impishly. "You're too kind. But people don't look at a degree from Nevada-Las Vegas in the same light as one from Harvard."

"Just out of curiosity," I said, taking a sip of coffee, "I know you grew up in Vegas. But your dad could have afforded to send you anywhere. Why did you stick around there for college?"

"Love," she said almost wistfully. "Or what passes for love at eighteen. And boy, did I get burned."

"Now you have my full attention."

She threw back her head and laughed, smoothing her thick, dark blonde hair and fashioning it into a pony tail. "I was actually accepted at UCLA. My boyfriend in high school was a football star. A tight end. UCLA was recruiting him heavily. But then they up and signed a five-star tight end out of Newport Harbor at the last minute. That guy was projected to come in and start right away, he was super good. So UCLA pulled Kurt's offer. And by that time, most of the big-name colleges had given out all their scholarships. He ended up signing with UNLV."

"And so you stayed home. Out of love and devotion."

"Big mistake," she admitted. "But what happened next was so unexpected. The five-star kid out of Newport got busted for sexual assault, and UCLA pulled *his* offer. Then their backup tight end got injured in spring practice, out for the season. And their third-string guy was partying too much and flunked out of school."

"Which left a big-name college program without a tight end on scholarship."

"They worked out some deal with UNLV so Kurt was released from his commitment and signed with UCLA."

"And I'll bet you had already turned UCLA down."

"I did. I think Dad might have been able to pull strings and get me in, but I was incredibly upset at Kurt. The love of my life accepted the offer without even talking to me. I found out through the internet."

"Says a lot about Kurt."

"I felt totally blindsided. Left me with a really bad feeling. Even with Dad and his multiple divorces, I wasn't expecting to be dumped like that."

"And you stayed at UNLV."

"I did, and it actually turned out well. I played on the college basketball team, even started at point guard. That was something I never could have done at UCLA, those girls were just too good. We even made the NCAA tournament one year. And in the end I wound up with a degree in hotel management, and it led to this gig at Disney. I'm running marketing for the Disney hotels."

"Which brings me to why I'm here," I smiled. "Gary Wynn."

"Ah, yes. My old boss. He was the one who promoted me, although he's since moved over to head up consumer products. Gary's worried about his son. I hear Trevor's marriage is, well, unstable."

"Uh-oh," I sighed, thinking that wayward wives were my least favorite kind of case. When a man is cheating, he may be perfectly happy with his lady, and he simply wants variety. When a woman is cheating, it often means something very different, that the marriage is on the rocks, and it's a question of when, not if, the relationship will crash and burn. For men, an indiscretion often had little to do with the marriage; for women, an affair typically had everything to do with it. Investigating an emotional crescendo like that was a groan-inducing chore. The one bright spot was it often came with a lucrative payday.

"Then why is the dad involved?" I asked. "It's usually the husband who's concerned."

"I don't think his son knows. Gary only found out because he saw her having dinner one night with another man. He's worried."

"All right. Anything else I need to be aware of?"

Honey shook her head. "Gary takes himself very seriously. Like all executives. But him more than most. And I think he has a strained relationship with his son.

He'd like to rebuild it."

"Okay. Good to know. I'm having lunch with him tomorrow."

"Well, he has excellent taste in restaurants. I'm sure you'll go somewhere nice."

"I had ramen noodles for lunch today. Hard to top that."

"I forgot who I'm talking with," she smiled. "By the way, you should check out a place called Plan Check not far from you. It's by the Santa Monica Pier. I was there last week and the burgers are great. L.A. seems to be having a burger renaissance."

"I'll put it on my list."

"It's worth it," she smiled.

"Now, I have to get closure on something. Kurt. What happened? I know a lot about college football and I don't recall the name."

"Oh. Kurt had some problems at UCLA. They started him as a freshman, but he wasn't ready. Got benched by game three, they actually replaced him at tight end with an offensive tackle. Kurt started partying a lot. Endless stream of girlfriends. Didn't study much. Long story short, he lost his scholarship by the middle of sophomore year. He wound up back at UNLV."

"I hope you moved on from him."

"I did. Learned a lot about men. It's an ongoing education."

"We're not all that bad," I said and held up my hand.

"I know. I've just seen the worst side. And growing up in Vegas contributed. I spent summers working at Circus

Circus. Talk about an education."

"Vegas hotels probably could teach anyone a thing or two."

"Yeah. The people who worked there were nice enough. But some of the guests, oh my. I had to remind a few of them that I was an intern, not a hooker. One guy didn't want to take no for an answer. Good thing Dad taught me something about knees and just where to place them when things got a little, um, dicey."

"Speaking of which, how is your dad?" I asked, a little hesitantly.

"Dad is dad. He's fine. In fact, I'm seeing him tonight. He had four tickets to a play at the Pantages and I'm taking a guy I'm seeing. Ethan hasn't met Dad yet, and I'll need to warn him about a few things."

Indeed she would. Honey Roper's father was many things, a man who had been accused of everything from check kiting to murder, yet he had never been convicted of a single crime. He used people when he needed them, discarded them when their usefulness was gone. He was despicable in many ways, but he did do one thing right in his life, which was to treat his only daughter well. He was protective, doting, and unwaveringly proud of her. Unconditional love can lead to some good outcomes. Even bad people are capable of doing a few good things.

"I guess I can figure out why you haven't gotten married yet," I said.

"Well, it's partly career. But mostly the fact that my parents were poor role models. When it comes to marriage, anyway. Mom's been married three times. Dad four. It's tough to put trust in a relationship when you see so many end badly. Dad did a good job of being a parent and a bad job of being a husband. It's given me pause."

"You'll get there," I told her. "It took me a long time to find the love of my life. But it was worth the wait."

"When I look at you and Gail, I have hope," she said.

"Good luck tonight. Or maybe I should wish Ethan good luck."

"Thanks. Dad has high standards. But you know what?"

"What?"

"So do I," she smiled.

Three

It was a warm evening. I was working vice out of North Hollywood. There were three of us on my team, and I was working undercover. I drove slowly down Lankershim and caught the eye of an attractive young girl who was wearing next to nothing: a gold lame bikini top, denim short-shorts and high heels. She approached my car and leaned in as I lowered the passenger side window. Her ample breasts were on full display.

"Hi there," she smiled. "Want a date?"

"How much?" I asked.

"Depends," she said, her big blue eyes practically twinkling. "Can I climb in?"

I reached over and pushed the button to unlock the doors. She slid into the seat and smiled again. I couldn't be certain, her makeup was on thick, but it was entirely possible she could have been all of fourteen years old. I began to wonder if I should be getting ready to arrest her or drive her to a middle school prom.

"It's fifty for a hand job, a hundred for a blow job, and two hundred to go all the way," she said matter-of-factly, as if she were reciting the menu at a Burger King.

"You mind if I pull over into that alley?" I asked. "Give us some privacy."

"Okay," she said. "But I need to have the money up front. Get business out of the way and all. Then we'll have fun."

I shifted the Ford into drive and steered the car into an alley past another plainclothes officer, dressed like a deranged homeless person, with a newspaper wrapped around his head. The newspaper covered his head set. As I slowed to a stop, I watched my partner slowly approach through the rear view mirror.

"How old are you?" I asked.

"Old enough," she quipped.

"Come on. You don't look legal."

She shrugged. "Does it really matter?"

It actually did matter. Quite a bit. If she were eighteen, she'd be charged as an adult. If she were seventeen, she'd be considered a child in the eyes of the law. Either way, she didn't look like she belonged on the streets. She looked innocent, and maybe a little sad. If I were working solo, I might have told her I was a cop, and instructed her to leave. But that was not going to happen. There was no good way to handle this. I pushed the button to unlock all the doors again, and the girl froze.

"Hey! What are you doing?"

"You're under arrest," I told her as the passenger door was flung open and one of my partners grabbed her by the wrists. "You have the right to remain silent."

*

Early in my adult life, Saturday nights were focused around alcohol-infused tidings, usually in a loud bar, often accompanied by fellow SC football players, LAPD cops, and of course, women. Since meeting Gail, those outings became increasingly fewer, and since having Marcus, even the thought of any wild evenings of debauchery stayed within the confines of my own mind. I did not miss these extracurricular activities, a sign perhaps, of long-overdue maturity. And as the three of us spent this particular Saturday evening playing an enthusiastic game of Candyland, I needed to take a few calculated steps to ensure I lost and that Marcus won. I pointed out how well he played this game, a compliment he accepted with a perfunctory shrug, communicating the message that defeating me was a decidedly easy task.

I managed to sleep in on Sunday morning, and since my new client had made noon reservations, I was in no danger of missing my business lunch. I arrived early, informed the hostess I was meeting Gary Wynn, and was immediately whisked into the dining room. I looked around in wonder. Bistro Garden is simply a beautiful restaurant. It is the type of restaurant one might go to for a special occasion. Like to propose marriage. Or celebrate a milestone birthday. Or, glancing at the prices on the menu, the type of lavish place I'd frequent if I was exceedingly well-off. It was not the type of lunch spot I'd go to just to have a regular meal. But I wasn't the one who chose it, nor was I the one who was paying.

I got back to the menu and noticed it leaned heavily on seafood, and featured entrees I would have trouble pronouncing or perhaps even understanding. The Bistro breakfast sandwich included layers of shirred eggs, uncured ham, and a potpourri of discombobulated ingredients jazzed up with Dutch cheese, field greens, and a shiraz sauce, which all amounted to a gourmet chef's take on an Egg McMuffin. A breakfast sandwich was at least something I could say without feeling illiterate. This was not the case for the $25 Wagyu cheeseburger, made from a type of beef from cattle raised in a tranquil countryside ranch, where they were fed with beer and given daily massages. Burgers in L.A. may indeed be having a renaissance as Honey suggested, but even at trendy eateries, a $25 burger was eye-popping.

The room had an abundance of natural light, the pitched glass ceiling providing the feel of being outside. A few small trees in planters were tastefully inserted around the perimeter of the room, and a series of archways framed the hallway leading to the bar area, next to which sat a baby grand piano. The rattan chairs were comfy, with a dark green pillow, soft and thick, lining the seat. The tablecloths were white and silky. Overall, I had the distinct feeling I was basking in the lap of luxury. I thought back to a saying a former USC coach had told me a couple of years ago. If you can't be rich, have rich friends.

Gary Wynn entered the dining room at just past noon, looking as if he owned the place. He was tall, lean, and sported a thick head of silver hair. Even dressed in a white golf shirt and khakis he seemed to maintain a refined air about him. Walking over to me without any hesitation, he presented the image of a man who was in complete control. I knew that look, and it was usually bravado. He even waved to someone across the room. I glanced over and saw that no one was waving back.

"Mr. Burnside," he said. "Gary Wynn. Thank you for coming. I appreciate it."

I stood up and we shook hands. His grip was strong but his palm felt clammy, and I discreetly wiped my hand on a white cloth napkin as I set it down on my lap.

"I'm impressed you recognized me. We've never met before."

"I did a little research on you," he said as we sat down. He tried to smile, but he had trouble pulling it off. A waiter came by and asked if we'd like something to drink. I ordered black coffee. Gary Wynn ordered pineapple juice.

"I didn't recall seeing pineapple juice on the menu," I commented.

"Oh, you know, I believe in asking for what you want. A place like this, if they don't have it, they'll go get it. But you know, they normally have it."

Apparently they did, as the waiter returned three minutes later with our drinks, smiled, and said he'd give us some time to peruse the menu. Gary Wynn said that was all right, he didn't need any more time, without bothering to inquire about me. Maybe he was hungry. Maybe he was good at reading people's minds. Or maybe he felt whoever paid the bill called the shots.

"I'd like the broiled grouper," he said, leaving the menu

opened. "And could you substitute béarnaise for the garlic butter sauce?"

"My pleasure, sir," the waiter said, without exhibiting a single sign of any genuine pleasure. He then turned to me and waited patiently.

"Well, I'm torn between the breakfast sandwich and the burger," I said, not feeling very torn at all, but knowing waiters would sometimes steer you in the right direction. Unfortunately, some steered you toward the item the kitchen was overstocked with.

"The Wagyu burger is wonderful," he said perfunctorily, pronouncing it wag you. "You can never go wrong with that."

"All right. Medium rare would be good," I said, refraining from asking for extra ketchup just yet.

The waiter took our menus and departed swiftly. I took a sip of my black coffee. Smooth and refined, but without that strong bite I had come to enjoy in my cup of joe.

"So," I began. "You know Honey Roper."

"Yes. Honey. What a lovely person. Honey worked for me for years. She recommended you without hesitation. I consider that high praise indeed."

I nodded and said nothing. That normally kept the conversation rolling.

"Honey tells me you're quite a good private detective. I need help with something."

"Private investigator. But yes, I'm sure I can help you. What's going on?"

"It's my son," he said as he took a sip of pineapple juice. "Well, actually my daughter-in-law. I think she's having an affair."

"That's too bad," I said, and then asked the question I had been pondering for the past day. "Why is that your problem?"

He coughed on some of the pineapple juice and gave me an incredulous look. "Do you have children, Mr. Burnside?"

"Yes. I have a son."

"Then you should understand."

"He'll be four years old in January. So no, I don't understand."

Gary Wynn looked off at a corner in the room. He seemed to be deep in thought, but maybe he was just trying to hunt down our waiter for another hit of pineapple juice. His facial features revealed no internal machinations about what might be churning inside of him, not fear, regret, sadness, or even despair. Those were the typical emotions I would read on a potential client's face, the stark reasons a person would seek out a private investigator. These people found their way to me when they had run out of other options. But behind Gary Wynn's tanned, chiseled features was a blank slate. It was the type of face you see on good poker players, and on people well trained at keeping their emotions at bay.

"I don't have a great relationship with my son," he began in a matter-of-fact way. "We've never been close. And that's my fault. I've spent my life chasing a dream, to be the head of a large company. It meant a lot of late nights and too much travel. It also meant missing time with my son. I never saw most of his piano recitals or his

Little League games. I was more of … an uncle than a dad. I'd see him in passing. I'm sorry about that. I have deep regrets. But I don't want him to get hurt."

"And you think your daughter-in-law's cheating on him."

"I have a hunch that she is."

"Why is that?"

Wynn hesitated. "I used to be in charge of the theme parks and hotels at Disney. Well, the CMO to be exact. Chief Marketing Officer. I know a lot of people working in our Anaheim properties. And the other day one of them mentioned to me that they had seen Madison having dinner at their hotel dining room. With a man."

"All right. Why is that unusual?"

"They live … Madison and my son Trevor … in Studio City. It's an hour's drive."

"What does your daughter-in-law do for a living?"

"She's an attorney. Corporate law. Works for a firm our company does business with. That's how she and Trevor met. I got Trevor a job with Disney."

"And this couldn't have been a business dinner she was having?"

"She works in Century City. Nowhere near Anaheim. But the way my colleague put it, they were laughing and giggling and touching the whole time. He didn't provide too much detail, I don't think he was intending to spy on them. And I honestly don't know if anything happened beyond that. She didn't check in to the hotel. At least not under her own name."

"You looked into it," I observed.

"I do have that liberty."

"Anything else?"

"That's all I know."

Our food arrived, my Wagyu burger came open-faced, with two cute little silver cups next to it, one filled with thick ketchup and one filled with what might have passed for mayonnaise, although I recalled the menu describing some condiment called garlic aioli. I spooned a liberal helping of ketchup along the top of the burger, affixed the Bibb lettuce, beefsteak tomato and carmelized onions underneath the bun, and prepared to lift it and take a large bite. Then I looked around and saw that no one in the restaurant was using their hands. I decided to employ the necessary decorum befitting an upscale restaurant. I picked up my fork and the large serrated knife, and employed good table manners.

"How's the Wagyu?" Wynn asked, delicately arranging a specific number of capers onto a forkful of white fish.

"Very good," I lied, wondering what all the fuss was about, thinking a hickory burger at the Apple Pan offered surprisingly more flavor and infinitely more value.

"This is a wonderful place," he smiled. "I come here for business a few times a week when I'm in town."

I looked around and changed the subject. "Okay. Just what is it you'd like me to do?" I asked, knowing the typical answer of confirming infidelity, although this case came with a twist. Usually I'd be brought in by a spouse looking for evidence of cheating so they could divorce their partner and secure a large settlement, as per their marital contract. Prenuptial arrangements used to be limited to the rich and famous, but, like many things good and bad, they eventually went mainstream. And even though this type of lifestyle clause was unenforceable in California, a lot of high-profile spouses simply wrote a large check to keep image-bursting scandals out of the media. But this Wynn case was different. The parents rarely got involved.

"I'd like to know if she's cheating," he said, putting his utensils down on the plate and looking evenly at me.

"Naturally," I said. "And what do you plan to do with this information?"

"Why ... I'd want to intervene. I'm thinking I might want to confront her first, but I can't do that without proof."

"Really?" I said, cutting another piece of my Wagyu burger and taking a bite. "Why confront her?"

"I ... think this marriage can be saved," he said thoughtfully. He played with a piece of fish, but didn't bother to lift it off the plate. "And maybe if I inform her that I know what she's been doing, she might stop. People can change. And it might be better if my son didn't find out."

"Ignorance is bliss," I mused, wondering whether holding an incredibly intimate detail of another couple's marriage would be beneficial to anyone.

Gary Wynn shook his head. "There are times keeping secrets can be helpful. No marriage is perfect. If a partner strays and then comes back, it's sometimes best that this remain quiet."

"And you'd have something on your daughter-in-law."

"I don't look at it that way," he snapped, getting slightly annoyed. "I'm actually trying to help here."

"Helping them by lying," I said, starting to get a little unconcerned about losing a paying client.

"It's not a lie if no one talks," he said, the exasperation crossing his face becoming more visible. "But this is L.A. Haven't you ever been tempted to step out on your wife?"

"Tempted, yes. Acted on it, no."

Gary Wynn went back to looking down at the table and absently pushing his grouper across his plate. Perhaps in his line of work, especially in hotels, wayward spouses were a given. I had seen my share, arresting johns soliciting undercover policewomen who were dressed as scantily-clad prostitutes. After getting cuffed, the men's first words were often about how they were married and could they keep this transgression quiet. That was a legitimate concern a few years ago, as public shaming was considered a deterrent for married men who were thinking of paying for sex. But when one local police department posted mug shots of johns on their social media site, the local citizenry jumped in to add names, addresses, phone numbers, employers and even the names of their kids. It was one thing to get called out publicly, it was quite another to have their child subject to ridicule. Kids may absorb their parents' habits, but they should not have to pay a price for their moral lapses.

"Then you want me to follow her around," I said. "Catch her in the act?"

"Yes."

"I can provide a log of where she goes. And who she

goes to see if you really want that level of granular detail. But that's where it stops. I don't take lewd photos, and I don't peep through drapes. If you're looking for video evidence, that's not me."

"No, no, that's all right," he said, waving a hand. "A log is fine. I'm not a pervert, I don't need to see them in the act. I don't want to. But I do need some proof. Their walking in and out of a hotel or a home. Who the other person is. Basic details."

"All right," I said. "That I can do."

"Good," he said, seemingly a little relieved, and he resumed eating. I waited until he had swallowed another mouthful before bringing up the next topic.

"I need to tell you up front," I said, sizing him up as well as the type of job I'd be doing. Cheating spouses were my least favorite assignment and I usually added combat pay atop my normal rate of a thousand dollars a day.

"What's that?"

"I charge fifteen hundred a day," I said, watching him carefully. "And I normally require a two day retainer. Cases like these often take longer."

He looked down and casually placed a few more capers on top of another piece of grouper. "Done," he said absently.

I cut another piece of Wagyu and this time dipped it into some garlic aioli. Taking a bite, I chewed methodically, and began wondering if I would have been wiser to have raised the rate to two thousand. Gary Wynn certainly acted like he could afford it, and his involvement was curious. Maybe he was just a concerned parent.

Maybe he harbored an abundance of guilt about his lack of involvement with his son's upbringing. Maybe he really wanted to make amends, although this was quite a distorted way to do that. I wondered if Gary Wynn might try to confront his daughter-in-law violently, but he didn't strike me as an angry man. I tried to size him up, but had difficulty. Maybe the rich really were different.

We finished lunch, and I asked Wynn to provide details of his daughter-in-law's home and work addresses, as well as her car and license plate number, and a recent photo. A photo of his son, Trevor, would be helpful, too. You never know when some things come in handy. As we walked out of the restaurant, he said he'd arrange for those to be sent in a day or two. I suggested that would also be an opportune time to include a check.

The valet brought around my Pathfinder, albeit a minute after Wynn's silver Mercedes arrived. I handed the valet a ten, thinking I was generous, but he merely accepted it in a perfunctory manner, as if this were the going rate. I checked my messages as I pulled onto Ventura Boulevard, only two of them on a Sunday afternoon. One was from Gail asking if I could bring home some milk for Marcus, and another from a world-weary voice I hadn't heard in many years.

"Mister Burnside," said the haggard-sounding man. "It's been a long time. This is Barney Sack from the Santa Monica PD. Give me a call as soon as you pick up this message. That means now."

I punched the call-back button and heard the line engage. He picked up on the first ring.

"Sack here."

"This is Burnside. Long time."

"Not long enough," he said as he pulled the phone away from his mouth to shout some instructions before returning his attention to me. "We got some business we need to discuss, mister private eye."

"Oh we do, huh?" I said.

"Yeah. Get over here now. Condo building on 6th near Broadway. Address is 1440 6th Street. Unit 612."

"Why the rush?" I mused in that playful way cops hate when they're on the job. "It's been what, five years? Six? Can't wait a few more hours?"

"Need you now. Unless you want me to swear out a warrant."

"Why would you do that?" I asked, no longer feeling so playful.

"We got a stiff here. Your name came up. Or down as it were."

"How so?"

"We found your business card lying around, remarkably near the dearly departed. Looks like the residents here were running an escort service. You got some real nice clients."

Four

I had lived in the seaside community of Santa Monica for over a decade, but it had been four years since Gail and I had moved out. While I was initially sad at leaving my old stomping grounds, I had come to like Mar Vista. It was suburban, friendly, and unpretentious. And I had suddenly begun to feel out of place in Santa Monica, the small, sun-drenched beach town that people once referred to as Bay City. The place had changed. But I had changed, too.

While the community retained some of its coastal charm, Santa Monica was undergoing a rapid transformation. Old shops on the 3rd Street Promenade had been replaced by trendy boutiques and high-end chains, the soaring cost of rent pushing out many old-timers. Rare bookstores were closing and cool clothing outlets were opening. New office buildings were attracting a hipper work force. Eateries specializing in everything from Vietnamese pho noodles to a Hawaiian raw fish concoction called Poke were now materializing where a variety of pizza stands and coffee shops had previously flourished.

Brand new condos and apartment buildings were springing up everywhere, often sitting right above retail outlets. It was a 21st century version of a mini-Manhattan: a small, upscale, densely packed community. And just like the real Manhattan, the traffic was becoming nightmarish. After twenty minutes of searching in vain for a parking space, I finally pulled into the public library garage. There were always open spaces in the library.

The afternoon had grown cool and cloudy as I walked down 6th street. The multicolored building that Barney Sack directed me toward was a condo complex called the Ocean Vista, although it was questionable that anyone living there could actually see the ocean from six blocks away; a burgeoning cityscape was blocking nearly everything. There was a stylish burger outlet on the ground floor, and while their burgers didn't run in the $25 range, neither were they cheap. A very cool-looking staff, dressed in black t-shirts, stood near the entrance, whispering and laughing at what was most likely an inside joke. I walked by them into the condo lobby, rode the small, chrome elevator smoothly to the 6th floor, and then proceeded down a narrow carpeted hallway toward the din of activity enveloping unit 612.

A uniformed police officer blocked my path and informed me in that oh-so-serious cop manner, that this was a crime scene and to state my business. I handed him my card and said Detective Sack ordered me to come here. He fingered the card and gave me a reproachful glare.

"You mean Deputy Chief Sack," he sneered. "He's been promoted."

"I'll come with a present next time," I replied. "Okay if I go talk to him? Or do I need to make an appointment with his assistant."

"Smart alec," the cop said, and he stepped aside just enough for me to squeeze past. "Don't get your fingerprints on anything. Our work here isn't done."

The apartment was small by most standards, except if the standards were what's typical in a congested urban center. The living room was big enough to hold a sofa, an easy chair, a 40-inch flat screen, and not much more. The furniture had been moved back, and a sheet covering what was undoubtedly a very large dead body took up most of the open floor area. A medical technician worked nearby, trying to pull DNA off of whatever he could in the unit. A pair of plainclothes cops stood off in a corner sipping from Dunkin' Donuts coffee cups and cracking jokes, gallows humor that served to distance them from the bloody carnage laying a few feet away. I heard the overworked voice of Barney Sack barking orders to a small, rotund man in the bedroom. I waited for him to finish before walking in.

"Oh, would you look at this," Sack remarked as his eyes gave me the once-over. He wore an off-white shirt with the top button undone, and a brown rep stripe necktie pulled partway down. It might have been the same tie he had been wearing when I first met him, and that was some years ago. "Hey Callaway. Remember that business card you found? The one for the P.I.?"

The small man looked up at me. "I remember."

"Well, here he is," Sack said and turned toward me.

"You sure did get over here quick. I like your promptness. You still live in the neighborhood?"

"No. I decided to go make the streets safe in Mar Vista."

"Their loss, our gain. What do you know about what went on here?"

"I don't know anything. Other than you haven't bothered to move the body and draw a chalk outline yet. What happened?"

"I'll let Callaway fill you in on the details. And ask you to fill him in on everything you know. And it better be good."

"Yeah," I said. "I hear you're a big shot now. Deputy chief. You must have been next in line. Lots of early retirements?"

Sack turned to the smaller man. "Callaway, don't be afraid to smack this one around if he gets cute with you," Sack said as he sauntered out the door. "I'll back you up. And hey, Burnside ... "

"What?"

"See me before you leave. That is if we haven't slapped cuffs on you."

I turned to Callaway, who looked at me and shrugged. "Have a seat," he said, pointing to an unmade bed, the sheets slightly askew. Callaway was short and round and looked a few years younger than Sack, which might have put him in his late thirties. He had an impassive demeanor, neither smiling nor scowling at Sack's comments.

"I'll stand if you don't mind."

"Suit yourself," he said, taking a seat on a corner of the

bed and pulling out a small, spiral-bound notebook.

"Who's the deceased?" I asked.

"Name's Henry Knapp. You know him?"

"Nope," I said. "Never heard of him. What's his connection here?"

"Not sure. He works security at clubs. We think he's been moonlighting for a P.I. named Carl Hillebrand, although how he wound up here is still a mystery. We were hoping you might fill in a few details. We think the condo's being rented out, but it's owned by two people named Lucas Jerikoff and Owen Magid. Names ring a bell?"

"Sorry, no," I said, although Judy had mentioned the name Owen a few times. I didn't have any enlightening information on him, so I kept mum.

"Yeah, we can't find anyone in the building that's met them."

"Who lives in this unit?" I asked.

"Pretty much no one. Near as we can tell, it's a fuck pad used by an escort service. I think that's where you come in."

"Oh?" I said, arching my eyebrows as high I could. "And how's that?"

"You have a history with a Judy Atkin. We learned she's one of the escorts who does business here. We know about you and her, it's been a matter of public record forever. Did you have any contact with this girl recently? Or any of her associates?"

"Yup."

"Go on," he sighed. "Don't make me follow my boss's

directive."

"You try it, you might wind up on the pavement."

"You keep talking that way and I'll bring in four other cops, and you'll end up in the ER."

"They all as big as you?"

Callaway put down his notebook and stood up. He didn't look angry, but he did look annoyed. He wore a holster with a Beretta clipped to his waist. He fingered his belt buckle demonstratively.

"You really need to give us a hard time today? You really want to spend the rest of your Sunday behind bars?"

I shook my head. No, I didn't. But there was a lot about this case that was already turning my stomach and dredging up nasty feelings from years past. Being arrested by the LAPD for a crime I didn't commit. Being tossed into a cell with the type of lowlife perps I had previously busted, hoping none pegged me for a cop. The flood of bad memories was washing over me and I was having a difficult time keeping my equilibrium. Being in this environment, knowing Judy Atkin had a connection to this scene, and hearing that the police suspected my involvement in a capital crime were all rocketing me into a very vile mood. I had yet to learn ways to calm myself from these dark places, fortunately they didn't emerge much anymore. But they were throwing shadows over me again today.

"Sorry," I forced myself to say. "It's not your fault. I just don't like where all this is going. And my being drawn into a murder investigation just because someone happened to drop my business card."

"Yeah," Callaway responded. "About that. How do you think it got there?"

"Judy Atkin," I said. "She came to my office yesterday. Looking for some help. Looking for me to protect her."

"From what?"

"Some guy her boss was trying to blackmail. I gather the boss has a video recorder somewhere in here and he's been snooping."

"Where was this recording done?"

I shook my head. "No idea. Could have been right in this space," I said and began glancing around the sparse bedroom. There really wasn't much here, just a bed, a night table holding an open tube of KY jelly without the cap, and a small bookshelf on the other side of the room. On it were a few porn DVDs lining the top shelf, one end held up with a brick, the other with a soft, golden teddy bear. I picked up the teddy bear delicately by his ear, and took a good look at him. One of the eyes was brown, the other was missing. Behind it was a mechanical device of some sort. I pointed out the bear to Callaway.

"What do you think?" I asked.

Callaway nodded. "Clever," he said. "I'll get this checked out. Who is this guy they're blackmailing?"

"No idea," I lied, not sure that the football player, Walter Anawak, actually had anything to do with this, and not wanting to implicate him based on the word of a prostitute whose word had no currency. The NFL takes a dim view of its players getting involved in anything sordid, much less illegal, and even the whiff of scandal could end a career.

"Okay," Callaway continued. "What'd you say when she asked for your help?"

"I said no."

"How come?"

"You have to ask?"

"I have to ask."

"Judy Atkin helped end my career with the LAPD. She got arrested for turning tricks, and said I was involved in pandering. I wasn't, but I took an awful lot of crap over it. Still taking it, or so it appears."

"I don't know everything about your history," Callaway said. "But it looks like Sack does. You guys have an issue?"

"Not really. I helped him on a case a few years back. Wayne Fairborn's murder. Wayne was a friend of mine."

"Oh, yeah, I remember," Callaway said, nodding, eyes half-closed. "You were *that* P.I."

"Uh-huh. I do have a checkered past," I said, thinking back to the case. Wayne had been shot dead in his office, ironically with the business card of a hot young blonde lying nearby. The similarities were a little more eerie than I cared to recall. Having my business card sitting provocatively near a murder scene wasn't the type of notoriety I wanted. And it also meant I was now a person the Santa Monica PD would be taking a close look at, no matter what I told Callaway or Sack. And as long as Judy Atkin wasn't around, there would be no one to back up my story. If Judy backed it up at all.

"Any idea where we can find this Judy Atkin?" he asked.

"No. People like her live in the wind."

"Uh-huh. How do you think she ended up bringing in this Henry Knapp?"

I shrugged. "I told her there were a lot of private investigators around. Said to find one in Santa Monica and explain in detail what was needed. At some point, she'd find a guy who's willing to bite. Especially since she was offering two large for what might have been a few minutes of standing there looking tough."

"Nice payday," Callaway said. "You must be doing okay financially to pass that up."

I looked out into the living room, and my eyes focused on the big lump lying underneath the sheet. I extended my arm and pointed to the body. "The job came with a pretty high price tag. Don't you think?"

Callaway took a breath and looked down at his notes. He asked a few more things, then handed me over to another detective who asked me a bunch of perfunctory but largely irrelevant questions, which would lead them nowhere near the killer. Finally the two of them guided me over to Sack and told him they were done with me. For now.

"So Burnside," he said, leading me out the door and into the darkened hallway. "I was hoping I wouldn't be seeing you at another murder investigation."

"But here I am," I smiled.

"Pretty cocky," he shook his head. "You don't seem to realize you're implicated in this."

"Because some whore left my business card lying around?" I said, my irritation starting to rise again as I thought of Judy and the hell she put me through.

"That's right," he said. "Your card was here. You're involved somehow."

"No, I'm not," I said evenly. "I'm not implicated in any way."

"Well, you are. At least for now, and at least by SMPD standards. You still have good detective skills left, so you might want to use them."

I stared at him. "Meaning you're going to try and hang this on me?" I asked incredulously. "Unless I help you?"

"I'll let that go unanswered for the time being. But you're someone of interest. Consider that."

"And you should consider I have a stone cold alibi for last night."

"Oh, really?" he yawned.

"Yeah. And have you bothered to check for surveillance video in the building? Although the word of my wife, who works in the City Attorney's office, should be enough."

"We're checking video, don't you worry. There are cameras everywhere. You'll be the first to know if we see anything with that mug of yours featured. Or anything that kind of resembles it."

I shook my head. "And how did this Henry Knapp die?"

"Blunt force trauma. Got walloped over the head a few times. Not sure with what, other than it was hard enough to crack his head open. Might have made it if he had been driven to a hospital right away. But whoever did this last night just took off."

"How inconsiderate."

"Yeah. But the wounds are unusual. The M.E. said there were cuts in the skull and the instrument couldn't have been very wide. Didn't think he'd ever seen anything like it. Murder weapon had to be pretty heavy. But it's unusual."

"And I take it they didn't leave the murder weapon lying around behind them."

"Nope. We're scouring the area. But I'm not optimistic. We've got our work cut out on this one. Maybe you do, too."

I looked up at the ceiling and said nothing. Deputy Chief Barney Sack took that as an opportunity to walk away and let me stew in my own juices.

*

I stopped at the supermarket before I went home, picked up milk for Marcus, some flaming-hot Cheetos for Gail, and a 6-pack of Blue Moon ale for myself. Can't forget about the basics. I absently listened to the end of the Rams game on the way back. The Rams were losing to the Seahawks 31-0, and the announcers sounded demoralized. With a minute to play in the game, the Seahawks fumbled the football, the play-by-play guy's voice suddenly got a little animated. The ball was recovered by a player with a familiar name. Quentin Ware was a safety I had coached for one season at USC, my first year on Johnny's staff. They moved Quentin to linebacker the following year, as Johnny frequently shifted players around. He believed in putting players in positions where we could take advantage of mismatches in speed. A player like Quentin could effectively cover tight ends, and could also blow past heavy offensive linemen when we called for a blitz.

The NFL wasn't crazy about Quentin, but for the same reasons we liked him. Scouts called him a tweener, code for a guy they considered too slow to play safety and cover wide receivers, but also not big enough to be a linebacker, fending off run blockers and bringing down hulking running backs. They decided that all Quentin had were good football skills, which meant he was quick enough to get to most opposing ball carriers, and savvy enough to wrap them up and tackle them. The Rams drafted him in the final round last season, which was considered by some as a throwaway pick, but he managed to make the roster. Hearing Quentin's name gave me an idea.

The next morning was warmer, but the sky was still overcast. I made a phone call and drove up to a strip mall in Thousand Oaks, not far from the Rams practice facility. Thousand Oaks is one of those nice bedroom communities in the distant suburbs where not much happens. Nice, well-manicured housing tracts, nice clean shopping centers, nice schools with well-dressed kids. Everything was nice. Pre-planned, from the rows of date palm trees lining the sidewalks to the soft, curved streets that ended in cul-de-sacs. It was a 45-minute drive from West LA in clear traffic, but once I got there I practically felt as if I were in a different state. I didn't fit in there. And I'm not sure Quentin Ware did either. But here we were, approaching each other at a local Denny's filled with nicely dressed, smiling people. The restaurant was his choice, not mine.

"Coach B!" he smiled. "Good to see you again!"

We gave each other a hug and pats on the back. Quentin had added some thickness to his torso in the nine months since I had last seen him. His arms were now approaching the size of my legs. He wore a blue and gold t-shirt, and blue and gold workout pants. A few people glanced our way, pointing and smiling approvingly. That Quentin was dressed this way and was the only African-American in the place at 9:30 a.m. practically screamed he was a football player.

We sat down at a booth. I ordered pancakes and coffee, he ordered pancakes as well, along with four scrambled eggs, two sides of ham, and a double portion of hash browns.

"Good to see you you're staying nourished, Q. Have to keep your strength up."

"I'm celebrating," he smiled. "Got some playing time yesterday and came up with a turnover. But yeah, I kind of eat like this most of the time. Protein and carbs keep me going."

"You remember what we taught you at SC? Some of it, I hope."

"I know, I know. Go easy on the syrup and get a lot of salt. Before games I just eat chicken and bread."

"Good," I smiled. "And how's life in the NFL?"

"It's tough," he pointed out. "We're living in a fish bowl. Every move I make in practice is diagnosed. Got to watch myself off the field, too. One guy on our team got waived last week, somebody recorded him getting into an argument with this dude at a bar, there was some pushing and shoving, and it got posted online. He had some bad luck, but no place is safe."

"Life isn't always fair," I said, wryly.

"I know. You coaches helped drill that into us."

"How so?"

"Hey, in practice if one guy in the secondary dropped a pick, we all had to run laps. Nothing fair about that," he said.

"True," I smiled. "But the larger picture was it helped build unity among you guys."

"Yeah, I guess. We were all ticked at you. But it did help encourage us to hold onto the rock when we got our hands on it. And we mostly tried to stay out of the trouble off the field. Weird thing about that was not having you be disappointed in us. Almost like not letting your mom down."

I marveled at how well Quentin processed this. Some of the players I coached did not have their dads around, and their coaches became father figures. We took on that role as part of the job, but I could relate personally to it. My father had died before I was born, and as hard as my mother tried, I had to struggle with how to become a man. There was no one to guide me except my coaches. And while I had planned on making football my career, I needed to shift gears after my senior year at USC. My NFL aspirations were short-circuited by a freak injury before the draft, so I never played in the pros. Back then, an ACL injury was a career-ender, something that couldn't be fixed with surgery and a few months of rehab.

"I'm glad whatever we said worked. And in your case, it

looks like it's working really well. You know, you only have a narrow window to capitalize on this opportunity; pro football has a short shelf life. You have to make the most of it. When your playing days are over, that's it. The money spigot dries up."

"I know. And I'm kinda lucky to be here. In training camp, the guy ahead of me tore a hamstring in the last preseason game. If it wasn't for that, I'd probably have gotten cut."

"You never know what life has in store for you."

"Ain't that the truth. And I'm going to play as long as I can. Not just because of the money, but that part's good. I mean really good. But what I most like is playing in front of a packed stadium with people screaming their heads off. That's lit."

"The cheering can be addictive," I agreed, not bothering to add that for some guys, when it stops, it leaves a vacuum that never gets filled.

"It's worth all the hard work. My whole life was spent getting ready for this. Dreams are coming true. I have coaches like you to thank for it. Even if I didn't say it directly. I do appreciate everything."

"I just coached you for one year. It was Johnny's idea to move you to linebacker."

"Glad he did. The Rams like it that I can step into multiple positions. And hey, we're playing Coach Cleary in a few weeks. The Bears are coming into town. You going?"

"I will if someone gets me tickets," I mused. "Hint, hint."

"Yeah, I might be able to arrange something. Just don't

sell them on Stub-Hub."

I laughed. "That's the last thing I'd do. Why'd you even think of that?"

"Something that happened years ago. Guy I had beef with. Dude named Tony Longley. Found out later he knew you."

I shook my head. Not a name I wanted to hear. "How'd you hook up with that character?"

"My bad move. You know I grew up near the Coliseum."

"I know."

"Yeah, so I figured out a way to sneak into SC games when I was in high school."

"How'd you manage that?" I frowned.

"I used to walk in with the vendors. My cousin worked there once, selling lemonade or something. He kept his employee badge. I'd borrow it, flash it to security and walk in with those guys, usually a couple hours before the game. Then I'd wander around the Coliseum, hang out, watch the players warm up. Eventually I'd find an open seat somewhere when the game started."

"Clever. But it sounds like you got nabbed. That's how Tony Longley came into the picture?"

"Yeah. One day he caught me walking in, told me he was going to have me arrested, thrown in jail, kicked out of high school, you name it. Then I made the mistake of letting on I was a high school football player and had scholarship offers. Thought I'd appeal to the better angels of his nature. Turns out he didn't have any. He wanted me to pay him. Can you believe that?"

I thought back to my days when I knew Tony Longley. I

was in high school as well, and I was an actual vendor, not at the Coliseum but at Dodger Stadium, where Longley had worked. Longley was a thug and we had our run-ins. One time, a pair of his goons jumped me, and it led to a free-for-all outside of the Dodger dugout. The cops found out he was behind it, but instead of getting fired, he took a step up in what passed for a corporate ladder in the concessions world. Next thing I knew he was running things at the Coliseum. Certain people never change, and Longley was apparently one of them.

"He wanted you to pay him?" I asked. "Sounds like something he'd try and pull. What did you do?"

"I had a high school all-star game coming up, so I got him a bunch of 50-yard line tickets."

I frowned. "He didn't need you to get him into the Coliseum for free."

"Nope. He went and sold them online. Then when I got into SC, he'd try to hit me up for tickets too, said he'd inform the NCAA and get me to lose my scholarship. Dude was following my career, and not in a good way."

"Hey, Q, how come you didn't tell the coaches?" I asked, starting to get a little steamed. "We could have fixed this for you."

Quentin shook his head. "Guys like Longley, you just deal with. But he's in the past. A couple of my boys went and talked to him. Explained things. He got the message quick."

"You can take the guy out of the hood, but you can't take the hood out of the guy."

He nodded and smiled a little. "Yeah. Part of me wants

to forget where I'm from. Part of me wants to make sure I don't."

Our food came and we dug in. "So, what brings you out this way, Coach? Not that I ain't glad to see you and all. But Thousand Oaks is a drive. And you're not coaching any more. Or are you looking to get back in?"

"Nope," I said, pouring a little syrup carefully on my pancakes. "Loved you guys, but I love my wife and son more. The hours were too grueling. It's a 24-7 job being a coach. Hard to believe, but it's more demanding than I thought it would be. Being a cop was less grueling."

"That's right," he laughed, "you were on the LAPD. We used to talk about what you'd do if you caught us smoking weed. Kick us off the team or bust us."

"You guys smoked weed?" I peered at him, knowing that in the end, the football players I coached were still college kids, some in their teens, and they simply did what their peers did.

"Not much for me. Once in a while, maybe. I was always in training. But some guys did it. It's part of being in college."

"Okay," I sighed. "Listen, you know I'm a private investigator again."

"I heard. You lookin' into me?"

"No. But I am looking into one of your teammates. And I'm trying to find a way to approach him."

"Who's that?"

"Walter Anawak," I said, looking at him closely.

Quentin frowned. "Walter? That's the last guy I'd expect to be in trouble. Seriously. What'd he do? Sit on someone?"

"Can't get into the details. And there's some holes in the story I'm hearing. It might be nothing, it might be something. But his name's come up in connection with an incident. I'd just like to talk to him."

Quentin shrugged. "We're not close. But I'm sure I can introduce you."

"What's Walter like? I remember when we played against him in college. He was the best lineman on Washington's team."

"Yeah, he's becoming the best lineman on the Rams, too. That big man works hard. He's a serious dude."

"Tell me about him."

Quentin scraped some eggs onto a piece of ham, lifted it smoothly into his mouth. He chewed enthusiastically as he thought about Walter Anawak, his eyes looking off into a corner of the diner.

"He's very quiet. Comes from a small town in Alaska. His nickname on the team is Eskimo. I think he belonged to some tribe once. Doesn't say a lot, but you can tell he's taking everything in. And he's smart. Really smart. Got to be to play O-line. Those dudes are big, but they need to work as a unit and know what the guy next to them is doing. Walter picked all that up fast."

"I remember when we played the Huskies. He'd just steamroll whoever he was blocking. Even you."

"Nah," Quentin winked. "I was too elusive. That's my favorite word now. Elusive. But I know what you mean. You couldn't out-muscle Walter and he's got surprisingly quick feet. Good athlete for a guy that big. He probably goes 330 pounds, could be 340. Depends on the day."

"What does he do in his off hours?"

Quentin frowned again. "I don't know. He lives out in Malibu Canyon with a teammate from Washington and a few other guys. They share a house. I thought that was strange at first, the canyon area's kind of isolated. But the more I think about it, the more it makes sense. Small-town guy like that wouldn't be comfortable living in the big city."

"Not like you."

"Nah, I'm a city kid, I was born into it, Coach. I live over in Santa Monica now. It's nice, but it's still a city. Just a small one. Guy like Walter would be lost without a bunch of trees and dirt roads and stuff nearby. Funny what you get used to, huh?"

"Yeah," I said, taking a sip of coffee. "Funny."

Five

The freeways slithering through the San Fernando Valley were gorgeously wide open by mid-morning, and driving back to the Westside became a pleasure rather than a chore. On the way, I thought of my next move, only to discover that I had none. My one paying client had me tracking a cheating wife to whom he was not married. From all I could tell, she was safely ensconced at her high rise office in Century City, and if she were cheating there, somebody else would have to uncover that today. I decided to go back to Santa Monica. A crime scene often held witnesses, or maybe people with a few interesting stories to tell. At the very least, it was a place to start.

I found street parking and waited outside of the entrance at 6th and Broadway for fifteen minutes. There were police cruisers parked out front, sitting noticeably in a red zone. The pungent smell of hamburgers wafted over from the burger joint next door, but the cool-looking staff still seemed more interested in laughing and joking amongst themselves. A few patrons seemed to be trying to get their attention but to no avail, so I made a mental note to avoid the place going forward. Getting a good hamburger in L.A. wasn't hard, getting good service often was. And for now, my stack of pancakes would hold me over just fine.

A few people came in and out of the building, but none felt like giving up a few minutes of their day to chat with a complete stranger, and certainly not about a recent murder. Most said they were in a hurry, and oh-by-the-way, they had already been interviewed by the police, and had nothing further to add. At about 12:15 p.m., a middle-aged man in a light gray suit and burgundy tie approached, a pile of keys jingling in his hand as he searched to find the right one for the front gate lock. I took the opportunity to step in front of him.

I flashed my impressive gold shield, the one that came complete with an authentic-looking sunburst and the number 4040 on it in royal blue. Had I given him time to look carefully, it would not say I was a police detective, but rather that I was a special investigator for an unnamed city. It was a badge that looked impressive but was completely fraudulent. I needed to use this trick judiciously; while I never identified myself as a police detective, it was perilously close to impersonating an officer. This was technically a misdemeanor, punishable by up to six months in county jail. While rarely enforced against private investigators, the local cops still took a dim view of this and could make my life miserable if given the opportunity. Considering Barney Sack had implied I was being scrutinized as part of a murder case, I decided the larger value of clearing my name in this mess was worth the small risk of actually running afoul of the law.

"Good morning," I said in a serious, authoritative tone. "Do you live in this building?"

The man stopped and look up apprehensively. "Well, yes and no," he said.

"That covers most of it. What part of yes would you like to extrapolate on?"

"Oh," he said, and looked mildly flustered. "Well, I live down in Orange County. Laguna Beach. But I work across the street at Bolton Capital. I stay here a few nights a week. Saves on the commute."

"Interesting. They won't let you work from home?"

"Oh, well, no. I have too many clients in this area. I grew up in the Palisades. But my wife works down in San Diego, so we picked a halfway spot. Over the years the commute home has gotten worse and worse. Takes three hours some nights. That's why I bought a condo here."

"Sweet," I said. "Were you around this weekend?"

"No, not at all. I was at home with the family. We have two teenagers. They go to school in Laguna. I was home with them. I had nothing to do with what went on here the other night."

I studied the man's nervousness and considered making a crack about the French saying, that he who excuses himself, accuses himself. But he might indeed have had nothing to do with the carnage on Saturday night.

"You heard about it. What did you hear?"

"Just that there was a man murdered. Hit over the head with a blunt instrument. Terrible thing."

"Sure. What floor is your unit on?'

"Fourth floor. I'm in number 401. I think the sixth floor is where this incident happened."

"Have the police talked with you yet?"

"No, no," he said and wiped his brow. "It's Monday, so this is the first I've been here since the tragedy. Heard about it on the news. I was actually just going to pick up some mail and have lunch."

"You say you're in ... 401?"

"Yes."

"Did you know any of the people who lived on the sixth floor? Where this, um, tragedy, happened?"

"I don't know a lot of people in the building. Like I said, I only stay here a few nights a week. But I have heard a few neighbors complaining about the people in that unit. And, well, it's hard to miss those girls who hang out there. They dress pretty, uh, revealing, I think they're strippers. I was in the elevator with a couple of them once, we were leaving the building at the same time. I heard them talking about working at the Pleasure Cove over on Pico. In West LA. It's a strip joint, so I assume that's what they do for a living."

I nodded. "You ever go there?"

"Oh, goodness, no. I'm a married man."

"Uh-huh. Anything strike you about the girls? Anything at all."

The man sucked in some air. "Well, like I said, I've heard they're a pain. There are a lot of guys coming in and out; I think the guys are the real problem, they're usually loud and usually drunk. At least from what I've been told.

Seems like it's party central up there. Doesn't matter to me, I don't live near them, I don't hear anything. But I know some of their neighbors have complained about the noise. Young people, shouting, boisterous. That kind of thing."

"You know any of the girls' names?" I asked.

"I think one was named Candy, hard to forget that one. Sounds like a stripper's name, huh? Another was Farrah. She had the biggest blue eyes. Those were the two I met on the elevator. I don't think I interacted with any of the others. Like I said, they came and went. Lot of them. Different girls, different guys. Hard to keep track."

"All right," I said. "Appreciate your time."

"Sure," he said, using his key to enter the doorway and go into the building. I waited a few minutes more and a short, heavy-set, middle-aged woman wearing frameless glasses approached. She had a small mouth and looked annoyed. I flashed my fake badge and she rolled her eyes.

"Not again," she said disgustedly, her exasperation smoldering out of her like a cigarette that was stabbed out inexpertly and still spewing smoke. "How many of you cops are working on this?"

"I don't know. Why do you care?"

"Why? Because I've already spoken to four or five cops. I've said everything I know. Four or five times. The guy that got killed, well he didn't live here. I don't know who he was. I don't want to know, either. I just want this whole mess to go away."

"You live in this building long?"

"I don't live here. I'm the property manager."

"What's your name?" I asked, taking a keener interest.

"I'm Toni. Toni Marinelli."

"Well, Toni, I hate to keep you. But I have a couple of questions. Strictly routine. The unit involved, number 612. We know there were some prior incidents. Complaints. Were you trying to do anything about them?"

"Look, these are condos. It's not like we can evict people. We don't even know the girls in that unit, they're not the owners. I told the other detectives that the owners are off-site, they just rent out the place. We've been in contact with one of them, but he doesn't care. Why should he? He doesn't have to put up with the noise and the commotion and all the foul language being used. And now this."

"Okay," I said. "Can you at least tell me about how long these guys have owned this unit?"

Toni shrugged. "Maybe a year."

"They live in the area?"

"One of them lives over in Mar Vista. I guess there's no harm in telling you that."

I sucked in some air. I knew Mar Vista all right. That one of my neighbors was involved in running a house of ill repute in Santa Monica bothered me more than it should have. The owner of the business certainly had to live somewhere, but it annoyed me that he resided close to where I lived with my wife and 3-year-old son. Mar Vista was a relatively quiet, safe neighborhood. I thought about it for a moment and calmed down, realizing it could be worse, he could be running this sort of business in my neighborhood.

"I know Mar Vista. Anything you can tell me about him? Anything at all might help."

"Nothing to tell really. I saw them when they first bought the place, after that it's all been by phone. Can't say I was impressed, but I didn't think they'd turn out to show such lack of consideration for their neighbors. But that's what you can get when a buyer purchases this as an investment property. The home owners association is going to take action against them, but I'm not sure what they can do, aside from levying a fine that probably won't get paid. Their next-door neighbor is talking about filing a lawsuit, but those things rarely amount to much. I'm hoping the publicity might get these guys to rent to normal people. This whole incident was reported on CNN, and you know, murder in a swanky, beach-front town is news. Listen, I need to get upstairs. Your colleagues are still mucking around on the 6th floor. I need to make sure they know someone's going to have to clean up their mess. Probably me."

I wished her good luck with that and watched her walk through the entrance. I wasn't used to hearing Santa Monica referred to as swanky, but makeovers happen, even for cities. I waited another half-hour and was getting ready to leave when a pretty, well-dressed woman about 30 walked toward the entrance. She had blonde hair and green eyes and wore a cream colored business suit with a low cut red top. I flashed my badge and asked if I could have a word with her.

"Oh, is this about the murder?" she asked casually.

"Yes, I'd like to ask you a few questions."

"Oh, I don't live here," she said as she brushed past me.

"Ever been here before?" I asked, following her over to the directory where a chrome intercom system was installed.

"Yes, a few times," she said. "I have a friend who owns a condo. But I haven't been here since last week. I don't know anything about what happened. And I'm in a bit of a hurry, to be honest. I'm late for lunch."

I stood back and watched her punch 401 on the intercom system. There was no verbal response, only the shrill buzz that also served to unlock the front gate. She swung it open and walked into the building.

*

The pulsating sound of a bass guitar reverberated in my gut as I walked into the Pleasure Cove. Located in a little triangle near Pico and Gateway, there was a grimy auto repair shop on one side and a tattoo parlor on the other. There were a few more businesses shoved into storefronts, but these were the more respectable establishments on the block.

I entered the darkened club and forked over my $20 entrance fee to a fiftyish man wearing Ray Bans and a long beard with haphazard gray streaks. I couldn't fathom what possible light he could have been trying to block out with the sunglasses, but he was most likely wearing them for effect. I walked in and sat at a table that was about 30 feet from the stage, which was something akin to a long catwalk strung with outdoor holiday lights. It was a runway of sorts, the type that fashion models might walk down, except this one featured floor-to-ceiling silver poles on either end.

Two busty girls with long blonde hair and no clothes on danced rhythmically, or perhaps absently, to the thundering beat of the music. One of the girls grabbed onto a pole with both hands, and hoisted herself up, a few feet off the stage. She did an acrobatic twirl, exposing her genitals to the small crowd for a moment, and removing the slightest shred of mystery regarding her well-shaved private parts. There were a dozen men sitting in the audience, and one of them began to applaud. A fat man with a walrus moustache told him to shut up. It was that kind of a place.

A slender woman with an olive complexion quickly approached. She wore an orange bikini and sported long, silky brown hair. She sauntered up to me in a sexy way, and promptly sat down in my lap. She smiled at her boldness and told me I was cute. I agreed.

"You look like you could use a lap dance," she purred excitedly in my ear.

"I could use a lot of things. But right now, no."

"Why not?" she pouted. "Am I not pretty enough?"

"You're super pretty. But I'm taking things slow."

She made a face and started to get up but I put my hand on her shoulder. "What is it?" she asked.

"I'm looking for a girl named Candy," I said.

"Hmmm. Candy, Candy," she said slowly, the way a bad actress might read her lines robotically. "Doesn't seem to ring a bell."

I sighed a pulled out another $20 bill. "Think harder."

She was about to grab the bill when I moved my hand six inches away.

"Hey!" she protested.

"Share your thoughts first," I said.

"Oh, okay. You probably mean Candy Pence. I think she's in the back. I can get her. If you really want me to ..."

I handed over the bill. There was no upside to paying on delivery in a place like this. And while there was a chance she might take the money without coming back with Candy, I didn't imagine I had much choice. A few minutes later, a tall, shapely woman with a black bob haircut, sauntered over curiously. She wore a low-cut one-piece bathing suit that was very red and a size too small. Her breasts seemed to struggle to stay hidden.

"Hi," she said, bending over and offering me a close-up view. "You were looking for me."

"You're Candy."

"I am," she said, a slight wariness in her voice. "But I don't think I know you. Have you been here before?"

"I'm on the job. Investigating what happened in Santa Monica the other night," I said, not wanting to flash even my fake badge in this place. "You know. At the condo on 6th and Broadway."

Her eyes widened. "Are you a cop?"

"I'm not with Santa Monica PD. But I am looking into it. And I'm mostly looking for Judy. My name's Burnside."

Her eyes narrowed suddenly and she licked her lips. "Look. I go on break in fifteen minutes. Meet me at the Saloon."

"The Saloon?"

"San Francisco Saloon, across the street. Catty corner. You can't miss it."

"I know where it is," I said.

She gave a quick look around the room and walked past the stage and disappeared through a door that presumably led to a dressing room. A waitress who looked like she was barely out of her teens approached just as I was getting up and told me there was a two drink minimum. This time I did flash my fake badge, and asked her if she minded if I left without ordering a beverage. Her mouth dropped and she said nothing, which I took as a tacit agreement to my suggestion.

I walked across the street and entered the San Francisco Saloon, an unusual name for a bar in West Los Angeles. It had been around for as long as I could remember, which spanned more than four decades. On the outside, it vaguely resembled a cable car, but on the inside it was just another watering hole. Years ago, I would occasionally come here with a date. It was, at the time, a quiet sort of fern bar with colorful tiffany lamps hanging from the ceiling. A nice place to just go and talk. They served a good Irish coffee, a concoction which had been falsely rumored to have been invented in San Francisco, not Ireland. The only part of this drink that might have actually been invented in San Francisco was the name. I once asked a waitress here what they called an Irish coffee in Ireland and she laughed and said "breakfast."

It had probably been fifteen years since I had been in

the San Francisco Saloon, and while they probably still served a good Irish Coffee, I decided to just order a Coke. I had changed, and so had the Saloon. The Tiffany lamps were still there, but the hanging ferns were gone, replaced by a remarkable number of flat-screen TVs spread out around the bar. A Dodger playoff game was on and every TV was tuned to the baseball game. There were only four other people sitting around, and two of them were waitresses. I sat at a table and nursed my Coke for a while as I waited for Candy to show up, which she did in about half an hour.

"Hi," she said, sitting down next to me. She had put a black tank top and tan shorts over her red bathing suit, which was still somewhat visible, as was her considerable cleavage. Dressed this way, she looked like any other twenty-something L.A. girl. No one would have surmised she worked, at the very least, as a stripper, which may have said as much about her as it did about L.A.

"Thanks for coming," I said. "I was starting to wonder."

"I know. It's sometimes a little difficult to get away. The manager wanted me to work another shift. I told him I'd be back in a few minutes."

"This shouldn't take long," I said, eyeing Candy and trying to figure out her role in all this. Strippers don't necessarily become prostitutes, but a lot of prostitutes work as strippers, especially when business is slow.

"You're the famous Burnside. What can I do you for?"

"Just want to talk about the other night," I said. "And I'm looking for Judy."

"So's everyone."

"Sure. Tell me what happened on Saturday."

"Nothing much to tell."

I took a sip of my Coke. It was about half empty. "When a man gets murdered, there's always something to tell. I know a little bit about what went down there. Or what was supposed to go down. And there's video cameras everywhere, so it's probably best to come clean and tell me what you know."

"You're not the police."

"Nope, but I'm looking into this, too. Personal reasons. And it may be better for you to open up with me rather than the cops."

"Do what?" she frowned.

"This is a high-profile case, Santa Monica doesn't get a lot of murders. The cops want to apprehend a suspect quick, just to put the community at ease. I don't think they're real selective right now. I'm sure you're on their radar. And if I can find you, the cops can, too. It just may take them longer."

"Are those cops that bad?" she asked.

"No, I'm that good."

She stared at me. "And if I don't talk to you, then you'll pass my name to the police."

"I didn't say that," I pointed out. "But maybe I was thinking it."

"Okay, look," she said, hesitating, and peering at me carefully. "You go first. You think you know something about what went down there. Tell me what you know."

"I show you mine, you show me yours?" I asked, a little incredulously.

She nodded slowly. "Yeah. Something like that."

I shrugged. This might be the best deal I could negotiate from her, especially if it meant gaining some semblance of cooperation. "Judy came to my office on Friday," I started. "She wanted my help."

Candy looked at me. I continued.

"Long story. We go way back. Sounds like you might know a little about us. Judy wanted some muscle on Saturday night because her, ah, boss, I believe his name is Owen, was involved in a deal that might go bad. It involved a guy who looked like a football player. And apparently Judy was told to be there to broker the deal. Turns out things did go bad, and the guy she brought in as muscle wound up dead."

"Um ... okay," she said slowly.

"Look I know Judy turns tricks. That's what she does. And that's what got her into this latest mess."

"You seem to know a good bit," she managed.

"And how do you know Judy?" I asked.

"Florida," she said, her body easing back into the chair. "Miami. South Beach. I was working at a bar. Must have been a couple of years ago. Judy hooked up with me there, we became friendly. I had some money issues. Credit cards, you know. She told me how I could make a lot more cash, and it would be way easier than hustling drinks."

I let out a breath. I hadn't bothered to look for Judy after she skipped town, I had no reason to, and was simply glad she was gone. That Judy ended up in Miami was not a surprise. I figured when she left L.A. she'd wind up in another big city, a place with money and energy and excitement. Anything that was different from Des Moines.

"And after Judy told you about this gold mine of an opportunity you figured since you liked sex and were giving it away for free, why not get paid for it."

She shook her head. "Something like that. How did you know?"

I shook my head. It was an age-old story, especially here in L.A. Lots of girls come out to Hollywood to break into acting, but most never make it. Some get other jobs in entertainment, anything from makeup artist to production assistant. Some go into another line of work, a few go back home. But some just don't have a place to go back to, or pride keeps them here. And when they run out of money and can't borrow anything more, they open their legs to the oldest profession. Poverty draws them in. The money's good, and it's easy at first. Then it becomes complicated, for a myriad of reasons. These included the need to have sex with men who disgusted them, the fear of violence that might occur with each transaction, and the ultimate realization of just how degrading it all is. Some get out quickly. Others simply adapt.

"I've seen this a lot," I said. "But that's not exactly what happened to Judy. She got roped into it by a very bad *hombre*."

"Yeah, I guess. And she told me about you. About how you tried to help her. She said you were a good guy."

I frowned. "She tell you anything else?"

"Nope. Just that you were a guy who helped her. Along the way."

"Right," I said dryly, wondering if Judy had related the

entire story of how she betrayed me. Certain details get left by the wayside, especially when they do not add to whatever narrative she may have been creating in what she told Candy.

"Look, I don't know where Judy is," she said, looking back over at the Pleasure Cove across the street.

"But you live in the condo on 6th and Broadway."

"No. I live with somebody. Not in Santa Monica."

"Boyfriend?" I asked nosily.

"Kind of."

"What do you know about what happened on Saturday night?"

"Just that Judy gave the recording to the football player. Walter, I think his name was. He gave her the money and left. What happened after that, I have no idea. Just what I heard on the news."

I looked at her and decided to take a shot. "There's a technology called license plate readers. They photograph your license plates when your car crosses certain intersections. Yours were picked up on Saturday night at Lincoln and Broadway. So I know you were there."

Her wide-eyed, deer-in-the-headlights look told me I had hit some pay dirt. In reality, I had no idea whether Candy's car had been there or if there were plate readers at Lincoln and Broadway. But there are times when employing a lie will propel the other person to come forward with the truth. It's funny how the two can be crookedly intertwined.

"Wow," she said. "Look. Judy's car wasn't running, so I was giving her a ride. But I can't help you with how that guy got murdered. I wouldn't know."

"Okay," I said, pondering this for a moment. "Who was there on Saturday night? Judy must have said something about it to you."

"Just that something bad went down. The side of her face was all red, like she had been hit. But she wouldn't tell me much about it."

"And to your knowledge, it was just Judy, the guy she hired for protection, and this big football player who she was collecting money from. That's it?"

Candy shook her head. "Judy told me there was also a girl in one of the bedrooms, she had a client. But they weren't part of this."

"What's her name?"

"Sadie. Judy said that Sadie never came out of the room."

"Okay. Go on. What else did Judy say?"

"Once that football player handed over the money, Judy said she gave him the recording. It was on some kind of little device, a thumb drive I think it's called. Then he left."

"And Judy stayed behind with the guy protecting her. Who turned out not being so good at protecting himself. Why did he and Judy stay behind?"

"I think they had an arrangement."

I shook my head. So much for offering one or two thousand dollars for standing around. Especially when you can pay someone off with a freebie.

"But Judy got smacked in the face. Who do you think did it? The bodyguard?"

"I don't know. Again, she didn't tell me," she insisted.

I tried another tack. "The bodyguard was named Henry Knapp. You know who he was?"

"Nope."

"Who do you think killed him?"

Candy shook her head. "Look, I have no idea."

"Ever hear of a private investigator named Carl Hillebrand? Sounds like that's how Knapp got involved with this."

"Nope."

"What can you tell me about the other owner of the condo. His name's Lucas Jerikoff."

Candy looked past me. "He and Owen have some kind of a deal. Not my concern."

"Have you been back to the condo since?" I asked.

"No, of course not. I mean, would you? With all those cops around?"

"Cops, yeah, who would want to be around them," I said aimlessly. "And did you hear anything from Owen after this?"

"Yeah."

"How did that go?"

"Not too good. He told me Judy never delivered the money to him. She was supposed to. But something went wrong."

I nodded. Famous last words.

Six

It was 4:00p.m. and I was approaching the North Hollywood police station. I glanced to my right, just past a cheap beige-colored stucco apartment building. I saw the two of them sitting on a bus stop bench arguing. She was still wearing the same skimpy clothes from last night. The young man sitting next to her was lecturing her angrily and pointing his finger in a threatening way. I stopped my Pathfinder and got out.

"There a problem here?" I asked.

"What's it to you, Jack?" the young man snarled. "Take a hike. Before you get hurt."

I flashed my LAPD badge and drew my jacket back to reveal the butt of a .38 tucked away in my holster. "Sorry, Jack. You take a hike. Before I run you in."

"On what charge?" he asked, standing up, not looking nearly as tough.

"Being a jerk for starters. But if you push me, I'll come up with something. And you'll be out of circulation for a while. Now beat it."

The young man turned to look at the young girl. He was about to say something, but thought better of it. He began ambling down the street. I watched him until he looked back, like I knew he would. I moved my hand and rested it on my .38. He turned back, kept walking, and did not turn around again.

"You're Judy, right?" I asked.

She nodded apprehensively, the blue eyes looking worried.

"Where are you from?"

"Iowa. Des Moines."

"How long have you been in L.A.?"

"A few weeks," she said.

"You do this type of thing in Des Moines?"

"Nope. I wasn't planning to do it here, either."

"You come out here to be an actress?" I asked.

"No," she said. "I came to get out of a bad situation."

"And now you're in a worse one."

Her big eyes lowered and faced the pavement. I had seen girls like this before, but never one who looked so young and innocent, so pretty and waif-like. When I booked her last night, a search showed she was just seventeen, too young to be on her own, and a candidate to go into foster care. But at seventeen that was a stop-gap which would soon go away. And foster care was no picnic for anyone.

"You have family you can call?" I asked.

She shook her head. "That's what I'm trying to get away from."

"Friends?"

"None out here."

"And that guy?" I asked, jerking my thumb at the figure growing smaller and smaller.

"He's just a guy."

"Your pimp."

"Yeah. I guess that's what you'd call him."

I sighed and tried to think of some options for her. None came to mind. I thought of leaving her here, but I knew her pimp would return. I thought of buying her a bus ticket back to Iowa, but she'd probably get off before the bus reached San Bernardino.

"Come on," I said and motioned for her to follow me into my Pathfinder. I had a funny feel I might regret this. In no way could I have imagined just how much regret I would come to have.

*

I didn't bother to press Candy for Lucas's address; the internet was an easy way to locate just about anyone. Lucas Jerikoff owned the condo on 6th Street in partnership with this Owen Magid. Jerikoff was also listed as a member of a trust that owned a house on Butler, just south of National. This was part of the Trousdale section of West L.A., not to be confused with the Trousdale Estates in Beverly Hills, a more prestigious neighborhood, but built by the same developer. The one in West L.A. was a tract of well-maintained post-war homes tucked away in a quiet, serene neighborhood. Driving through there made me feel like I was in a secluded suburb, more resembling

Mayberry than Tinseltown. But Los Angeles was full of hidden nooks like this, the Trousdale tract just happened to be one of the nicer places.

The Jerikoff house was a two-story that looked like it had been remodeled fifty years ago. The exterior was in dire need of a paint job, and the overgrown lawn hadn't been cut in a few months. Tears of rust had streamed down from the side window ledges, and the roof should have been replaced years ago. A screen from a window facing the driveway was slightly off of its hooks, hanging precipitously in the air. The appearance of this house was in stark contrast to the other homes on the block, which were all well-manicured.

I rang the bell, and even though I heard noises from a television inside, no one answered. Then I knocked a few times, before progressing to rapping and then pounding. Eventually I heard footsteps. The door opened and an elderly woman wearing a pink bathrobe appeared.

"Yes?" she asked pleasantly. "How may I help you?"

"I'm sorry to bother you," I said. "I'm looking for Lucas."

"What?"

"Lucas," I said a little louder. "Lucas Jerikoff."

"One moment," she said, and walked to a table a few feet away. Pulling something out of a drawer, she had gotten a device inserted it into her left ear, and walked back to me.

"I'm sorry, young man. I didn't have my hearing aid in."

"No problem," I smiled. "I'm looking for Lucas."

"Oh, yes. Lucas lives around back."

"Around back?"

"In the garage. We had it converted. This way he can still live with us but have his own space. Kids, you know."

"Yes," I said. "Kids. Just how old is Lucas?"

"Oh, he just turned 38."

"Ah," I said. "Thank you."

I walked to the side of the house and across a black asphalt driveway with a myriad of cracks in it. Opening a squeaky white gate, I noticed the garage and heard music coming out of it. There was a side door with a doorbell, but this time I skipped the preliminaries and just pounded a few times. The door opened and a tall, skinny man looked at me. He had rust-colored hair and what looked like a four-day-old stubble. Part of his chest was covered by an assortment of stupidly designed green tattoos.

"Yeah?'

"You Lucas?"

"Who the fuck are you?" he asked pleasantly.

I flashed my fake badge at him. "I need to talk to you about Santa Monica."

"Huh?"

"The condo," I said. "What went down there on Saturday night."

"Oh, yeah, I heard about that. That was weird," he said, scratching his ribs. "I don't know nothing. Got nothing to tell. I'm just the landlord."

"Oh, you're the landlord, huh? Is that what you call managing an escort service?"

He looked blankly at me. "What do you know about the escort service?"

"What I know is you're running an illegal business."

He processed this slowly. "Look man. There's no law against running an escort service. It's a legitimate line of work."

"That's a bunch of crap," I snarled. "Women may have the right to rent themselves out for dates. But once it extends to sex, it's as illegal as hell."

"Hey, man. Two consenting adults and all. We just put 'em together on a website. It's all cool."

I stared at him. People shouldn't be this ignorant. "Let me explain something," I said slowly. "There are laws against pandering. And pimping. And we can probably get you for human trafficking too, if I ask enough girls."

"Trafficking?"

"Forcing girls into prostitution."

"Hey, I'm just a businessman. I don't force anyone to do anything."

I sensed this conversation was going nowhere fast and decided to ratchet it up a notch. "Tell me about that blackmail plot you were trying to hatch. Or do you think it's perfectly legal to charge a guy $20,000 after recording him on a sex tape? And threaten to post it on the internet and ruin his career."

Lucas's mouth opened and didn't close right away. I thought of asking him if he was trying to catch flies. Finally, there was a glint in his eyes, and he spoke, albeit in a hoarse voice. "What are you talking about?"

"I know you were blackmailing a football player. Or it could have been a former player. And I know you were too chicken to show up and make the exchange yourself, so you and your partner sent your girls to do your dirty work. Brave guy. I ought to nominate you for a medal of valor."

"Get out of here," he said, his voice rising. "I don't know anything and I don't have to talk with you."

"I think you had something to do with that guy getting killed in your condo. I don't have proof yet, but I'll get it. You don't know me."

"Yeah, I don't want to know you. And this ain't Santa Monica, it's West L.A., so you're out of your district. Screw off, pig."

I felt I had entered a time warp and had returned to the 1970s. No one had ever called me a pig before. That type of reference ended around the time the Vietnam war wound down. I took a confrontational step toward him.

"Watch your mouth," I said.

"Or what?" he said, starting to enjoy himself. "You're not going to do anything here. You're not gonna risk getting kicked off the force. Pig."

"You think you're tough?" I asked, my frustration starting to boil over.

"I'm not scared of you, you p ..."

My first punch was a left hook to the mouth, which sent him reeling back against the door. Lucas put both hands over his mouth, which left his midsection vulnerable. I slammed my right fist into that soft spot just underneath the rib cage, and he grunted in agony and dropped to one knee. I took a step back, not to give him the opportunity to get up, but because there was no reason to hit him again. He wasn't going to respond. In fact, he had already started to cry.

"What'd you do that for?" he whimpered, still keeping one hand over his mouth, the other holding his abdomen. "I wasn't going to hit you."

"You don't get to say anything you want without repercussions. This isn't the internet. You don't get to hide behind a screen name."

"I told you everything I know," he said, brushing a couple of tears away. "Leave me alone."

"Where's Judy Atkin?"

"I don't know any Judy Atkin," he said, his breathing coming in spurts.

I ignored him. "Who's Owen Magid?"

He looked up at me, wincing. "How do you know about Owen?"

"There's no secrets any more, pal. The internet took care of that. You bought a condo together."

"Yeah, he's my business partner."

"Where does he live?"

"Hollywood."

"Where?"

"I don't know."

I grabbed him by the scruff of his neck. "Look. You are already up to your eyeballs in trouble. Maybe you're in over your head. But you better stop stonewalling. You're already looking at doing some prison time. And if you can't take a punch from me, the inmates at Pelican Bay are going to mess you up but good."

"Okay, okay," he said and stumbled into the garage. I followed him. The garage was a mess, it looked like it hadn't been cleaned in forever. On the back wall there was a bed and a dresser and a TV tuned to ESPN; a panel of sportscasters were discussing the Dodgers chances of going to the World Series. Lucas Jerikoff sifted through some papers on a folding table before coming up with a note written on a piece of scratch paper. He grabbed a business card from a gardener named Jesus Rodriguez and copied Owen Magid's address on the back. He handed it to me, his breathing starting to return to normal although he did keep massaging his waist.

"If this is wrong, I can come back."

"That's his address, I swear," he said, then started to back up. "And I don't know anything about no $20,000. I'm going to ask Owen, though."

"Yeah, you go do that," I said.

"Man, you shouldn't have hit me. Just for calling you a name?"

I looked at him and softened ever so slightly. "It's all about what you said. Words have consequences."

*

It was almost 4:00 p.m., that bewitching time in L.A. when offices and schools emptied out, and streets and freeways became flooded with cars. Any drive to Hollywood this time of the day would remove over an hour from my life, not counting the time it took to get back home. And with no guarantee that Lucas had provided the correct address or that Owen Magid would even be there. I decided I had clocked nearly a full day already, on a case which was paying me absolutely nothing, and one where the only end game might be the avoidance of a felony murder charge. That I was just five minutes from home made the decision to knock off work even easier. The fact that it had started to drizzle cinched the deal. The quilted clouds from Saturday were indeed a harbinger of wet weather.

Gail was home early from work and was busy shooting baskets with Marcus on his four-foot-high hoop in the den. I watched quietly as Marcus managed to sink ten baskets before Gail got to five. I wasn't convinced that she was actively trying to lose the match.

"Well, good job," I said to him as I walked up and gave both of them a kiss. "You're developing quite a touch."

"Daddy, I think I can beat you!" he exclaimed.

"I think he can, too," Gail said as she handed me the light, orange rubber ball that was about one-half the circumference of a regulation basketball. "I'm going inside to start on dinner."

I let Marcus beat me 10-9, making sure he managed to engineer a come-from-behind victory, even though I almost sank a late basket by accident, clanking it off the rim, a shot that came much closer to going in than I had intended. I taught him how to play H-O-R-S-E, and he beat me in three straight. At that point, Marcus got bored and apparently decided I wasn't much competition and told me so. He also wanted to watch TV. After setting Marcus up with a video on sea creatures, I went into the kitchen, where Gail was chopping vegetables. I took a bottle of Blue Moon from the refrigerator and opened it.

"What's cookin', good lookin'?" I asked, snaking an arm

around her waist as I took a small swig from the bottle.

She stopped and leaned back against me. "I got off early today. The judge moved our case up, and the defendants decided to take a plea bargain at the last minute. Good move on their part. Saved themselves five more years in prison."

"The types of defendants you like," I said, putting the bottle down and nuzzling the back of her neck.

"You'll have to wait," she smiled.

"For what?"

"For whatever it is you're looking for."

"Ah. I was just supervising dinner. What are we having?"

"Costco chicken and roasted vegetables. The chicken is ready, the vegetables will take a while. And sourdough bread. Did you know Marcus has acquired a taste for sourdough bread?"

"California kid," I mused.

"How was your day?" she asked, and noticed a swollen knuckle on my left hand. "Uh-oh. I think I may know part of the answer to that already."

"Yeah. Things got a little dicey with an upstanding citizen who didn't appreciate the fine art of being interviewed."

"He start some rough stuff?"

"No. But he called me a pig."

Gail stopped and looked at me. "And you hit him? For calling you a name?"

"Ah, yeah, um, it got a wee bit out of hand."

"I see," she said curiously, looking me straight in the

eye. "You know, sweetie, you can't just do that. Even when you were a cop, you could have been charged with battery."

I nodded, more solemnly than I wanted to. "You're right," I said. "I'm a little out of sorts today."

"Is this the case that Honey Roper referred to you?"

"No, I won't start on that one until tomorrow morning. This is about Judy Atkin. She's involved in that homicide over in Santa Monica on Saturday night. The deputy chief there, he and I have some history. It turns out my business card was found at the scene, and when he learned of my previous involvement with Judy, I suddenly became a person of interest."

Gail shook her head and returned to chopping vegetables. "That's nonsense and we both know it. You were home with us on Saturday night. Oh, I hate it when the police pull this stuff. Who's this deputy chief?"

"Name's Barney Sack. Not a bad cop, just perpetually overworked. And some of this stuff comes with the territory. He wants me to help investigate, but he can't say it and he can't authorize it. He has to distance himself. But he knows I'm good and I can get to Judy. And I can do things his detectives can't."

"That doesn't make it right."

"I know. But sometimes you just have to play along. Give something back to the community, as it were."

"That's a heck of a way to look at it. Nice civic spirit, but this is why cities hire detective squads."

"I've met their lead investigator, Callaway. Not quite sure about him. Seems astute, but you never know. I don't think they have a ton of resources."

"What have you uncovered so far? I heard some guy was found bludgeoned to death. But if Judy Atkin was involved, it probably had something to do with prostitution."

"And blackmail. Sorry we haven't had time to catch up on this. I told you Judy approached me on Saturday morning. Wanted me to accompany her to a drop. Her boss was blackmailing someone and she wanted muscle."

"And of course you said no."

"Of course. But she gets a hold of this guy Henry Knapp, he's done some work for a local P.I. although mostly he's a security guard."

"What was the blackmail scheme?"

"They had a football player, or maybe it was a former player, on tape, getting rough with Judy. And one of Judy's bosses, more accurately referred to as a pimp, had recorded the session and was trying to monetize it. He wanted $20,000 to keep it quiet."

"Bad investment," Gail observed. "No way to control digital copies."

"And these are not the most trustworthy of souls. Anyway, they all meet at this condo the girls work out of at 6th and Broadway. The football player supposedly paid up and left. What happened after that is undetermined. Other than this Henry Knapp gets his head bashed in."

"And everyone scatters."

"Yup. I'm hoping to find Judy. I talked to a friend of hers who seems involved in this, but I didn't get very far. I also had a give-and-take with her other boss, mostly me giving and him taking. That's what led to this, uh, cut on my knuckle."

"You know, sweetie, you're a father now. You can't be getting into these scraps like when you were younger. You shouldn't have been doing it then, either. I worry. And you've got an example to set," she said, motioning to the living room where Marcus was camped out watching his video.

"I know. I try. I can't always contain myself, sometimes the demons come out. It's difficult to control."

"Try harder," she said, turning to face me.

"All right."

"And I was chatting with one of the LAPD detectives today in the courthouse. We were waiting for our hearing. This guy knew a little something about what happened in Santa Monica the other night."

"Shop talk?" I smiled.

Gail shrugged. "For LAPD, I imagine this is what serves as chit chat. You know. His name's Albert Rocca, he works out of the Pacific station on Culver. I gather he knew this Henry Knapp, he had busted Knapp last year for assaulting a girl at some strip club. In fact, Knapp has had a few instances like that, and was out on bail. Some people can't stay out of trouble."

I nodded. "Reminds me of an old saying."

"What's that?"

"When you ride the back of a tiger," I said, "you sometimes end up inside of it."

Seven

Gary Wynn had a messenger deliver a packet containing what I needed on his daughter-in-law, which included a recent photo, her home and work addresses, and a description of her car. A check for three thousand dollars was surreptitiously inserted within the papers, almost as an afterthought. I rose early the next morning and was out the door before 5:00 a.m., which, in mid-October, would allow me to work under the cover of darkness. It also afforded me a 22-minute drive into the Valley, something that would take three times longer if I had waited a couple of hours and left home during morning rush hour.

I arrived in Studio City and exited the 101 Freeway at Coldwater Canyon. Driving south about ten blocks, I turned onto Dickens, a quiet, tree-lined residential street. Most of the homes were modest but well kept up, and I noted there were no sidewalks; the street began where the grassy patch of lawn ended. I found the residence of Trevor and Madison Wynn on the second block. It was a nice, ranch-style home, surrounded by leafy trees and a now-trendy fence made from distressed wood. But as I parked in front of their next-door-neighbor's house, something unusual struck me. Gary Wynn had informed me that his daughter-in-law, Madison, drove a late-model navy blue BMW 5-series car. Sitting in the driveway were not one, but two identical blue BMW 5-series cars. Their license plates were one digit apart; they had obviously bought the vehicles at the same time. I wondered how the couple figured out which car was which, although a quick glance at the interiors told me one driver was a neatness freak, and the other was a careless slob. While my gut told me the odds were the wife was the neat one, this was never a sure bet.

Fortunately, I had the good luck to have brought not one, but two GPS devices with me. The price of these had dipped to well under a hundred bucks, so I normally carried an extra in case one was not working properly. Today I'd need to hope both were functional. I fastened sections of sticky, double-sided foam tape to the devices and quickly walked over to the vehicles. It had rained overnight, and the streets were still damp. Regardless of how careful I was, the knees of my khakis were going to get dirty. Bending down underneath the trunks, I secured a device under each one of the BMWs. They stayed in place. All good, except for the fact that I would have no idea which car belonged to whom. I rectified this by writing down the license plate of each vehicle. Then I backed my Pathfinder up about 50 feet and sat there doing what P.I.s mostly do for a living: waiting and watching. At some point, Madison or Trevor would exit the house and drive away.

It took three hours of mindless endurance. I helped pass the time by listening to sports talk on the radio, hearing the outraged calls of Ram fans demanding their coach be fired and their starting quarterback be benched, if not waived out of the league. At least there were no complaints about USC's football team, they were off to a good start, having won 5 of their first 6 games. The only complaints about the Trojans revolved around how ticket prices had soared, and that parking near the Coliseum was expensive. Finally I got a reprieve. The Wynns' front door opened, and a young man in his late 20s walked out, wearing a sport coat and a nice oxford cloth shirt, a black gym bag slung over his right shoulder. I watched Trevor Wynn climb into one of the BMWs, gun the engine, and back quickly out of the driveway. Noting which vehicle he had taken, my work here was done for the morning, and I waited a few minutes before driving up the street.

I found a Starbucks a few blocks away on Ventura Boulevard, the main commercial artery that cuts across the floor of the Valley. I spent the next hour sipping on a *venti Sumatra*, eating a maple scone, and combing through various apps on my iPad, everything from the *L.A. Times* to *Bleacher Report*. By the time the clock reached 9:30 a.m., I decided traffic had died down enough for me to drive back into the L.A. basin. Although Hollywood was a small detour on the way to my office, I decided to stop and pay Owen Magid a visit. I didn't know if Lucas Jerikoff's partner would be as ornery and insulting as to spit the word "pig" at me. Gail's words from last night continued to wash over me, and I tried to inure myself from reacting too strongly to minor insults. Easy in theory, hard in practice.

The address Lucas gave me for Owen Magid led me to a dilapidated three-story apartment building just north of Sunset Boulevard, a few blocks east of Gower. The exterior was pre-fab stucco, puke yellow in color, although the peeling paint revealed it had previously been a light blue. The windows on the first floor all had bars on them. This was not uncommon in L.A. now. At one time, security bars were mainly a feature in downtrodden neighborhoods. But as the level of home burglaries rose, so did the unfortunate preponderance of these iron bars. They were ostensibly used to keep intruders out, but also had the unintended side effect of making residents feel mildly imprisoned.

No one had bothered to install a security gate here, so I breezed inside and immediately noticed all the apartments faced an outdoor courtyard. A stone fountain in the middle sat forlornly, no longer working, just a small, dirty puddle on the bottom, indicating what it once had been. I found apartment 4 on the ground level. A living room window was situated about two feet from the door. As I approached, I looked inside. A solitary figure was asleep on the couch, her long blonde hair slightly disheveled. A pale blue blanket was draped over her legs, the upper part of her body clothed in a low-cut t-shirt that revealed a shapely body. Even when she was sleeping, there was no way I could not recognize Judy Atkin.

My gut tightened. I positioned my body so my back was

flat against the outside wall, adjacent to the door. Even if they looked out the window, my face would not be visible. I drew my Ruger .357 and rapped on the door. There was no answer. I rapped louder, and then I started banging on it. I heard a sleepy voice ask who it was.

"UPS," I said hoarsely. "Got a package."

"Just leave it by the door."

"Need you to sign for it. Company rules. It'll just take a second."

I heard the lock turn, and just as the door opened a crack, I threw my shoulder into it and the door sprang back. I heard Judy yelp, but before she could protest too much, I shoved her back on the couch, pinning one arm behind her in a hammer lock. She was wearing white boxer shorts with the t-shirt, and I couldn't help but notice a few needle marks on what once was a lovely arm.

"Keep quiet," I warned, as I took out a pair of plastic handcuffs and yanked her other arm behind her back. Tying her wrists together, I noticed movement out of the corner of my eye. I turned to see two figures approaching. Whirling around, I pointed the pistol at them and ordered them to stop. Two nubile young girls stood there, neither one fully dressed. They saw the gun and froze in their tracks.

"Who are you?" asked an olive-skinned girl in her early twenties, long black hair hanging down her back. She was wearing an oversized Raiders t-shirt, some tattoos on her arm, and nothing else.

"I'm one of the good guys," I said, climbing off of Judy and feeling mildly ridiculous as I said this while holding a

.357 in my hand.

"You've got to be kidding," the other countered. She had thick auburn hair and was dressed in a red running bra and skimpy panties.

"Okay, look. Anyone else in the apartment?"

They looked at each other. "Um, no," said the girl with the long black hair, a bit apprehensively.

"Uh-huh," I said. "Get down on the carpet."

"Hell, no," the auburn-haired girl responded. "I'm not lying down on that."

I walked over and put the .357 to her temple. If Owen Magid were indeed hiding here, there might soon be trouble, and there might even be gunfire. My approach was harsh, but if bullets end up flying, people have a far better chance of survival lying prone on the ground.

"I said get on the carpet. And no more talking for now."

The two gave a panicked looked at each other, and the auburn-haired girl began to quiver as she slowly moved her body down onto the floor. The other one followed my directive without any more words of protest. I walked slowly down the hallway, pointing my gun ahead of me, and taking an occasional glance back at the girls to make sure they were still on the floor.

I heard a noise in the back bedroom and crouched as I eased the door open with my left hand, aiming my gun slowly across the room as the door gradually opened. I saw movement in a bed pushed up against a far wall. There was a young girl all curled up, blankets pulled up to her chin, staring at me. She was probably eighteen, but not by much.

"Lower the blankets," I ordered, "and let me see your hands."

She did as she was told. There was nothing in her hands, and no clothes on her body. I noticed a pair of jeans and a sweater tossed on a chair. I pointed to them and told her to get dressed.

"Promise you won't watch?" she asked innocently.

"I'm not a perv," I said, "but I've seen a few situations go sideways because a guy showed good manners. Just put on your clothes. I'll only keep an eye on your hands."

She slid out of bed and quickly put on her clothes, and I tried, with a modicum of success, to merely make sure she wasn't retrieving a weapon. As she tugged the sweater down past her midriff, I told her to go into the living room and lie down with the other girls. She did so without a word.

"Okay," I said. "Let's make this quick. Where's Owen?"

"Who?"

I sighed. "Owen. The guy who rents this place."

"You mean Tommy?" the black-haired girl asked.

"Tommy?" I frowned. "He also own that place in Santa Monica? On Broadway?"

"Yeah. We sometimes call him Screech because he's always screeching the tires on his car. Says he likes to leave rubber on the road. Weird, huh?"

"Yeah, weird to have so many names. Where is this Tommy?"

"He was here last night for a while. Then he left. He kind of comes and goes."

I looked around and didn't like what I saw. I also didn't

know what to do about it just yet. Four girls sleeping in an apartment was no crime. What they did to earn a living could very well be. But I knew they'd never admit to it, and frankly that wasn't my concern, I had more pressing business. I walked over to Judy, grabbed her by the elbow and jerked her up.

"Let's go," I said.

"Where?" Judy said with a frown.

"We'll talk about it in my car."

"You can't arrest me. You're not a cop anymore."

"Call it a citizen's arrest. And I'm the one with the gun, so you'll do what I say."

"What about us?" the dark-haired girl said, a bit of trepidation in her voice. "You mean you're not a cop?"

"Not exactly," I said, as I stepped over them on the way to the front door, my hand still clutching Judy's elbow. "But I can be a lot worse. And I want you to count to a hundred before you get up. I'll be listening."

I opened the front door, led Judy out, and closed it quickly. I holstered my weapon, and I moved her rapidly away from the building, down the street and into the back seat of my Pathfinder. I jumped in, fired up the engine, and roared down the street. After about eight blocks, I glanced in the rear view mirror. No one was tailing us. I pulled over into an alley and turned to Judy. In the light of day, I saw she had an ugly purple bruise surrounding her right eye.

"That shiner looks a few days old. You get it the other night in Santa Monica?"

"I don't remember. Like I told you, pain isn't a big deal

to me."

"Sure," I said, recognizing that what she told me was probably true. Some people are just into things like that. "Tell me what happened on Saturday night."

"I don't know what you're talking about."

I shook my head. "Oh, okay. You bring some muscle to this drop, his name was Henry Knapp. The muscle ends up dead, and my business card is sitting on the table next to him. And you don't know anything."

"Look, I'm really sorry ... "

I waved my hand. "Enough with the apologies. I'm sick of them. At the very least, you're an accessory to murder, if not the murderer herself. Although how you smashed that big guy's head in is a mystery."

"I didn't murder him, I swear," she insisted.

"What happened then?" I demanded, knowing I probably was going to be listening to yet another lie.

"We made the swap. I gave this Alaskan guy the recording. He gave me the money. Then we all left."

"Candy said you stayed with Knapp after she left."

Judy's eyes widened. "You talked to Candy?"

"I did. What happened? Better off telling the truth."

"Okay, look. I stayed behind. I did this guy, Henry, whatever his name was. He worked for some private eye in Santa Monica. The whole thing was quick, I just sucked him off. Then I left."

"He stayed behind?"

"Yeah."

"And you let him?"

"Why not? There was another girl there in the back

room. It's not like there's anything there to steal."

"What happened to the money this Alaskan guy paid you. His name was Walter Anawak, right?"

"How do you know has name?" she asked, bewilderedly.

"You told me. Or did you forget that, too?"

Judy took a deep breath. "I guess I did forget. And in all the confusion, I left the money behind. I was in a hurry to get out of there."

"And that's it?" I asked.

"That's it."

"So how did this Henry Knapp end up dead?"

Judy shrugged.

"Did you pay Knapp any money for being there?"

"I gave him three hundred up front. Seemed fair, seeing as I didn't know anything about him."

"How'd you hook up with him?" I asked.

"Candy found this private eye on the internet somehow. He directed us to Henry."

"And you don't know anything about how Henry Knapp got killed."

"Nope. Look, can I go now? I don't know anything else."

"Your story sounds like complete crap," I told her. "And because you left my business card lying around, I got roped into this mess. The cops are looking at me now as being part of a homicide. So I'm involved. And you're going over to the Santa Monica PD to tell them your story."

"Oh, no. Please. I've had it with cops. They won't

believe me."

"Maybe they shouldn't."

"Look, it doesn't have to be this way. I'll do whatever you want. Right here. I'll fuck you, I'll suck you, whatever, you name it. Anything. I'm really good, too."

I stared at her in mild disbelief. Whatever innocence I had once seen in Judy was long gone. The waifish teenage girl with the angelic face and the bluest of eyes had morphed into a hardened woman. Even the eyes had deteriorated, rimmed with red, they no longer gave off the innocence of youth, but rather they exuded the desperation that comes from seeing too many bad things over the years. I turned away from her, tossed my .357 into the center console, put the Pathfinder in gear, and pulled back onto the street.

It was mid-morning, and the drive to Santa Monica only took 20 minutes. I parked in the lot outside the remodeled police station complex, which was now shared with the fire department. The new building was made from a gorgeous gray stone, lined with glass, and had long horizontal slats that gave it an art deco tinge. An actual working fountain, which struck me as more of a sculpture, recycled a continuous waterfall into a shallow pool. A variety of green plants seemingly floated along the top of the pool. A lot of real estate money had streamed into Santa Monica over the past few years, and the city had wasted no time using it to modernize their civic structures. And there were plans in place to remodel it once again into something that would be environmentally friendly enough for the 22nd century.

I walked Judy in through the front door, my grip tight around her forearm. She struggled a little as I dragged her to the front desk, where a uniformed officer, middle-aged, balding, and looking like he desperately needed that first cup of coffee, greeted us unpleasantly.

'What the hell is this?" he exclaimed, his nose wrinkling in annoyance.

"Delivering a package to the deputy chief. Would you mind telling Barney Sack that Burnside is here?"

"Who the hell are you?"

I sighed. "Like I said, I'm Burnside. Do I need to repeat it again for you?"

The officer glared at me for a long moment and then called a female uniform over and ordered her to watch the front desk. He picked up the phone and made a quick call before hanging up, shaking his head, and telling me to follow him. Grasping a metal detector wand, he swiped it across our bodies before being satisfied we were unarmed. After leading us through a maze of hallways, he finally deposited me in a holding room, where he told me not to move. He took Judy by the arm and led her somewhere else. The walls in the room were painted white, the linoleum was white, and there were white ceiling tiles overhead. There were no windows, but the room was plenty bright. About forty-five minutes later, Barney Sack waltzed in.

"Well, just the guy I wanted to see," Sack said.

I looked at my watch. "You have a funny way of showing it."

"We got important business here," Sack said, taking a

seat across from me and loosening his already loosened tie. Today he had on a pink and brown striped number that looked as cheap as the one he wore the other day.

"I can only imagine. But you saw the witness I brought in. Maybe she's something more. She didn't bother to tell me much."

"We'll get it out of her," Sack said. "Judy Atkin, huh? You should bring me up to speed on your activities over the past few days."

"I'd be delighted to, chief. I mean deputy chief."

"Go on. And ease up on cracking wise."

"All right. I went back to the crime scene yesterday."

"Wonderful," Sack groused. "You get your prints all over everything?"

"I didn't go into the unit. Just spoke with some neighbors. Learned one of the girls who works there also dances at the Pleasure Cove. It's on Pico. You probably know it."

"I do, but not for the reasons you're insinuating. Some of our best clients hang out at that flesh pit."

"Sure. I went over there and talked to the girl."

"Name?"

"Candy Pence."

"Cute. You verify it with a driver's license?"

"We didn't get that intimate. It was hard enough to pull anything substantive out of her. I did, however, find the owner of the condo. Lucas Jerikoff."

"Uh-huh. You get anything else?"

"I got Owen Magid's address in Hollywood. Lucas Jerikoff gave it up."

Sack's eyes widened. "How'd you manage that. We got nothing from Jerikoff."

"Let's just say the private sector can be a bit more, er, agile than the police."

Sack gave the hint of a smile. This was clearly his reasoning for bringing me in on this. The police normally have a strict protocol. I don't.

"Write it down," he said, handing me a notepad. I jotted the address from memory and handed it back to him. He looked at it. "Okay. Keep going."

"So I get to Magid's apartment, he's not around, his name may actually be Tommy, who knows. But I found four girls there, and Judy was one of them."

"The rest of them were pros, too?"

"They were attractive young ladies," I replied. "We didn't get into where they were in their career paths."

"How'd Judy get that black eye? The private sector at work again? Or you just let your emotions get the best of you."

"Take another look at it, Sack. It's not fresh. It's a few days old, it's become discolored. If she got hit in the last hour, her face would just be red."

"The great medical expert. Thanks for the lesson. And who were the other girls?"

"I didn't spend a lot of time talking. Once I saw Judy, I cuffed her and got her out of there," I said. One of the problems with being a lone wolf is when you encounter more than one possible assailant. I knew nothing about these girls, and young people can sometimes throw caution to the wind. If they all attacked at once, things could get dicey, even if it's just four girls barely out of their teens. I didn't know if they were on drugs, and one-on-four situations are never good, even if I was the one holding the gun. The last thing I wanted to do was shoot anyone today.

"Judy say anything to you?" Sack continued. "I mean something I might want to hear?"

"Aside from propositioning me, no, not a lot. Henry Knapp was hired because Judy wanted a guy who looked tough. She paid him a few hundred, and apparently fellated him as part of their agreement. How he got his head bashed in is still a mystery."

"She tell you anything about the Alaskan guy?"

"Just that he paid the blackmail money and left. The money itself seems to have disappeared."

"Uh-huh."

"Judy thought he was a pro football player, but there's a hole in that story."

"How's that?"

"If he were an NFL football player, he wouldn't be available on a Saturday night. Even for a home game. The Rams are like every other team, they take all the players to a local hotel for the night. The coaches do a bed check, make sure the guys get a decent night's sleep and don't go out clubbing. Also means they don't have to worry about a player oversleeping his alarm clock on Sunday morning and showing up late for the game. Everyone is right there on Saturday night, and the coaches keep them relatively sober as well."

Sack nodded. "Okay. You know your stuff. I'll give you

that, Burnside."

I got the feeling there was something more coming, so I kept quiet. Sack's style was not to shower people with compliments. I waited, as Sack looked down at the white linoleum.

"We haven't released this to the media yet, but it'll be out soon enough. There was another murder last night. In the alley behind the King's Head. Body was found early this morning. A couple of joggers thought it was just a homeless guy sleeping there until they saw the pool of blood."

I frowned. "The King's Head? That British pub off of 2nd street?" I asked. This was not the type of place that ever encountered much trouble. My main recollection was they offered a wide range of beers and served a pretty good plate of fish and chips.

"Yup. We found a body in that alley between 2nd and Ocean. Big Alaskan guy. Shot twice in the back of the head. Looked like execution style. We have video evidence, but somebody popped the flood light in the alley, so everything's grainy. We picked up a few things but we just can't make their faces out."

"Sounds like a certain someone was planning this ahead of time."

"You figure, huh?"

"And let me make another guess. The big Alaskan guy wasn't a football player."

"Uh-uh."

"Then it wasn't Walter Anawak of the Rams," I said, deciding there was no longer any need to keep his name from the police. When things spiral into double murder, it's best to keep the local cops informed.

Sack's mouth opened ever so slightly and he gave me a long, curious look. "No," he said. "It wasn't. The victim was his cousin, Rolf Anawak. Lives with him, but you're right. Big Alaskan guy, although not the one who plays football."

Eight

I spent a few more dispirited hours at the Santa Monica police station, much more than I had anticipated. Barney Sack spent a solid hour grilling me, before giving way to a young detective who fumbled over similar questions. Still, he did manage to provide some insight into what happened behind the King's Head pub. Rolf Anawak was said to have left the bar soon after he arrived, departing with a man who apparently walked him into the alley. The big guy acquired two bullets in the back of his head when an unidentifiable accomplice snuck up from behind and shot him from point blank range. The video only revealed that the shooter wore a dark baseball cap and had long hair, most likely blonde, streaming halfway down their back.

The young detective allowed me to leave at 2:00 p.m., which was hours after my stomach first began grumbling that a maple scone was insufficient nourishment for the day. I drove north on 4th street, thinking of taking the freeway home, when I suddenly decided to hatch a different plan. The King's Head was only a few blocks away, and it was worth a detour, even if only to confirm they still serve a pretty good plate of fish and chips.

The police were finishing up at the crime scene, and had just allowed the pub to open for the day. The King's Head was divided into three parts: a bar, a restaurant, and a gift shop, together taking up half a city block. The restaurant had grown into the largest of the three, but it was the bar where Rolf Anawak had apparently met the man who led him to the alley and helped seal his fate.

I walked in to the darkened bar area, a relatively small space with a black linoleum floor augmented by dark pine paneling on the walls. Dart boards were set up across the room. Three large TV monitors hung from the ceiling, each one tuned to a different soccer match. I sat down on a stool next to a lean man in his thirties who was nursing a beer and looking up at one of the screens. I asked the barmaid for a menu, glanced through the offerings of Cornish Pasty, Bangers and Mash, and various Meat Pies, before reverting back to the original plan. Icelandic cod and chips.

"Would you like a pint with that, love?" the barmaid asked casually, her soft London accent providing a nice touch to the surroundings.

"Why not?" I said, figuring I had put in a full day's work already. "How about a Bass ale."

"Coming right up," she said, and thirty seconds later, a frosty glass of amber ale was placed neatly in front of me. I turned to the guy on the next barstool.

"Quite a commotion here today," I started.

"You got that right, mate," he said. "I wasn't planning

to get off to such a late start to me day."

I smiled. "This how you normally begin things?"

"Mostly. Except when I have a meeting or two. But, bloody hell, who'd've ever thought a murder would happen here? Place like this?"

I nodded in agreement. "You come here a lot?"

"Most days. Some nights."

"Were you here last night?"

"I was. And you know what? I didn't see a bloody thing, mate. Didn't hear no gunfire, nothing. Just another day at the office."

"You recall the big guy who got killed?"

He rolled his eyes. "You couldn't miss him! I swear, what do you all put in the water here? This joker looked like a bloated whale. But fair's fair, I wasn't paying too much attention to him. Just another Joe Bloggs. Like I told the five-ohs a little while ago. Seen him hanging around, he didn't order anything, but I didn't think much of it. Some people just stand at the bar until their table is ready. Apparently he was waiting for someone."

"They call police five-ohs in England?"

"This ain't England, mate. Gotta learn some of the local jargon if you want to chat up a girl and not sound stupid."

"Okay. He was waiting for someone. Apparently he found them."

"Yeah, right? Waiting for someone to come down and blow his head off? Ha! Might have given that one a second look if he could do it again."

"You didn't see any arguing or anything?"

"Nah. And you don't see much fighting in this place.

Nice pub, nice people. Mostly regulars, but you always get a few lowlifes coming through. Every once in a great while two guys might get pissed about something, so they step into the alley and sort out their differences."

"This time it went a little further."

"Sure did. Can't say as it surprises me though. You Americans love your bloody guns. Seems like everybody has one." He took a swallow of beer and looked at me. "You carrying, mate?"

"No comment," I said, remembering I had left my .357 in the Pathfinder.

"Figures. Bunch of sissies over here. Back in the East End, if some bloke pisses you off, you take 'em outside and rough 'em up a bit. Over here, you call someone a name and next thing you know they're waving a nine in your face, threatening to spatter your brains all over the wall. Americans are a bunch of cowards. Anyone can be tough if they're holding a gun."

I mulled this over, taking a long swig of my Bass ale. I began wondering if I needed to set the record straight and defend my country's honor by inviting my new friend into the alley and demonstrating our prowess with fisticuffs. Then I began to hear Gail's voice, reminding me of my need to set an example for Marcus, not to mention keeping her from the dreary process of bailing me out of jail. Angel on one shoulder, devil on the other. Story of my life.

My fish and chips arrived, and after giving the plate a quick douse of malt vinegar, I dug in. I had never been to England, but I couldn't envision that they had better fish and chips than what I was eating right now. I took another swig of ale and ignored my new companion until I finished and paid the bill. I tried to get the barmaid talking about last night, but she just shrugged and said she hadn't seen a thing. I asked a few others at the bar and got much the same answer. Finally, I pulled myself up before I got sucked in to having another pint or two and re-litigating the revolutionary war.

"Nice talking with you," I said to my new acquaintance.

"Cheers, mate. You sure do ask a lot of questions. I had you pegged as a five-oh. Am I wrong?"

"You're off by about eight years. I used to be LAPD. A lifetime ago."

"Guess some things never leave you. Bet you've got a lot of stories."

"More than I care to tell."

"Too bad, I could use a guy like you."

"Oh? What do you do?" I asked cautiously, knowing the city in which we lived.

"I just signed a two-picture deal with Paramount. I'm writing a screenplay about life and death in L.A. I might even put last night's scene in the film."

"So you write in the morning and drink in the afternoon?"

"Normally the other way around," he said, taking another swallow. "But when that big bloke got done in, it kept the pub closed for a while. Messed up my routine."

Shaking his hand, I told him to break a leg, and deep down I meant it. I strolled out of the pub and around the corner. The police had put up the yellow tape to block any looky-loos from waltzing in and wreaking havoc with their crime scene. I noticed Detective Callaway finishing up with a man in an SMPD windbreaker, who may have been working Ballistics. Callaway noticed me and walked over.

"Burnside. Interesting to see you here," the small said as he gave me the once over. "Been doing some gardening?"

I looked down at the stained knee on my khakis. "Just taking care of business."

Callaway continued to give me an odd look and pretended to sniff carefully. "And you're starting happy hour early, I see. You're a real credit to your profession. Whatever that is."

"I've got an easygoing boss. Lets me get away with a lot," I said, and made a mental note to stop off and buy some peanut butter before going home. People think mints hide the smell of alcohol, but nothing beats peanut butter for masking beer breath.

"Uh-huh. You're better off not being on the police force."

"One could say that about a lot of cops."

"Smartass. But hey, thanks for bringing Judy Atkin in. Couldn't get much out of her yet, but until she starts talking we're holding her indefinitely."

"How so?"

"She's all we got. Closest link to the Broadway killing and now this. Both tied in to Rolf Anawak. And we got her on video with him from last week. She was getting slapped around by Anawak before he did her. Judy said it was all pre-arranged, play acting and such, but we're not buying it. This looks like a revenge killing."

"How'd you get the video?" I asked.

"Thumb drive in her pocket. Said it was a copy, yeah, we know she was part of a blackmail scheme, looks like she didn't give up all her copies. Blackmailers never do. But it wouldn't have mattered much, that video's already on the web."

I frowned. This didn't add up. "You're thinking of charging Judy with this shooting?"

"We don't know yet. We get the feeling she was hitting Anawak up for more money last night and the deal went south. Who knows. But unless she cracks and tells us different, she's our prime suspect and she's going to rot in jail for a long time. We need to reassure the community that we've apprehended the killer."

"Sure," I said dryly. "Got to make sure everyone thinks the police are doing a bang-up job."

"You know the drill. Two killings in four days in a city like this? Got to show everyone we're taking action. This isn't L.A., where they got more stiffs than they can count. We'll see where all this goes. At the very least, Judy has to give up her accomplice, the guy talking with Anawak before he got, ha-ha, whacked. Thanks, buddy. Always glad to see you P.I.s helping out the real cops."

Whatever annoyance I had with my newfound British pal inside the King's Head had increased twentyfold at the gist of Callaway's remarks. My hand absently balled into a fist before I relaxed it and took a few deep breaths. The maturity process was not going to be an easy one for me.

"That's what I live for," I said. "Helping you guys out."

"So you're off the hook. But I'm curious. Why do you give a crap about Judy Atkin? With your history with her and all? Figured you'd be happy to see her in a jail cell where she belongs. All things considered."

I thought about this and didn't have a good answer. Judy betrayed me, destroyed my LAPD career, and any contributions she had made to society were going to be far outweighed by her indiscretions. I didn't quite know why I cared, but I did. And it wasn't as simple as seeing justice properly meted out.

I was about to provide Callaway with a not-so-heartfelt expression of appreciation for my feelings when my phone rang. The area code was unfamiliar, and I considered letting the call go to voice mail. Too many telemarketers were trying to sell me handyman services lately. But rather than get into another snit with a police detective, I walked away and picked up the call. The voice on the end was deeply masculine and he sounded very serious. He also had an unfamiliar accent.

"Mr. Burnside?"

"Yes."

"I'm wondering if I can meet you in a little while. We have a mutual friend who said you wanted to speak with me."

"Who's that?"

"Quentin Ware. I'd like to speak with you, too. My name is Walter Anawak. I think you probably know why we need to talk."

*

Not surprisingly, it took the better part of two glasses of cold water to wash down a large spoonful of peanut butter, but my breath held no evidence of alcohol when Walter Anawak entered my office. Offensive linemen are imposing figures, and Walter looked as tall as he was wide, and boy was he ever wide. Standing at least 6'7", he wore a gray t-shirt and khaki shorts, and his skin was deeply tanned. He had a round, placid face that revealed little, and the mass of black hair atop his head was pulled up into a man bun. But most striking was simply his girth. Every part of him was supersized, from the massive shoulders to the imposing gut, to a pair of legs that better resembled tree trunks than human limbs.

"Mr. Burnside?" he asked politely, but with a deep voice.

"Mr. Anawak."

"Please call me Walter," he said as he eased inside the door frame.

"Call me Burnside," I responded, and pointed to a chair across from my desk, hoping it wouldn't crack under the extreme weight. I took a final swallow of cold water and asked if he'd like a drink. He declined.

"Thank you for meeting me," he said, his tone serious, his dialect slightly resembling that of a native American.

"No problem. And my condolences about your cousin Rolf. That was tragic."

"Yes," he said, as his mouth curled painfully. "It's very disturbing. I hope Rolf's in a better place now."

I nodded my head as if I understood, but in reality I did

not. When a person dies, a lot of us like to believe they go to heaven. It makes us feel better to imagine they have moved on to someplace safe. In reality, we don't know, we simply need to have faith that this will transpire. No one who's ever departed for the great beyond, at least for more than a few minutes, has ever come back to gush about what it's like.

"Tell me about Rolf," I said, not wanting to delve too deeply into a religious discussion.

"Troubled guy. Familiar story, at least where I come from. His mother was a single mom, she drank too much, he learned from her. People in remote areas drink a lot, there's not much else to do. Some people handle it okay. But Rolf's drinking always seemed to get him into trouble. Not the drinking itself really, just that it led him into doing foolish things. Fights, mostly."

"You grew up with him?"

"Not exactly. I grew up in Barrow."

I frowned. "That's pretty far north, isn't it?"

"Yeah. Northernmost part of America. Our beach faces the Arctic Ocean. Not that anyone ever swims in it, Barrow is still really cold most of the year. And during the winter it's like constant twilight, you can go months without seeing the sun. Spent my first sixteen years there."

"Why'd you leave?"

"My parents. They went out hunting one day and never came back. A freak snowstorm hit. They must have got caught up in it and couldn't get out. It happens. Almost happened to me once when I was a kid."

"How so?"

"It was late October, right around this time of year. I was out walking around with a friend after school, but even now it gets dark early. We were a few miles outside of town when this squall hits. Big winds, driving snow, getting real cold. Even in October it can get down close to zero at times. Tough to walk in a blizzard. We were about thirteen years old at the time, should have known better but we didn't. The snow finally stopped but it was bitter cold and the winds really picked up. And there was no moon out, so it was pitch black."

"Sounds ominous. But you must have made your way back to Barrow."

"Yeah. You ever hear of the Aurora Borealis?"

"Heard of it, I think they call it the Northern Lights? Supposed to be really incredible to see."

"It's pretty freaky. These waves of green light moving across the night sky. And in this case, it saved our lives. It lit things up enough so we could navigate our way back to the village. Never felt so good to be home."

"Sounds like your parents weren't that lucky."

"No, they weren't. We never saw them again. We told the sheriff, but the storm was so bad, he couldn't go out until the next morning. He took a plane and scoured the area. Couldn't find them."

"Sorry."

"Yes. I had an aunt who lived outside of Anchorage, she eventually took me in. Rolf's mom. We're Iñupiat, it's a tight-knit community in Alaska, we look after each other. Rolf was about my age, a year younger than me. We became close."

I nodded. "You both play football?"

"We did. I played in Barrow but didn't get much attention, it's so isolated. They didn't even have a football field until a few years ago, there's no grass there. They finally put in field turf so we could play. When I moved down to Anchorage, a few schools started noticing me. I got a bunch of scholarship offers, mostly Division III colleges, I wasn't on the radar of any big-time schools. But during my senior year, a scout from the University of Washington visited, he was recruiting this running back from Juneau. I got noticed. Wound up getting a scholarship offer to play for the Huskies in Seattle."

"Let me guess. The running back from the other school didn't get an offer from Washington."

Anawak looked at me curiously. "Yeah. How did you know?"

"That happens more often than you might think. Scouts check out one player, but another one just catches their eye. I used to coach college football at USC. I worked with the defensive backs for three years. Left after last season."

"Wow, so you must have .... "

"Yeah, I coached against you a couple of times. You always gave us problems. I know you're good. Very good."

"Thanks."

"But tell me more about Rolf. Was he a good player?"

"Rolf was tough. Maybe not quite as good as me, but he had talent. He was big and he was quick. The drinking messed him up, though. He cut classes in high school, didn't do any homework. To be honest, he flunked most of his classes. He wanted to play in the NFL, but he wasn't willing to sacrifice to get there."

I sighed. This was also not an uncommon story. Football players weren't typically the best of students. At USC, Washington and other big-time schools, there is a certain minimum level of academics that players have to adhere to. I used to remind high school recruits that if they wanted to make it all the way to pro football, they first had to play in college. And to play college football, they first had to graduate from high school. You can't get into college without a high school diploma.

"It sounds simple," I said. "But for some guys, it's just not easy."

"Yeah. Rolf came down to Seattle to hang out with me. He worked part-time, got his act together, and I helped him with his GED. We were able to get him into a junior college in Idaho, they had a good football program, guys who graduated from there could sometimes transfer to a Division I college. He had the talent to go to the next level, but he started drinking again and it all fell apart. He flunked out after the first year."

"What did he do?"

"Rolf went back to Anchorage, which was not the best move. Fell in with a bad crowd, got arrested for a few things, mostly assaults against women. Usually happened when he was drunk. Put that firewater in some guys and they just can't handle it. I don't know what he had against women, but it was getting ugly. I got drafted this past May, so after I signed with the Rams, I moved down here. Asked Rolf to come down and live with me. Get him out of

Anchorage. Fresh start and all."

"Nice of you."

"He's kin," Anawak said, and suddenly began to wipe his eyes. "You do what you can to help your family. I couldn't turn my back on him."

I reached into my desk drawer and handed him a box of tissues. "Okay. He moved into your house. You support him?"

"Sort of," Anawak replied, reaching over and grabbing three tissues in a hand that looked like it belonged to a giant. "I gave him a place to live, free room and board, didn't charge him anything. But I also told him he had to get a job if he wanted spending money."

"Fair enough. What did he work at?"

"He was a mover. Worked for this guy Felix Montoya, he had his own truck. It kept Rolf physically active. He's almost as big as me, so lifting furniture is no big deal. Plus, he had to be on time, so that meant he couldn't stay out all night drinking. Seemed to be working out okay. But things changed last week."

"What happened?"

"Rolf said he needed $20,000. Told me he had run up some gambling debts. Told me he had been betting on the Rams."

"Not a good bet this year."

"We're improving," he pointed out, raising a big hand. "The Seahawk game was tough this week, they're really good. But we're getting better. Just takes time. Lot of young guys like me and Quentin on the team."

"Did you give him the money?"

Anawak paused for a moment and looked down at the floor. The tears had stopped, and his face tightened. "Yeah. I didn't want to do it at first. But he told me that these people were going to kill him if he didn't pay. I couldn't live with myself if I said no and something happened to him. I was a first round draft pick, so I've got a big contract. Twenty grand isn't much to me. Losing a cousin, that's different."

"Okay. So you gave him the money."

"I did. Gave it to him on Friday. I went with the team on Saturday, and didn't get back home until Sunday night. I was too tired after the game to do much more than eat and go to bed. I didn't see him on Monday, I got up late, and figured he had gone to work. But this morning ... I got the call from the police. They found him in an alley in Santa Monica. Two bullets in his head. No reason. A couple of detectives came out to talk to me, they said they had a suspect in custody already. A girl."

I nodded slowly. "They think she had a role in this."

"Yeah. Said they were working toward bringing charges. But then I got this call a little later. From some nut. Said he had a video of me raping a girl and that it was on the internet. Told me it was on a restricted website. He gave me the site and the password so I could see it."

"And he wants money from you."

"Yeah. Said it looks like me, but I can assure you it's not. It might be Rolf, it probably is Rolf. But he said he'd tell the world it's me if I don't pay him $50,000."

I let out a low whistle. "And you and your cousin probably look a bit alike."

"Yes."

"And it would be easy to confuse the two of you."

"Yes."

"And if the NFL thought you were involved in sexual assault, that could be the end of your career."

Anawak's mouth scrunched up. He said nothing, but shook his head definitively up and down.

"What did you tell him?"

"Said I didn't know. He told me he'd call me in a couple of days, and if I didn't pay him, the video would go viral. With my name all over it. Might end my career. Even the hint of it could get me suspended."

"Are you going to pay him?" I asked.

"I don't want to. But I don't want my career ruined. And I want to get this guy who killed Rolf. He needs to be dealt with."

I looked at him cautiously. "I can help you try and find this guy. But you can't take matters into your own hands. If you mess him up, it's a felony. And the NFL isn't going to look kindly on that, either."

He continued to nod, more vigorously this time. Finally he spoke. "Quentin said you were looking to speak with me. You were a private investigator. I had a feeling you might be working on this."

"I have been. Let me bring you up to speed on my involvement here," I said, and told him the part about Judy coming to my office wanting help, the blackmail scheme against Rolf, the murder of Knapp, and my apprehension of Judy. I left out the specifics about the Pleasure Cove and my brief interaction with Lucas

Jerikoff. I didn't know Walter Anawak or what he was capable of. A big, angry man looking for revenge could not be fully trusted with all the details, even if he knew the dire consequences.

Anawak listened carefully, and when I was finished, he spoke. "I came down here to hire you. But it seems like you're already on the case. You've been putting in work."

"I have."

"What's your rate?" he asked, pulling out a checkbook.

"It's a thousand dollars a day. I normally ask for a two-day retainer. It may end up being more, we'll see."

Walter Anawak wrote out a check and handed it to me. It was for five thousand dollars. I looked up at him.

"This is a lot," I said.

"I'm paying you for your time. You're already invested. I want you to find this blackmailer, and if we can't mess him up, we have to bring him to the police. And I'm paying you to find my cousin's killer, they could be one and the same. I can't go to the police. I just can't risk having any of this become public."

"Understood. I'm discreet."

"And these people are obviously dangerous. I'm putting you in a tough situation. If you had accepted that girl Judy's request, it could have been you that got hit over the head the other night."

I thought about that for a minute. "I imagine that's possible," I smiled. "But if I had been there, I'd bet someone else would have gotten hit over the head."

Walter Anawak gave a small chuckle, but he did it without smiling.

Nine

"It's a two bedroom apartment " I told her. "The second bedroom has a couch. You can sleep on that."

She looked around nervously. "It's a nice place," she finally said. "But why are you doing this for me?"

I took a breath. I didn't fully know the reason myself. Judy was a teenager, a runaway, a damaged child whose history I knew little about. I was an LAPD cop who should have known better. Mixed together, the combination was combustible.

"I guess it's because I know what it's like to have no one in your life you can turn to," I said. "But some very good people helped me. They didn't need to. But they did."

"Did you run away from home, too?" she asked, innocently enough, those big blue eyes evoking sympathy.

"No," I said. "My mother died of cancer when I was eighteen. I never knew my father, he was killed in a car accident before I was born. I had relatives, but they lived in the Midwest. I was all alone."

She sat down at the kitchen table. "What did you do?"

"I got lucky. I played football in high school. Over in Culver City. I was good, but not good enough to attract a college scholarship right away. But then one of the players USC had recruited failed to graduate high school. He played safety, just like me. It was June and they suddenly had a football scholarship available. My high school coach reached out to USC and told them my situation. And since most other high school players had committed to other schools by then, SC didn't have a lot of options either. They looked at my tapes and decided to bring me on board."

"Wow. So you played football. Were you good?"

"Yeah. But I worked hard and I stayed out of trouble. That was the key. In the back of my mind, I was always afraid something would happen. I'd be in the wrong place at the wrong time. I didn't go to many parties. I studied, I played football. And I focused really hard at doing both of these things well."

"Did you play pro football?" she asked.

"No, I got hurt after my senior year. It never quite healed properly."

She looked at me curiously, the way a person might look at an animal in the zoo that they had never seen before. It was as if she were trying to figure me out, and struggling to do so.

"I'm still not quite sure how this all relates to me," she said. "Or why you're helping me."

I sighed and turned away from her. This wasn't going to be easy.

*

Gail texted me she would be coming home late and asked if I could pick up something for dinner. I stopped by the Zankou near my office and bought some rotisserie chicken, along with their garlic sauce, hummus, and the softest, fluffiest rice I had ever tasted. British food for lunch, Middle Eastern cuisine for dinner. In L.A. there was nothing unusual about that, in fact, I didn't even think about it until I was pulling into my driveway.

I played a round of Leaners with Marcus as we waited for Gail to come home. Leaners was a game I had played as a child. We took a deck of cards, sat across the room, and tried to toss the cards so they would land standing up, or "leaning," against the far wall. For every deck of cards, we'd managed to get a few leaners, and when Marcus went up 3-2, I had to remember to avoid tying the score. It was, like many things about parenting, a rule I needed to constantly remind myself of. The competitive spirit does not yield easily.

Gail arrived just past 7:30. We ate and tried to get Marcus to tell us about his day, but he was more interested in eating bites of chicken. My day was rarely grist for dinner table conversation, so we mostly talked about Gail's. Marcus would occasionally ask me what I did, and I'd give a generic response that I was helping people with their problems. The gnarly particulars, such as assaulting people, looking into the activities of prostitutes and investigating homicides, were the sordid details I didn't like sharing with anyone, much less a 3 year-old.

After dinner, I went onto my computer and checked the locations of the GPS devices I had attached to Trevor and Madison Wynn's vehicles. Trevor's car was at an address in Burbank, which turned out to be a gym. Madison's was inching along the northbound 405 Freeway, most likely she was on her way home. I checked again an hour later, and both cars were now safely ensconced in their house in Studio City.

The next morning, Gail was hurrying to get out the door, and asked me to drive Marcus to preschool, although she didn't say why. On the way over, he talked about Frankie and he asked me what Antarctica was like, although he still needed help with pronouncing it correctly. I told him it was really cold and mostly covered with snow and ice.

"That sounds like fun," he said, reminding me that a child's vision of the world can be idealistic, and that wasn't such a bad thing at times.

"Your new friend is still planning to go?"

"Frankie, yeah. Hey, Daddy, can I go over to his house today for a play date? Mommy said I could."

I answered with a long "Hmmm." But when we arrived at the preschool drop-off area, Frankie was at the front entrance waiting for him. Marcus bounced out of the Pathfinder and ran over to his new friend, and they raced inside together. I was about to pull back out into traffic when a tall, slender blonde woman approached the car and waved to me.

"Oh, hi there," she called. "Remember me? I'm

Brittany."

"Of course," I said, scanning my memory quickly. "We met for ramen last week. You're Frankie's mom."

"Right. It's Francis, actually. Listen, Gail called and said your nanny was out sick today. And the kids have been asking for a play date, so I was wondering if today would be good."

I hesitated. "Sounds okay, but let me double-check with Gail."

"Sure," she said, and handed me her business card, that had the name of a production company on it in raised letters. "Our office is in Venice. Right by the boardwalk. Not far from here."

She turned and walked over to a black Mercedes, which she unlocked with the push of a remote button. I wasn't all that comfortable with Frankie or Brittany or especially Antarctica, where we were definitely not going next month. But I also knew the slippery slope, even if it involved a preschooler, of telling somebody who they could or couldn't have as friends.

I went home and spent the rest of the morning trolling the internet, looking for escort services that might feature Judy or Candy, or any of the girls I saw yesterday in the Hollywood apartment. There were dozens of sites and hundreds upon hundreds of escorts, and I began to wonder just how oversexed L.A. really was. And this cavalcade of scantily clad women didn't include the numerous streetwalkers who utilized a low-tech apparatus to generate business.

I drove over to Owen Magid's apartment in Hollywood,

but no one answered the doorbell. Nor did anyone respond to the knocking or the pounding. I did encounter a neighbor who yelled at me to knock it off, but when I flashed my fake badge at him, he backed off quickly. I tried a few other neighbors, but no one else was home. I drove over to the Pleasure Cove, but the doorman with the sunglasses and streaked-gray beard told me Candy wasn't working today. Nothing productive was emerging this morning, although the sun was starting to burn through the cloud cover, and that always felt like a good sign of things to come.

I finally decided it was time for lunch and drove to the Santa Monica Pier to try Honey Roper's suggestion, Plan Check, a cool, new burger joint. My order came with a fried egg, a special type of cheese, and a few oddly concocted items I could not identify without referring back to the menu. It was a pretty good burger, and while it lacked the comfort-food reassurance of the Apple Pan, it was probably better than the Wagyu burger I had with Gary Wynn the other day. It was certainly cheaper. I wasn't sure if L.A. was really in the midst of a burger renaissance or just a new way of conjuring up an old favorite. Either way, I had seen the future and was convinced it would come stuffed with candied bacon and ketchup leather.

After my lunch, I took a walk over to 6th and Broadway, and stood as unobtrusively as I could near the front gate of the condo entrance. I looked repeatedly down at my phone and tried to appear as if I were waiting for someone, which I ultimately was, although it was merely any random stranger who happened to be walking in or out of the building. Ten minutes later, a middle-aged man emerged and patiently held the door for me without bothering to ask if I lived there. Thankfully for me, there were still some people who just wanted to be polite.

The 6th floor appeared to be back to normal, and there was no yellow crime scene tape in view. I knocked softly on unit 612, but before I could escalate to rapping and pounding, the door opened and a pretty girl with wavy brown hair stood there looking quizzically at me. She wore a tight t-shirt and volleyball shorts, not unattractive, but not exactly what a call girl would be wearing if she were on the job.

"Can I help you?" she asked.

"I'll bet you're Sadie," I guessed.

Her confused expression grew deeper. "How do you know?"

I put a foot inside the unit in case she tried to slam the door in my face. Pulling out my fake badge, I flashed it quickly and said I'd like to talk for a few minutes. She hesitated, looked down at my foot, calculated there was little sense in resisting, and invited me inside with a shrug of her shoulders.

She closed the door. "I know what you're going to ask me. But I'm not sure how I can help you."

"Well, let's play it by ear," I grinned. "You never know."

She sat down cross-legged on the floor. I sat across from her on the couch.

"I know you were here on Saturday night," I said, and watched carefully as my words sunk in. I was getting tired of people lying to me, and sometimes presenting the bold-face truth can halt dishonesty in its tracks.

Sadie looked at me and processed this slowly. "You know that?"

"Yes. You were in one of the bedrooms, with a client. Tell me about what went on in here in the living room."

She took a deep breath and let it out, all the while looking down at the floor. "There were a few guys here. And a couple of the girls."

"And Judy was one of them," I said, hoping to impart that I actually knew something.

"Yeah, she was there, she asked me to just stay in the bedroom. But the conversation they were having got a little heated so I opened the door a crack. I didn't know what it was about at first. Still don't, not entirely. This one really big guy, looked like he was an Indian or something, I think. He was pretty intense. Said this was a one-time deal. If anything went up on the internet, he'd be back and mess people up."

"Okay."

"The other guy told him to shut his mouth, and that no one was getting messed up on his watch. Judy actually stepped in and tried to defuse things. It must have worked because people started to leave."

"And Judy stayed behind. With this other guy. His name was Henry."

"Yeah. Anyway, I was finished with my client, but when we started coming out of the room, I heard Judy arguing with someone. She must have promised to blow him or something. But the guy wanted straight sex."

"And how did they settle that little point of disagreement?"

"He smacked her in the face. Hit her pretty good, knocked her onto the couch. Then he jumped on top of her and began taking her clothes off."

"And what happened next?" I asked.

"Well, I couldn't very well call 911. And after he hit Judy, I wasn't going to jump in and break it up. He was big and I'm not stupid."

"What about your client?"

Sadie shook her head. "He's a mouse. When Judy started getting hit, he flew back into the bedroom and told me to shut the door. I think he's married, but still, he wasn't exactly a profile in courage."

"And you listened until they were done."

"I listened while he did her. And every now and then I'd hear a slap and a curse. Then I heard some weird noises and he grunted loudly. I figured he was done. My client insisted I not even open the door until I was sure they were gone. I waited until we heard the door slam, then we came out."

"And you saw Henry Knapp on the floor," I said.

"Actually he was still partly on the couch," she said. I looked down at where I was sitting and made a mental note to get my pants dry-cleaned.

"And then?" I asked.

"And then we stared at him for a second, and my john freaked out. He said he couldn't be caught here, where was the back exit, all sorts of crazy stuff. I told him no, there's only one exit. He insisted that he leave first and I wait a few minutes before I followed him."

"Which you did?"

Sadie shrugged. "Didn't matter to me. That Henry Knapp guy looked dead to me. Didn't think he'd get any deader. I waited a minute and then left."

"So there's a dead body lying there and you didn't call the police?"

"Nope, I'm not crazy. I know who I work for, and I'd like to live to see my next birthday. I guess someone else called 911 eventually."

I thought about this. Rolf Anawak and Judy Atkin were here with Henry Knapp. And Sadie and her client. Rolf left but he could have come back, he sounded pretty angry. Judy had been sexually assaulted. Sadie could have been lying about her role. Or her client's. But Rolf was dead, Judy was in jail and Sadie wasn't telling me much. I needed more answers, and they weren't materializing.

"When a client comes here," I started. "What's the process? How does it work?"

"You've never done this?" she asked, with the same curiosity that might be displayed for somebody who had never ridden a bicycle in his life.

"Believe it or not, no," I said.

"Oh. Well, a guy starts by going on our internet site."

"Which one?'

"They use a lot of them. Changes all the time. But anyway, the john picks a girl he likes and calls to make an appointment and agree on the price. When he comes over, we check him out," she said, pointing to a window across the room. "If he seems okay, we buzz him in and tell him we're up in unit number 612."

I walked across the room and glanced out the window. Looking down, even from the 6th floor, I had an unobstructed view of the front gate and the intercom.

"And you're looking for what exactly?"

"Mostly making sure it's just one guy. And that he's not acting weird. You can only tell so much, but we've turned away a few dudes."

I had an idea. "Give me your cell phone," I said, in as authoritative voice as I could.

"What?"

"Your phone. I want the number of that client that was here on Saturday. I need to talk to him."

She considered this for a moment, then pulled out an iPhone in a pink gold case that was studded with rhinestones. She opened it up and began swiping through her phone list.

"Let's see ... here's Saturday evening," she said and showed me the number. I wrote it down and then glanced up at her.

"Just one client that night?"

She shrugged. "We usually get a lot of business travelers. Sunday and Monday evenings book up. Saturday's not our busiest time. Date night. You know."

*

Asking Sadie for her client's name would be a fruitless endeavor, he almost certainly provided an alias; men who buy sex usually don't even give their real first names. After leaving the condo, I placed a call to the number I lifted from her phone, and after being routed to voice mail, I learned the john's name was Stuart. I wasn't sure he'd ever pick up, so I tried to invoke Plan B, but that got derailed when I learned my old pal Captain Juan Saavedra was not in; he was on vacation for the next two weeks. I phoned Roberto De Santos, but he was in a special ops training class. I finally conjured up another idea.

The LAPD's Pacific Division was on the corner of Culver and Centinela, not far from our home. It was like any other police station: sterile, bureaucratic, and humming with activity. I asked for Detective Rocca's desk and was directed to it near the back wall. Albert Rocca had a stocky build and his black hair was short and cropped. Wearing a light-blue shirt and a light blue patterned tie, he was leaning back in his chair, phone lodged between his ear and his shoulder, scribbling notes on a pad. He noticed me but did not bother to make any sort of acknowledgement. After a few minutes, he ended the call with a curt "uh-huh" and turned to give me a bored look.

"Help you?" he asked, with a placid demeanor.

"Name's Burnside," I said.

"That supposed to mean something to me?"

"My wife is Gail Pepper. She works for the City Attorney. I gather you've worked on a case together."

His expression changed and a smile crossed his lips. "Oh, sure. Gail. Just finished putting a perp away with her. Smart lady. Cute, too. You're a lucky man."

"I am indeed."

"She told me her husband used to be on the job. Out on

your own now."

I nodded. "P.I."

"I wouldn't mind doing that one day."

"It has its ups and downs," I said. "But don't discount a steady paycheck and decent health insurance."

"And a pension," he smiled. "I'm 16 years in. You know the saying. Do your twenty and take your forty."

I smiled at the standard cop line. It referred to qualifying for a pension after twenty years and then getting forty percent of your salary for life. If an LAPD officer started early enough and stayed healthy, that pension could extend for a good four or five decades.

"I never made it far enough to qualify for that. I'll be working until I keel over."

Rocca took this in. "So what can I do for you, Burnside? It's a shame Gail didn't take your last name. But Pepper is pretty catchy."

"I think she wanted to maintain her own identity," I said, leaving out my other thought, that she might not want to be publicly associated with a husband who treated the law as a suggestion rather than a set of rules to follow assiduously.

Rocca nodded and said nothing. I continued.

"I was hoping for a favor," I said. "I'm looking for this guy, his name's Stuart, no last name available. All I have is a cell phone number. It might be a disposable, but I'll bet the number can be traced. Just need his last name. An address would be a bonus."

Rocca continued to nod and then asked to see my P.I. license. I showed it to him. He glanced at it and handed it back to me. "Why are you looking for this Stuart?"

"He's a principal witness in a murder case. Happened over in Santa Monica on Saturday night."

"I know the one. Nest of hookers. What's Stuart's involvement?"

"One of the johns who was there at the time. Not sure if he saw anything, but I'm running out of leads."

"How come you aren't working with SMPD?"

I looked down at my hands and rubbed my thumb and index finger together for a moment. "Let's just say I'm not impressed with their detective work. They're closing a case too fast. I'm not sure they have the right suspect in custody. And I have a client who needs this thing unpacked."

"I heard they caught someone," he said. "Pretty quick, too."

"Uh, right," I said, not bothering to mention I was the one who caught Judy, brought her in, and in a bizarre fashion, was now actively working to get her released. I didn't explain all the details to Albert Rocca. I wasn't so sure I understood them myself.

"Also heard that the suspect was involved with that other homicide, the one behind the King's Head."

"I think there may have been a rush to judgment," I said.

Rocca considered this. "As a favor to Gail, I can check the phone number out for you. Give me a day or two, I'm a little busy right now."

"Working on anything in particular?" I asked nosily.

"Mail fraud," he shrugged. "Bunch of goofballs have

been following UPS trucks around. They wait and see if the delivery guy leaves a package by somebody's front door. After the truck leaves, they go and lift the package."

"Nice guys."

"Yeah. Half the time they wind up with a box full of mouthwash and shampoo. Or books they can't read. All they do is waste everyone's time, including their own."

"Great world we live in," I observed.

"Keeps me employed. Say, since we've been discussing her and all, how'd you get so lucky to wind up with a woman like Gail?"

I shook my head and gave him a truthful answer, the kind of answer I had spent many a night pondering myself.

"Darned if I know."

Ten

The Plan Check burger was sitting well. I thought of getting another cup of coffee. Caffeine had that magical ability to spark ideas when none were forthcoming, and I had no idea what to do next. Aside from Stuart the john, anyone who had any scintilla of knowledge about these murders had already been interviewed, was currently in jail, or had burrowed underground. Speaking to the victims would have been an ideal opportunity, except for the inconvenient fact that they were both dead. I finally decided the next best thing would be to speak to people familiar with the victims.

Carl Hillebrand had an office near Ocean Park and 30th Street, tucked away above a cluster of retail outlets that included yet another upscale burger joint called The Counter, an Italian restaurant, a draw-your-own frozen yogurt shop, and, fortunately for me, a Starbucks. I sauntered in and ordered a *grande* iced coffee, stirred in two packets of stevia, and walked upstairs to the third floor. A chrome sign that said "AAA Investigations" was glued to the door. I knocked a couple of times and tried the doorknob. It was open.

The office was like mine in that it was one large room with a desk near the window. Unlike mine, this one had a Persian rug, real artwork on the walls, and a mini-refrigerator and microwave sitting off in a corner. I made a mental note to consider upgrading my space soon.

"Hi there," I said to a balding, bespectacled man in his late fifties. He looked up from his keyboard. He appeared affable and mildly mannered. A large, 25-inch monitor took up a good part of his desk. The man leaned back in his chair, revealing a large paunch around his middle. He didn't strike me as an ex-cop, but admittedly, some retired officers let themselves go after they leave the force.

"Yes, can I help you?" he asked.

"Name's Burnside," I said, and handed him a business card.

"Nice to meet you," he said pleasantly, giving my card a long once-over. "Call me Carl."

"Carl, then."

"You're a P.I., too," he observed.

"I am. Former LAPD. Been out on my own for almost ten years. You?"

"I've been doing this for about five."

"Ever on the job?" I asked.

"No, never had anything to do with law enforcement. I actually used to work in accounting for Toyota. Took early retirement. Detective work always interested me. It's kind of like a puzzle."

I looked around his dapper office again. This was not an unusual story. He probably took a few classes at a detective agency and picked up a P.I. license along the way. My field did not have a high bar for a motivated applicant to hurdle.

"You take classes at Pinkerton?" I asked.

"No. Did it online. Wasn't too hard."

"So I've heard. And now you're a licensed P.I."

"Uh-huh. Hey, don't get me wrong. I'm not a cop. In fact, I rarely leave the office. A lot of the work I do is from here. Skip traces, mostly, you know, people looking for their birth parents, an old girlfriend from high school that they never got to bang. Occasionally I get a real missing persons case, or some meth addict jumped bail. But I mostly work here. I'm pretty good with computers."

"I take it you don't carry a weapon," I mused.

"No way," he said and raised his shirt slightly to reveal a can of pepper spray attached to a holster. "I'm no Phillip Marlowe. Just want to make sure I can get out of a situation if I have to."

"Ever need to use it?" I asked.

"Ha. Once. Some valet parking attendant took my BMW for a joyride when I was at dinner. When I confronted him, he got tough and shoved me, so I sprayed him. Kind of regret it though."

"How's that?"

"He pressed charges. I got off, but it cost me a bundle in legal fees. Good thing I wasn't packing. Getting off a homicide charge is a lot trickier."

"Good thing indeed," I echoed. "Speaking of homicide.

Henry Knapp. I hear you knew him. How'd you guys come into contact?"

Hillebrand smiled. "Over time, I'd meet a few bouncers and security people. I'd keep their names in case something came up I couldn't handle."

"Like Judy Atkin."

"Yeah. She called me on Saturday. The whole thing sounded sketchy."

"She find you through the internet?"

"Most likely. I paid one of those search engines to pop my name up first when a prospect googles L.A. detectives. But having a name like AAA Investigations usually gets you listed first anyway. Honestly, getting business really isn't that hard. A few tricks of the trade."

"I'll keep that in mind," I said wryly. "So you passed on Judy."

"I don't do security," he said. "Like I said, I'm more of an inside guy."

"And you sent her to Henry Knapp."

He shrugged. "He's big, he looks tough. That's what she wanted."

"You get a cut?"

"Usually I get a ten percent finder's fee," he said. "In this case I wasn't planning to charge Henry. He's had money problems."

"Legal fees?"

"You know something about that?"

"I heard he's had problems with the law."

Hillebrand looked at me, duly impressed. "You really are a detective. Yeah, he had a few scrapes. Maybe more than a few."

"And you didn't think sending him off with a hooker might lead to another issue?"

"Hey, whoa, cowboy," he said, putting his hands up. "I don't do background checks on every referral. Judy wanted muscle, she got muscle. I didn't know she was a whore."

"I believe the phrase is 'sex worker,' but let's not get stuck on that," I said. "I gather the SMPD paid you a visit."

"They did. Little guy named Callaway came by on Monday, it took him a couple of days to figure out how Knapp was connected back to me. Probably scanned his phone. Hey, that guy Callaway, I don't think he stood even 5'4". I thought there was some kind of regulation on minimum height for cops, 5'8" or something like that."

"The LAPD used to have a height requirement, but that was from another century. I don't know what other cities require," I said and tried to get the conversation back on track. "Anyway, what happened with you and Callaway?"

"Ah, he mostly asked questions about Knapp and Judy. Not that I could answer much, just what Judy told me initially. Knapp obviously never came back."

"Callaway relate anything specific about what happened Saturday night?"

"Well, just that Henry got hit with a blunt instrument. Oh yeah, he asked if I knew whether Henry ever carried a weapon. Whoever killed him used something unusual."

"Oh?"

"Yeah, they said it wasn't a bat or a pipe or a stick. Nothing like that. Those would have left a different kind of mark, long and narrow. Callaway must have gotten the coroner's report. The fatal blow came from something else. A more compact weapon, I think."

I pondered this and threw out something to keep the conversation going. "Maybe an ashtray? Or a stone of some kind?"

"I don't think so. He said in addition to Henry getting his head busted open, there were some deep cuts. Like whatever it was had a sharp edge to it."

I considered this. Knapp was bludgeoned to death with something that had to be heavy enough to crack his skull, but also able to dig gauges in the skin. An unusual murder weapon was often a good thing for investigators. If they could figure out the weapon involved, it dramatically narrowed the pool of suspects.

"Callaway have any thoughts as to what it was?"

"No," Hillebrand responded. "To be honest, it sounded like he was just going through the motions when he was talking to me, checking off a box. I'm not sure he even cared."

*

I gulped what remained of my iced coffee and checked my phone as I walked downstairs. There was a message from Gail, asking if I could pick up Marcus from his play date at Brittany's office. I texted her back and said okay, although the address did not sound like it was in a commercial structure. It turns out it was not.

Brittany's "office," as it were, was a three-bedroom

bungalow, situated along a walk street in Venice, half a block from where the asphalt ended and the sand began. It was about as eclectic an office as one might imagine, steps from the beach, and close to where a growing homeless population camped out on the boardwalk. Venice was always a cool and hip neighborhood in which to live, but the burgeoning real estate market now made it a cool and expensive place. The homeless added an element of urban grit to it.

The house looked like it was about a hundred years old, but nicely kept, a throwback to another era of Los Angeles, when Venice was more of a vacation spot than an sunny, urban paradise. The one-story wooden bungalow was painted a dark green, and it stood out because the other homes on the walkway were now mostly two-story glass-and-steel behemoths. A small fence surrounded the tiny front yard, providing a safe haven for a teaming garden of succulent plants.

I drove around the block three times before pulling into a parking space on Rose Avenue. It was technically a red zone, but I assumed my brief pickup would not take long enough for the crackerjack L.A. meter maid crew to zoom in and zap me with a ticket. I walked up to the bungalow, and after ringing the bell, I knocked on the door and waited ten seconds. I wondered if I'd need to begin my usual rigmarole of pounding, but Brittany popped her head around the side of the house and called to me.

"Oh, we're out back. Come on, follow me," she said.

I walked around the side of the house and saw, next to the shimmering dark blue swimming pool and hot tub, was a small trampoline. Marcus and Frankie were joyously bouncing up and down, letting out a whoop whenever they reached their apex and began to descend.

"Daddy!" Marcus called as he climbed off the contraption. Frankie continued to bounce up and down, shrieking with delight as he edged higher and higher.

"Hey there," I said, giving him a hug. "Have fun today?"

"Yeah. Wow, can we get one of these for our house?" he asked excitedly.

"We'll see," I replied, uttering the indispensible words parents learn to say, the phrase that's employed when neither yes or no is a good option.

"They had a blast together," said Brittany. "We're so glad Marcus could come."

I took a look at her house. "This is your office?"

"Oh, yes! Isn't it a great space?"

"It is," I admitted. "But I didn't realize you worked out of your home."

"Oh, we don't actually live here, we're just renting this place for a few months. The owners are going to tear it down next year and put up a new home, but they can't get financing yet, so they're renting it out for now. We actually own a place in the Palisades, up on the bluffs. It's beautiful, but we can't walk to the water. This is so nice for Francis."

"Ah," I said, recalling Brittany and her husband were working on a movie, and well aware that people in the industry often had more money than they knew what to do with. Even as a wildly compensated pro football coach, Johnny Cleary, my old boss at USC, only maintained one residence. Maybe he needed to renegotiate his contract.

"It really works out quite well," she gushed. "Clark's movie is in pre-production now. So it's nice we can be together part of the day while he sets everything up for the shoot. We're headed to Antarctica in a few weeks and there's a ton of stuff to do."

"Antarctica, yes, I remember," I mused and let my curiosity get the best of me. "Do you mind if I ask you something?"

"What's that?"

"If you can afford an office at the beach," I said, thinking rent on this house, teardown as it might well be, had to be a staggering figure, "why are you at the Mar Vista preschool? It's a good school and all, but it's out of your way. Applewood is closer."

"Well, we tried to get in at Applewood, but it was booked solid, no wiggle room. We even offered a twenty-thousand dollar donation and they still turned us down. They even seemed a little miffed."

I smiled to myself. They probably didn't offer enough. "Well, I hope you like Mar Vista. It's a nice preschool."

"Oh, it is. But like I told Gail, we're looking at enrolling him at Mirman next year. It is rather competitive, though. Lots of bright kids in L.A."

"There certainly are," I said and scooped Marcus up in my arms. "Ready to go home, kiddo?"

"Aw, do we have to?"

"Yup," I said and turned to Brittany. "Thanks for having him."

We said our goodbyes and walked down the street, and

as if the gods decided to laugh at me today, a ticket was indeed sitting underneath my windshield wiper. I looked around, but no parking enforcement scooter was within sight. it was as if the ticket had simply come down from the heavens and landed on my Pathfinder.

We drove home, inching through the start of rush-hour traffic. When we arrived, I lifted Marcus out of the car seat and we started walking from the driveway to the front door. I heard a voice call out my name and turned to see Beverly Pine walking toward us. Beverly was our next-door neighbor, a nice, gentle woman in her mid-seventies.

"Hi there, I'm surprised to see you home so soon," she said.

"Oh? Why's that?"

"Your dog walker came by. He said you and Gail were working late and he needed to feed Chewy and take her for a walk."

I stared at her. "What did he look like?"

"He was tall and a little thin and had reddish brown hair. He was so nice and I could hear Chewy barking. I guess you didn't want her to be cooped up all day without going and relieving herself outside. Or not eating dinner."

I nodded warily. We had given Beverly a set of keys to our house in the event of an emergency, or if we couldn't be home when a repairman came over. She was beyond reproach, but it was suddenly obvious she was way too trusting. There are downsides to being a nice person.

"And you let him in," I said slowly.

"Yes, and Chewy was very excited to see him."

"When was this?"

"I would think about an hour ago," she said, looking at her watch.

"Can you describe him any further?"

"Oh, well, he had the start of a black beard and he was wearing a blue baseball cap, Dodgers I think, and sunglasses. Kind of tall, like I said. Funny thing now that I think about it, the hair I could see under the baseball cap seemed red. You don't see red hair too often on people with a black beard. Why do you ask? Did I do something wrong?"

"I'm not sure. Has he gone?"

"Oh, yes, apparently, it didn't take long."

I licked my lips. "Mrs. Pine, would you be so kind as to watch Marcus for a few minutes for me? I need to do something."

"Why, of course."

"Go ahead and take him into your house. I'll be by in a couple of minutes."

Marcus went with Beverly Pine, and once they were safely inside her house, I moved quickly to our front door. Unlocking it carefully, I reached for my .357 Magnum and held it pointed upward. Walking inside, I glanced around and then methodically went through every room in the house. Opening closet doors, and pulling shower curtains open. I glanced into the back yard and saw Chewy walking around, sniffing a few leaves. Finally, I reached the master bedroom.

There was no one inside, but a brown paper bag sat obtrusively in the middle of our bed. I stepped closer, moving slowly and deliberately before carefully opening the bag and peeking inside. Before I called any authorities, I wanted to make sure this wasn't just something Gail had left behind. But inside the bag was a cluster of four chrome pipes, each about eight inches long and an inch in diameter, the ends of the pipe jammed shut. The pipes were tied together with rubber bands and connected to a series of wires that had been taped to a battery. I let go of the bag gently, and began moving quickly out of the bedroom, my walk changing rapidly to a run as I sprinted toward the front door.

Eleven

The LAPD bomb squad arrived within minutes, screeching their tires as they parked their SUV haphazardly in my driveway. They were, in no short order, followed by three black-and-white cruisers with their sirens wailing as they approached, but at least their drivers understood the basics of parallel parking.

I spoke briefly with the two officers from the bomb squad and gave them directions to the master bedroom, alerting them to the brown paper bag. The two men carefully put on their garb: thick khaki jumpsuits that were no doubt fireproof, chest protectors that would make a baseball umpire blush, knee pads, and an oversized silver helmet with a clear plastic shield. One of them carried a thirty-foot pole with an elongated device at the end, as well as an enforced steel box, no doubt for carting off whatever incendiary material they discovered. The officers walked slowly and methodically into my house, giving the entire scene the bizarre touch rarely found outside of a science fiction movie. Neighbors meandered out of their houses to gawk, but most were careful not to stray too far from their own property line.

After about forty-five minutes, the squad emerged and pronounced the house safe again. They told me the steel container held what I already knew to be the case, a crudely made pipe bomb, but they also told me something I did not know, that the explosive device was woefully inoperable. Whoever devised this knuckleheaded contraption had created a legitimate pipe bomb, but they attached it to a battery that was at least fifteen years old and had long since lost its juice.

A different officer on the scene asked if I had an idea who might have done this. I told them about Lucas Jerikoff, my investigation into the Henry Knapp killing, and Beverly Pine's description of the red-haired man who came to her door this afternoon. They asked me why Lucas Jerikoff might want to plant an explosive in my home, and I related my physical altercation with him. I was admittedly vague on the details of how the fisticuffs began, who threw the first punch and how it ended, employing an ex-cop's knowledge that self-incrimination was not a good thing to invoke.

The officer spent a few more minutes asking me for additional details, ones that included a physical description of Lucas, as well as his home address in the garage behind his mother's house. I told them about a video camera I had set up to record anyone approaching our front door, but if Jerikoff were wearing a disguise, that might not yield much. I then asked Beverly Pine to come outside and have a word with the officer while I kept a watchful eye on Marcus, who was busying himself watching TV.

Part of me wanted to deal with Jerikoff swiftly and directly. It was one thing to target me; it was quite another to endanger my family. And that was where it became personal, and where, on the surface, it seemed perfectly reasonable to have justice meted out in a swift manner. But I had apprehensions about going down this path. The anger boiling within me might not end in a good way, even if the target of my fury was the person who put the lives of my wife and son at risk.

"You got lucky," one of the bomb squad guys remarked. "Maybe this guy was just trying to send you a message. That, or he couldn't afford to buy new batteries."

"My guess is he just grabbed whatever was handy," I responded, and considered that if Lucas Jerikoff wanted to send a message, it was an awfully strange way to do it. The only message it conveyed was that he, Lucas, was a complete and total idiot.

"I'll tell you something," he continued. "Half the time the guys assembling these things just blow themselves up. Pipe bombs can be tricky. This one was loaded with shrapnel, mostly nails and screws. Would've been ugly if it had gone off properly."

Gail arrived just as we were finishing up, her expression stoic but her eyes were blazing, probably more with fear than with the seething anger I was feeling inside of me. After taking her through the mindless madness of what could have happened, we thanked the officers and went back into Beverly Pine's house. Beverly had ordered two pizzas and they showed up a few minutes later. I tried to pay, but Beverly would have none of that.

"It's all my fault," she wailed, her voice cracking as she got out some plates from her cupboard and set them around the table.

"You couldn't have known," Gail said slowly and reassuringly, providing the mature insight that we were unable to change the past, but we should guard against an incident like this ever happening again. Gail also added an admonishment, to please call one of us and confirm we were expecting a visitor before ever letting someone into our house again.

"Oh my, I will, I will," she said. "I seem to trust people too much. But I'm by myself all the time these days, I just don't always think straight. You know, ever since my kids moved up north a few years ago, it's been hard."

I put a slice of cheese pizza on Marcus's plate and two slices of veggie pizza on mine. I thought of trying to get Marcus to try the veggie one, but today was not a day that needed to be further upended by an argument.

"Daddy, what were the policemen doing at our house?" Marcus asked as he picked up his pizza, and sunk his front teeth in. He pulled it away from his mouth, tearing a small piece off in the process, and began chewing methodically.

"Well," I said, thinking quickly, observing that the slice I had just picked up was starting to droop back down toward the plate. "There are times the police need to do a check on someone's house. Make sure everything's okay."

"When you were a policeman, did you check on people's houses?" he asked.

"Sometimes. The goal is to keep people safe."

"Were we not safe?"

"It never hurts to be sure."

"Okay," Marcus replied, and seemingly satisfied with the answer, he turned to Beverly Pine. "How come you don't have a TV in your kitchen?"

"Marcus," Gail jumped in, "that's a little rude. We don't ask people that. And not everyone watches TV when they eat dinner."

"Why not?"

Beverly Pine gave a small laugh. "I have a TV in the bedroom. But if I have people over, I prefer to talk with them."

"Oh," he said, trying to process this, shrugging, and taking another bite.

"How do you like your preschool? she asked.

"I like it," Marcus answered as he chewed. "There's fun things to do. And I have a new friend named Frankie."

"Is Frankie a nice boy?"

Marcus stopped chewing for a minute and thought. "He's nice to me. But not so much to everyone. The teachers, I don't think they like him."

"Why not?"

"Today he told one of our teachers he was smarter than she was. Said he heard it from his mom, so it had to be true."

Beverly gave him an odd look. Gail and I glanced at each other.

"And Frankie's going to Ant ... where was that again, Daddy?"

"Antarctica," I said and turned to Beverly. "His parents are making a movie. Doing some filming there."

David Chill

"Well that's exciting," Beverly said.

"And I'm going with them!"

"You know, Marcus," Gail began slowly, "we haven't decided anything. And you don't travel anywhere that we don't go."

"That's not fair!" he exclaimed.

"Marcus, can I show you something?" Beverly asked, and carefully winked at Gail and me, a surreptitious act which Marcus did not see.

"Um, okay."

She took him by the hand and led him over to the refrigerator. Pulling out the bottom drawer, which held the freezer, she directed him to place his hand inside and then asked how it felt.

"Wow. That's cold."

"Yes," Beverly said. "That's what zero degrees feels like. And that's what it's like in Antarctica. In the summertime."

Marcus's eyes widened. "In the summer?" he asked incredulously.

"Yes. And in the winter it gets even colder. And it's very windy, too."

Marcus suddenly did not look happy. "That's not sounding like fun. How do you know this?"

"My son is a scientist. He travels to different parts of the world. He went to Antarctica many years ago. Said he'd never go back."

"Oh," Marcus said, and then looked up at her. "How come he doesn't live with you?"

Beverly smiled. "He's all grown up now. Grownups

160

usually live by themselves or with their own families. He lives near San Francisco and he has children of his own. They've been asking me to come live near them. I might."

Marcus walked back to the table, looking a little dejected. We finished eating, and after letting Beverly go on with profuse apologies for letting a violent intruder into our home, we finally convinced her not to worry anymore, using a this-could-happen-to-anyone theme. After we walked back into our house, Gail and I placed Marcus in front of the TV and handed him the remote. That lasted about thirty seconds. He managed to find his way to HBO where there was a war movie featuring loud machine-gun play. Gail took the remote and turned the channel to Nickelodeon.

"Aw, how come I can't watch this? Frankie's parents let him watch anything he wants."

"Really?" Gail asked.

"Yeah. His mom said it was good for him. To see different things. How come I can't do that?'

"Marcus," Gail explained, "there are some things we don't think you are ready for yet. You may not be for a while. But we'll decide that. As for Frankie, well, different parents have different rules."

"But that's not fair. He gets to watch anything he wants. I don't."

"You get a lot of nice things, Marcus," I pointed out sternly. "You just don't get everything."

"I don't see why not," he sulked. "You're not the boss of me."

Gail and I looked at each other, and the unspoken

words between us were rather clear. Marcus needed to make some new friends.

*

After Gail took Marcus into his bedroom for an in-depth chat about what constituted inappropriate manners, I found myself looking up Lucas Jerikoff's address again. Then the thorny scenarios began to materialize, the possibilities that a slapdash solution to confronting Jerikoff could easily go sideways in a hurry. As much as I hated to cede responsibility here, I concluded, once again, it was best to let the police handle this. I also suspected Jerikoff would probably not be home. When a person commits a dreadful act, their most likely course of action is to go where no one would find them that night.

I decided to look in on my other case, the wayward spouse, Madison Wynn. I checked out where the GPS devices were, and learned something interesting. Madison's BMW was parked at a hotel in Burbank. I could have simply told this to her father-in-law, but a man like Gary Wynn would be expecting confirmation. I didn't blame him. And as much as I hated leaving Gail and Marcus tonight, I strongly doubted they were in further danger. Plus Gail, a former campus security officer, was well skilled in how to handle a weapon.

Walking into the other room, I told Gail I needed to leave. Work related. She gave me a strange look, as if to query why I had to go on this particular night. I took her aside and told her to double-lock the doors and call 911 immediately if anything unusual happened. But I also assured her that it was extremely unlikely there would be any more drama. Lucas Jerikoff had made it a point to approach our house when we weren't there. People like that do not come back if they think anyone is home. Nevertheless, I called Detective Albert Rocca, explained the situation, and inquired whether he would be so kind as to request a patrol car pass by our house a few times tonight. He said it would be no problem. He also added that he had not forgotten about my request to get background information on Stuart, the john who was in the Santa Monica condo. Rocca said he had been very busy but would try and get to it tomorrow.

It was after 8:00 p.m. by the time I arrived at the Burbank Holiday Inn. Many years ago, comedians poked fun and laughingly referred to this area as "beautiful downtown Burbank." Back then it certainly was a dreary eyesore, with lots of aging shops and small commercial properties creating an ugly landscape. The closest thing to fine dining were mostly taco stands. But over the years, Burbank took steps to build out the Media Center, later rechristened as the Town Center, an attractive outdoor mall with trendy chain stores, movie theaters and nice restaurants. The Holiday Inn was part of this commercial space, a pair of twin 19-story high rises that further helped usher in gentrification.

I parked and walked inside the attractive, but quiet lobby. A desk agent wearing a jacket and tie stood at the check-in area, but he did not bother to look up from what he was doing. I knew better than to try and pull any guest information out of him, they were trained to deflect such requests. Taking another glance at Madison's photo, I noted she was blonde and cute and had a perky smile. I walked into the hotel restaurant and looked around. There were about a dozen tables occupied, but no woman there matched the photo. I went back into the lobby and found a house phone, picked it up, and asked the operator to connect me to Madison Wynn's room.

"Hmmm ... I'm sorry, sir, but we don't have a guest by that name here."

I took a breath. That an hour-and-ten minute drive might have been all for naught was the first thing that buzzed through my mind. It was possible Madison's tryst could have been with a man who registered under his name, thus making it next to impossible to ferret her out. I checked my iPad again and saw the vehicle was still here, parked in the general area of the garage.

"Is it possible Madison is using her maiden name?" I asked curiously.

"Nooo," came the slow response, "no Madison is registered here. But there is another guest registered under the name of Wynn. Should I connect you?"

"Please," I said, grateful I didn't need to tick off the names of any more Wynns.

A few seconds later the line was buzzing and a male voice picked up the phone.

"Yes?"

"Hello," I said, trying to pivot quickly and add some time. "Mr. Wynn?"

"Who is this?"

"Oh, this is the front desk, sir," I said, rapidly trying to think of a workable plan. "May I speak with Madison, please?"

The long silence that followed could be felt in the pit of my stomach. I had hit pay dirt somehow, struck a nerve, but I needed to figure out how to proceed. There was no handbook, and my copy of Dick Tracy's crime stoppers did not include a section on what to do when a sexual liaison you're investigating turns out to be different than you first imagined.

"What is this regarding?" he finally asked in a low voice.

"Oh," I said, thinking wildly. "We have a package here for her. Should we bring it up to your room?"

Another brief moment of silence. "No. I'll come down and get it."

And with that, the line went dead. I sat down on a long, uncomfortable couch and pretended to check the email on my phone, glancing up occasionally to see who might pass by. It took about ten minutes, but Trevor Wynn exited the elevator in a hurry and dashed quickly across the lobby, a black leather suitcase slung over his shoulder. He stopped at the front desk, spoke with the desk agent in hushed tones, and then walked briskly out of the hotel. I waited a few seconds after he left before following him outside. He strode hastily into the parking garage and disappeared.

There was no reason for me to follow him, but there was every reason for me to see if anyone else was coming out of the hotel. I walked back inside. A few minutes later, a tall, leggy woman in her 20s walked toward the front door. I pretended to fiddle with my phone as I snapped a photo. Gary Wynn wanted some photo evidence. The woman had straight red hair that went a little past her shoulders. She was clearly not Madison Wynn. Following her outside, I moved into the next step of my hastily arranged plan and called out.

"Mrs. Wynn?"

She turned and stared at me, mouth agape. Finally she found her voice, which turned out to be rather high-pitched. "Who are you?" she squealed.

"Funny, I was going to ask you the same question."

"What do you want?"

I held up my hands. "Sorry, I thought you might be Trevor's wife."

"That's insane. Is this a prank?"

"I wish it were. But no."

"Why would you think I was Madison?"

"I apologize," I said, not wanting to reveal anything further, and feeling a strong desire to remove myself from this awkward situation.

"Who are you?"

"That's not important," I said, thinking I needed to be the one asking the questions.

She gave me a strange look. "If I didn't know better, I'd say you're spying on me."

I thought for a moment and decided I had nothing to lose by asking. And I was a little curious, too. "How long have you been seeing Trevor?"

"Seeing Trevor?! Who the hell are you to ask me a

question like that?"

"Just curious."

"Oh, good heavens. I don't know who you are, but you're such an idiot. Screw you," she sneered and stormed off toward the garage.

I waited a minute before walking into the garage and standing unobtrusively by the exit, out of sight from any passing cars. A minute later, a navy BMW roared past. I checked the license plate and it matched Madison's. Maybe Trevor took her car today. Maybe he took her car yesterday. Maybe they just took the first car closest to them. I didn't know if Madison Wynn was engaged in an affair, but it did seem pretty clear that Trevor Wynn was.

Pulling out my phone, I called Gary Wynn and left him a voice mail saying I had some new information to share with him on his case. I said I was available to speak with him whenever it was convenient. It was not something I was looking forward to, and not something he'd want to hear. That was one of the problems with my job. Delivering bad news was part of my routine.

I was about to start walking toward my Pathfinder when a silver Honda Accord came tearing through the garage. The angry woman with the red hair was behind the wheel, gripping it tightly, and sitting bolt upright. I looked for the license plate, but it was moving too fast. In one sense, that was a good thing, because I was pretty sure she didn't see me; if she did she might have swerved to run me over.

Twelve

*The banging on my front door began a little after 4:00
am. I grabbed my .38 and stumbled into the living room.
A glance into the second bedroom told me Judy was not
there. I approached the door and asked, in a hoarse
voice, who was there.*

"Police! Open up!"

*I glanced though the peep hole and saw two uniformed
Santa Monica police officers. One was tall and thin and
young, the other stocky and, grizzled. I went to the
kitchen and tossed the .38 into a silverware drawer
before going back to the door and pulling it open.*

*"You Burnside?" the grizzled one snarled, his right
hand fixed on the service revolver that still sat in its
holster.*

"Yeah. That's me."

"You need to come with us."

"Why? This about that parking ticket I threw away?"

The pair looked at each other.

*"A wise guy," the older cop observed. "Come on. We'll
let you get dressed. We know you're a cop, so just don't
do anything stupid."*

"Like opening the door at four in the morning?"

"I said get dressed."

"What's this about? You're right, I'm a cop. LAPD. So do me a solid. At least tell me why you're dragging me in at this hour."

The grizzled cop shrugged. "Didn't know what shift you worked. Plus, we need to take you in here. Santa Monica."

"You mind at least telling me what this is about?"

"You know a Judy Atkin?"

"Uh-huh."

"We busted her this evening."

I stared at them. Judy had been staying at my place for a week. We had talks about next steps. Getting her a job, a place to live, a way to settle in. Maybe go back to school here. Figure out what path her life could take from here.

"You busted her for what?" I asked.

"For what?" the younger cop snorted. "For streetwalking. What did you think? Mr. Pimp."

"Huh?" I managed, my jaw dropping.

"Cops like you make me sick," he continued. "She's only seventeen. She's a child. And you put her to work for you. Turning tricks. Doing other guys. And then you pocket the money. You're disgusting You're a disgrace to the badge."

*

I put my feet up on my desk and looked out the window

at a blue sky dotted with clouds. This was the extent of my schedule for the morning. There was no other place I needed to visit, no other person who I could talk with about either the Henry Knapp case or the Rolf Anawak case. I picked up an Italian roast coffee from Starbucks and went to my office. I sipped on it for a while and looked out the window, wondering how sending Judy Atkin away last Saturday morning had propelled me down a path like this. Two people had been killed, and while I would hardly called them innocents, neither deserved to be dead right now. Homicides were often the product of either love or money, sometimes both, and they rarely solved anything except sealing the fate of the murderer, and usually providing them with an extended stay at a federal prison.

I pondered this some more, concluded nothing, and was about ready to go and get a refill on my coffee when the office phone rang.

"Burnside!" came a familiar voice on the other end of the line. I smiled at the sound of Johnny Cleary. It had only been a month since we had last talked, but it felt like forever.

"If it isn't the legendary Trojan coach," I said. "Or former coach, to be correct. You've got a new life in Chicago. How's it going?"

"Well ... the NFL is just plain different. You know the pressure we were under to win at SC? Take that and turn it up twenty notches. If the Bears lose a game, everyone from the owner to the fans to the media gets to screaming. I stopped listening to sports talk on the radio. They dissect every play like we have unlimited time in the middle of the game to decide what to call."

"Life in the fast lane. But it's the life you chose."

"I know. I could have stayed at SC forever. Would have worked out well, we had a great system in place. But I couldn't keep putting off the challenge. Could I make it at the next level? It's tough to ignore that siren sound."

"Your competitive spirit," I mused. "Or as they say, pride goeth before the fall."

"Ah," Johnny said. "I recall who I'm speaking with. You should have come with me. I could use a pal nearby."

"Realistically, I probably wouldn't have stuck it out in coaching much longer, even if you had stayed at SC. The money was great and I liked working with the kids. But it was a strain not being able to see my own son grow up."

"And now you're back in your old world," he chuckled. "More free time, more opportunities to get into trouble."

"Oh?" I asked apprehensively. "How do you mean?"

"I read the article on Walter Anawak's cousin. Tough one. But then I read how they already had a suspect in custody, a local P.I. was involved, and the name Judy Atkin came up. I remembered. Long time ago. That's why I called. Figured you might want to hear a friendly voice."

"I do. And you have a good memory. You know, Judy paid me a visit the other morning. Wanted my help."

"Wow," Johnny said. "Some people have no shame."

"True. I turned her down, but I got sucked into the case anyway. The irony is I actually have a lot of doubts about Judy being the culprit."

"So now you're working to set free the girl who ruined your life?" Johnny said. "Burnside, how do you get yourself into these messes?"

"I have the gift," I said, smiling ruefully. "Trouble just seems to find me. And you know Walter Anawak even paid me a visit. He wants to know what really happened to his cousin. Tough thing for the kid to go through."

"Well, he picked the right investigator. Obsessive-compulsive sums you up. That's why I hired you a few years back. And why I asked you to come to Chicago. Offer's still open. Not pleased with my secondary coach. Or my defensive coordinator."

"Oh?" I said, surprising myself that I still had any shred of interest. Not that I was going to move to Chicago, nor go back to a twenty-four-seven life of non-stop football, and effectively abandon my family once more. But it's nice to be asked.

"Yeah, the DC's aggressive, a little too much so. Takes a lot of risks, blitzes too much. I even have trouble getting him to go into a Tampa Two defense when we have a lead late in the game."

I smiled. The Tampa Two was occasionally called Cover Two, or the pre-vent defense, where the safeties play fifteen to twenty yards off the line of scrimmage, and the middle linebacker drops back deep into pass coverage. It's easy for the other team to move quickly down the field with short passes. But it's hard for their receivers to get behind the secondary and torch them for a long touchdown.

The Tampa Two was named after a Tampa Bay Buccaneer coach who pioneered it decades ago. Head coaches like it because it's a risk-averse strategy. Fans hate it because they don't like seeing the other team march quickly down the field at the end of a close game. The reality is that if defenses have the right personnel, the Tampa Two works more often than it doesn't. It can also lull the offense into a false sense that their strategy of short passes is working. But the odds are good that the defense will usually hold off a score, so long as they don't do anything dumb. Most coaches like it because it helps ensure wins and, along with that, some degree of job security.

"The Tampa Two took a hit the past few years," I said. "One of our guys at SC asked if we called it that because the safeties play so far back they might as well be in Tampa."

Johnny chuckled. "That's almost as good as what one of my guys on the Bears told me. In the league, Tampa Two means bedding two different girls in the same evening. Some guy did it in Tampa and he reached legend status."

"Interesting how this stuff takes on a life of its own," I said. "But if you want to run the Tampa Two, you're the boss. And the defensive guru. You can always overrule your coordinator."

"I can," he sighed. "But you know a head coach these days is like a CEO. Chief Executive Officer. The system works best when I delegate. I can't call all the defensive signals, I have to keep my head in the game on offense, too."

"Plus, you need a scapegoat to blame in case you lose."

"Ah, Burnside, always looking on the tactical side of things."

"You know me well. Hey listen, I'm glad you called. I have an odd question for you."

"Not a surprise. Shoot."

"NFL players and girls. I assume a lot of them use hookers."

Johnny chuckled. "Well that's not a question I get every day. I'll have to remind our beat writers to come up with some topics like that."

"Just curious."

"Uh-huh. Look, about a quarter of my team are married with kids and they just go home to their families after practice. Some of them just don't fool around. The rest? Sure, there are guys who'll hire hookers, but there's pride in not having to pay for it. A lot of them will go onto Tinder, or some other app, and hook up with a girl for a night. Girl likes it, she gets to be with a pro football player, the guy likes it, it's an easy date. And some of these players are real divas. It helps their self-image to know they can be with a lot of women. You'd be surprised at how insecure some of these stars can be. They need constant adulation."

"And I bet a lot of these types of guys go to strip clubs."

"Ah, football players and strippers," he mused. "About half of those types start the evening getting drunk and they wind up at a strip club."

"And the other half?"

"They start at a strip club and just get drunk. Yin and yang. Why do you ask?"

"It's just a world I'm trying to figure out, is all," I said.

"Not much to figure. Rich young guys and strippers.

The man's goal is obvious. The woman's goal is to separate the guy from as much money as they can. Pretty simple."

"Any of your players get in trouble in that area? No need to provide names."

"Sure, a few. Mix alcohol, men, women, and lots of money, and you'll always have a few situations. As long as it doesn't get violent, the profile is typically low."

"Yeah, that was the problem with Walter's cousin. There was violence involved. Supposed play acting, but not confirmable."

"Violence against women," Johnny said. "Nasty thing, and the NFL's trying to clean the league up. Some of these girls don't fawn over players the way the players' moms did. And I think a few players just have an inherent dislike for women. But you know, a lot of this gets back to the need to dominate. We teach these guys to dominate the other team on the field, and that attitude can extend beyond the game. That's where stuff goes off-kilter. Each guy has a different story, but there is a pattern. When the league spots this, they try and make an example out of a player who physically abuses women. They hope it keeps other guys in line. Sometimes it works, but not always. I take it Walter's cousin played football?"

"Junior college. Had trouble with academics, so he never went any further. And with Walter's cousin, there was a video recording. And then blackmail. The thing is it seemingly had nothing to do with Walter. Except the video was grainy and he could have been mistaken as the abuser."

"Interesting. Walter just sought you out?"

"Not exactly. When this case first got going, I paid a visit to Quentin Ware. Asked for an introduction."

"Oh man, don't remind me of Q," Johnny said.

"Why not?"

"I had him in my sights. We were going to bring him in as a free agent at the end of the summer, he was one of those guys I thought would be flying under the radar. The Rams took him in the 7th round of the draft. I figured he might not make the team and I could pick him up on waivers when they cut him."

"Sounds like he got a break when the player ahead of him went down with an injury."

"That's the way the league works. And now he seems to be developing. Smart player, great kid. Wish I had a tweener like him right now."

"Hey, Johnny," I said, thinking of something. "You're not going to use any of this stuff against Walter when the Bears come into town in a few weeks, are you?"

Johnny chuckled. "I might, I might not. Everything is fair game in the NFL. It's all about winning here. But the reality is that Walter is pretty self-contained. Not much shakes him up, we found that out when we played Washington. And for some guys, the football field is their refuge. Lets them block out all the other junk in their lives. So no, in this case, I probably won't have our guys taunt him. Wouldn't work. He's one smart *hombre*."

"Good," I said. "And speaking of when the Bears come into town ... "

"Oh, no. You want tickets?"

"Well ... "

"Look, the problem with living in L.A. for all those years is I have about a hundred ticket requests already. You may have to look for another source. My sense is you probably already have one on the Rams."

"Yeah," I said. "Maybe two."

*

After my conversation with Johnny, I did manage to pull myself out of my office chair and go get a refill at Starbucks. Even after ten minutes, I was still blowing softly on the coffee to cool it before I took my first sip. All of a sudden my office door opened. In walked a man who appeared to be in his mid-thirties. He had long, sandy blond hair that looked like it might have been bleached by the sun. His face was distinguished by a blond goatee. He was lean, but his body type struck me as muscular. His hands were large, possibly like a UFC fighter, or more likely, by a guy who did a lot of physical work.

"Mr. Burnside?" he started. "Can I come in?"

"Sure," I said warily and pointed to a chair across from my desk. "What's your name?"

"Pete Atkin," he said.

I stared at him, my wariness growing by the second. "Atkin," I repeated. "Do I have that right?"

"Yeah," he said. "I'm Judy's brother."

"Her brother," I repeated, thinking that aside from the hair color, he and Judy didn't look much alike.

"Stepbrother, I guess," he added quickly, as if reading my mind. "Her mom died when she was young. My mother married her dad. For a while anyway."

"I know some of her history," I said. "Why are you here?"

Pete Atkin pulled up a chair and sat down carefully, looking blankly at a small spot on the corner of my desk that held a rack of pens. He was wearing a black dress shirt, untucked, a pair of faded jeans, and boots.

"I heard Judy was in jail. I came out to try and help."

"I didn't know she had a stepbrother. You still live in Des Moines?"

He gave me a funny look. "Yeah. Still live in the area. How'd you know?"

"Like I said. I know her history. You read about her in the media?"

"She called me. Wanted me to bail her out again."

"Again?"

"I've bailed her out before. Here, in Miami, other cities. Wherever she goes, it's just part of her life."

"You must have some money."

"I've got the house my grandfather left me. I use that as collateral. That way we don't have to pay a bail bondsman ten percent every time she gets into trouble."

"You know she's in some real trouble here."

"Yeah. Like I said, I'm the one she calls. Looks like the police are charging her with two counts of manslaughter. Unfortunately they decided not to set bail, they think she's a flight risk. They want her to take a plea. Admit to killing both guys and they'll give her twenty-five years. Beats life imprisonment. Beats a lethal injection."

I considered this. "Tell me a little more about her

background. Why she left home. That kind of thing."

"Well, she claimed her dad sexually assaulted her. But that wasn't true."

"Oh, no?"

"She seduced him a bunch of times. I know. I watched a few of them. Out of the way, top of the staircase kind of thing. She came on to him, climbing into his lap, that sort of stuff. A girl looks like that, I'm sure her dad had trouble resisting. When my mom found out, she tossed both of them out of our house. Guy doing that with his own daughter, didn't matter to her that Judy was the instigator. Pretty disgusting any way you look at it."

I nodded and started giving thought to this. I hadn't known Judy well, but this didn't fit any pattern of deviant behavior I had ever come across. Girls rarely try and seduce their own fathers. If there was sexual abuse going on in the home, it was almost invariably an adult male who was the catalyst.

"After your mom threw them out, you still stayed in touch with Judy?"

"Yeah. I did. She's a weird chick, but I like her. Could just be because she's pretty, I don't know. I probably had a crush on her. Her mom's dying young had a bad effect. And her dad didn't have his head on straight. All that stuff, it starts with the parents."

"She got dealt a poor hand."

"Poor, yeah. I was two years older than her. I looked out for her when I could. But some things you just can't fix."

"So," I said, getting a little more curious. "Tell me what

happened after she left L.A. ten years ago."

"I only know bits and pieces," he said. "She'd mostly call when she was in trouble. She started out in Houston. After her experience here, I imagined she was done as a streetwalker. Then she got work in some brothel. You'd have thought it would be better, but it wasn't. Lots of abuse there, too."

I agreed. This was not unusual. Streetwalkers I had arrested told me if a john who pulled over in his car seemed dangerous, they could just walk away. They felt that on the street they had some semblance of control, that they were their own boss. Working in a brothel meant doing what they were told, and if they turned down a client, they'd likely be fired or beaten. People who ran brothels couldn't afford to let the girls dictate terms.

"She stay in Houston for long?"

"Couple of years. Quite a lot of business there, so I understand. Then she had stops in Atlanta, Orlando, Tampa, eventually Miami. Spent a long time in Miami, she didn't want to come back to a cold-weather climate, and certainly not to a straight-laced city like Des Moines. Although there's hookers there, too."

"Oldest profession," I said. "Wherever there are men, there'll be women willing to service them."

"Yeah. I suggested she do something else, but the money's too good. She told me she tried working as a stripper, but she didn't like it. Felt vulnerable."

"Oh?"

"Yeah, strange, huh? She was okay being with one guy at a time, but having a bunch of guys leer and scream stuff at her wasn't her thing."

I looked at him curiously. "Why are you telling me all this?"

Pete Atkin considered this for a long moment. "When I went to see Judy, she seemed to know you were still investigating this."

"Right," I said, not bothering to add that I was the one who found Judy and handed her over to the police. Or that Walter Anawak was now paying me to figure out what happened, and find out who was blackmailing him.

"Judy heard you were still looking into stuff. Talking with girls who worked at that place in Santa Monica. You spoke with one of the guys running the show."

"She heard that, huh?"

"Yeah. I guess Candy came by to see her."

"Okay," I said, wondering how the Santa Monica police let Candy in to talk to Judy without realizing she had been standing outside at the time Henry Knapp got clobbered.

"Anyway, Judy appreciates everything you've done for her. But she's going to take the plea bargain and get this part of her life done with."

"Take the twenty-five years?" I asked incredulously.

"She'll get time off for good behavior. Be out before she's forty-five. Maybe sooner. Could have something of a life left. That would be nice if it happened. Anyway, that's her decision. She just wanted me to come over and tell you."

I nodded and thanked him. And then Pete Atkin got up and ambled out of my office.

Thirteen

I thought about calling Barney Sack. I was puzzled why Pete Atkin looked familiar. I wondered whether the temperature in Antarctica really dropped to zero degrees during the summer. I stared out the window pondering these issues for a little while, but mostly watched a large white cloud slowly dissipate into small puffs within the backdrop of a bright blue October sky. I waited for something to happen, an endeavor which normally disappoints. Then my phone rang.

"Burnside," came the somewhat familiar voice on the other end of the line. "Rocca here. Hey, I've got something for you."

"I'm all ears."

"That cell phone number you asked me to check out? We did a reverse lookup. It's registered to a Stuart Kolodney. Lives in El Segundo, down by the airport."

"Okay, thanks. Much appreciated. And hey, detective?"

"Yeah?"

"Thanks for sending a car around last night to check on my house."

"Not a problem. Looks like everything was copacetic. Give my regards to Gail," he said and hung up quickly before I could ask him for any more favors.

I did a search on Stuart Kolodney and found an El Segundo address for him. He was 41 years old and lived with a Melissa Kolodney who was 39, and most likely his spouse. I scanned through LinkedIn and discovered he worked in El Segundo as an engineer with a large defense contractor, Southway. He was even kind enough to post a photo of himself.

Approaching Kolodney at his home, with his wife, and perhaps even his children in viewing distance did not strike me as a good first step. An option to consider down the road, in the event he was uncooperative. Leverage might not be needed, and if Sadie's assessment was correct, Mr. Kolodney might crack easily.

I called the Southway corporate headquarters number and asked the operator for Stuart Kolodney. He picked up on the first ring.

"Hi, it's Stuart."

"Hello, Stuart, my name is Burnside. I'm an investigator and I'd like a few minutes of your time. Can we meet today?"

"What is this in regard to?" he asked, a slight hint of suspicion in his voice.

"It is in regards to that unpleasantness over in Santa Monica on Saturday night. I think you know what I'm talking about."

There was a long silence before he responded. "Just what do you know?"

"I know you were there at the time. And without getting into any more detail, I'd rather not do this over the phone. And I don't think you want me coming over to your house in El Segundo to talk about it, do you?"

"No, God no," he said quickly. "All right. Look, there's a little restaurant a few blocks from my office, called the Yabba Grill. It's on Kilroy, here in El Segundo. Park in the structure next door. I'll meet you there in an hour."

El Segundo is Spanish for "the second." A century ago, the city was named after Standard Oil's second oil refinery, which I imagined was as good a way to name a city as any. Los Angeles is Spanish for "the angels," and one could read into that what they will. The drive down to El Segundo only took about twenty minutes, but finding parking in the structure felt like it lasted almost as long. After winding my way up ten levels of parking and finding no spaces, I wound my way down most of the way before squeezing my Pathfinder into a space meant for compacts. I slowly opened the driver's side door, taking pains not to scratch the Toyota Camry parked little more than eighteen inches to my left. I shuddered at the thought of having to do this every day.

The Yabba Grill was more of a cafeteria than a restaurant, serving a hodgepodge of questionable looking sandwiches, wraps, soups, and salads, along with the daily special, which happened to be turkey meat loaf today. Photos of the different options were pasted onto a cardboard sign. They also claimed to proudly pour Starbucks coffee, but one sip told me it either wasn't Starbucks, or maybe they brewed it in a very different way. I sat down on a white plastic chair at a white plastic table and watched the entrance for Kolodney. At exactly one minute past the appointed time, he walked through the doors and looked around.

Stuart Kolodney was of average height, average weight, and wore a pair of silver-framed glasses. He had thinning brown hair that was combed back with the help of some pomade. He wore a nervous expression as he scanned the room, and I waited a couple of beats before acknowledging him; seeing someone this jittery was a concern. They could be more apt to talk freely, but they were also more apt to do something stupid.

I stood up and made eye contact with him, smiled, and gave what I hoped was a reassuring nod of my head, signaling that he should feel free to come join me. He walked over purposefully before stopping suddenly and looking around the room once more. Satisfied there was no one nearby who was familiar, and that no uniformed police officers were visible, he approached, introduced himself and shook my hand.

"Would you like some coffee?" I asked politely. Burnside, the generous soul.

"No, no thank you," he said and sat down across from me. "How did you find me?"

"I'm a licensed private investigator," I said, and handed him my card. The poor guy was so nervous I decided not to flash my fake badge and risk sending him into a full-blown panic. "I'm not with the police. But I am doing an investigation and I'd like your cooperation."

"I didn't do anything wrong," he said quickly.

"Didn't say you did."

"I was visiting a friend in Santa Monica. I didn't see what actually happened. I was in another room."

"Ah, yes. Visiting a friend," I said, suddenly thinking I may need a more stern approach if we were to get anywhere here. "Look, I know what you were there for and that you were with Sadie. We don't need to discuss those sordid details at length. I'm more interested in what went on in the living room. And I'm not going to stop until I find out. Don't hide anything, trust me, I'll be able to figure it out if you're not being truthful. Do you know what it means to be an accessory after the fact?"

"I ... I think so," Kolodney said as he licked his lips. It was easy to tell he wanted to wrap this up and get out of here.

"Let me clarify. It means aiding a person who has committed a crime. So by not divulging what you know, you could very well be an accessory after the fact. By not coming forward right away, you have placed yourself in jeopardy. The only way out, and I mean the *only* way, is to tell me everything you know about what happened on Saturday night. Right now. Again, I'm not the police, and I'm not looking to jam you up. But I will if I have to."

Kolodney took a very deep breath, leaned forward, and lowered his voice. "Okay. I was with Sadie. I paid her five-hundred dollars for sex. I don't want this getting out. I'm married with kids."

"Go on. Again, I'm more interested in what happened in the other room."

"After we finished, there was a commotion in the living

room. We walked out and I saw this big guy slap a blonde girl in the face and throw her on the couch. Then he began tearing her clothes off. The girl was struggling, but he was pretty big and he was on top of her."

"Uh-huh."

"I didn't know what to do. The guy was huge. I wasn't going to jump in and break it up and risk getting killed."

"Of course you weren't."

"Hey, I didn't know what the deal was. She was probably working there. Maybe that was part of what he paid for, their arrangement, who knows. Sadie told me there's a price for everything. I just wanted to get out of there. I was going to have enough problems explaining to my wife why I was late coming home from my poker game. Last thing I needed was to end up in the emergency room."

"Wouldn't want that. What's this about a poker game?"

"That's just the excuse I gave my wife. Anyway, Sadie and I go back in the bedroom and wait it out. We heard some more commotion and then it was quiet for a bit. And so we walked back out again."

"And that's when you found the body."

"Yes. Looked like he got hit over the head. There was this bright blue device lying next to him."

I frowned. "Device?"

"Yeah. I think they used to call it the Club. You'd snap it onto your steering wheel to prevent your car from being stolen. Even if a thief broke into your car and started the ignition, they couldn't drive it because the steering wheel was locked. I don't think many people use them these days."

I remembered how popular the Club once was. For a while, it did reduce auto thefts because it was a visual deterrent for joy riders. Then the more sophisticated thieves discovered that, with a hacksaw blade, they could simply cut through a steering wheel in a matter of seconds. They could then remove the Club and actually use it to break the lock on the steering column without having to carry extra tools to do the job. Thieves found they could actually use the Club to help them steal the car. The only people who still use a Club these days were those without a newer car, because the newer cars have an electronic ignition system.

"So the Club you saw was bright blue."

"Yeah. It was lying on the carpet, a few feet away from him. Looked like it had bloodstains all over it, too. The whole scene looked nasty. My guess is that this wasn't part of their arrangement."

Fourteen

I didn't elicit much more out of Stuart Kolodney, but I had pulled out enough. It was almost lunchtime and I was hungry, but the Yabba Grill wasn't going to cut it. Instead, I went for a wet burrito at a little hole-in-the-wall in Manhattan Beach called El Tarasco. An old USC buddy had introduced me to this hidden gem many years ago, but I rarely got down to the South Bay enough to revisit it. A wet burrito starts out no different from any other burrito: a flour tortilla stuffed with beef, beans and heaven knows what else. But then it is smothered with a spicy ranchero sauce and cheese, and baked in an oven until everything sizzles. At El Tarasco, they jazzed it up by topping it with sour cream and guacamole, and then naming it the Junior Super Deluxe Burrito. It was a mouthful to say, but a pleasure to eat.

There were no tables here, just one long counter that seated about a dozen people. I had gotten there early enough to get a seat without waiting; by the time I finished, there were a good two dozen people standing in a line that spilled outside. As I departed, I took a look at the blue Pacific, felt good about the warm sun shining on my face, and decided I had plenty of time to take a stroll by the beach.

Three blocks down a steep hill was the Strand, nothing more than a concrete walkway used by pedestrians, dog walkers, and an occasional bicyclist refusing to stay on a separate bike path. I thought about the Judy Atkin case and knew I was beginning to scratch through the surface. If Judy had indeed killed Henry Knapp, it could easily have been self-defense. Although it struck me as highly unlikely Judy killed Rolf Anawak. There was no motive, no incentive, and it was out of character, at least from what I had known of the Judy Atkin from my past. I suppose ten years working in a grizzly profession could change anyone. But while a woman could easily monetize her body and sell it for sex, it was a huge step to go from that to committing murder. And as Judy reminded me, she didn't seem to mind pain.

Rolf Anawak's killer had shot him from behind, in a darkened alley, and had executed him for reasons only related to money. It was a planned hit. Rolf had foolishly paid $20,000, a sum he had borrowed to try and protect his cousin from career ruin. Something had gone haywire in the deal, and he had returned to Santa Monica on that fateful night. He might have learned the identity of the blackmailers, the bad guys might have been trying to continue the shakedown, or it was conceivable they just wanted Rolf out of the way to cover their tracks. But nothing about this hit, save for the long blonde hair in that grainy video, pointed to Judy.

I needed to contact Callaway and Sack again, and I probably should have done so right away to alert them I had learned of the murder weapon that killed Henry Knapp. But I didn't have the bright blue Club in my possession, nor did I know where to find it, a vexing problem that would guarantee a short conversation. It struck me that Sack and Callaway might not even care, that they just wanted to wipe a homicide off the books and put a community at ease. By alerting the decent citizenry that all was safe, that the killer had been apprehended, everyone could go about their business peacefully. But as much as Judy had wronged me, as much as her actions had spun my career down a devastating path, I didn't think she deserved a fate that included a long prison term. Even if her stepbrother insisted that this was the road she was intent on going down.

I wanted to have another word, and perhaps another punch or two, with Lucas Jerikoff. But whatever his role might have been in trying to blow up my house, nothing in that encounter would likely lead me closer to Rolf Anawak's killer. Jerikoff could be pushed around, but I doubted he'd admit to anything or lead me to whoever was involved in these murders. I needed to let the LAPD handle Jerikoff, and I kept reminding myself of that, even though I kept thinking of going rogue.

I had an inkling that the path to cracking this case lay in finding Owen Magid, and I didn't know how to do that. Going back to his Hollywood apartment would probably be to no avail, the girls had undoubtedly told him about my last visit. And after hearing that Judy was dragged away in plastic handcuffs, I assumed Owen would not be returning there anytime soon.

There was one person I hadn't talked with yet. He seemed like a bit player in all this, even though both murders emanated from his involvement, coincidental as it may have been. And after lunch and a leisurely walk by the beach, I had little else on my calendar today. I phoned Walter Anawak and, after giving him a brief update on my limited progress, I asked for the number of Felix Montoya, the mover that his cousin Rolf worked for. Surprisingly, Walter had it in his phone, he mentioned that sometimes calling Felix was the only way he could get a hold of Rolf. I called Felix Montoya and asked if I could speak with him this afternoon. He sounded tired and hesitant, but I told him I was investigating Rolf's murder and he perked right up. Said he was working on a job in Van Nuys, and I could come by this afternoon.

I drove the twenty-five miles up to Van Nuys, an area of the San Fernando Valley that had established itself lately as more of a hotbed for drugs and crime than for containing exceptionally desirable neighborhoods. I navigated my way to the address Montoya gave me on Wish Avenue, a surprisingly pleasant street, lined with large, well-maintained, two-story homes. Not everything is as you'd expect, even in the Valley. I parked behind what looked like a converted UPS truck that had been painted slate gray. Two heavy-set men were sitting on a curb drinking from bottles of blue Gatorade.

"Hi there," I said, approaching them. "One of you must be Felix Montoya."

"That's me," said a man with an ample gut, wearing a dark blue t-shirt and jeans. He stood up and shook my hand, his grip strong and rather powerful.

"I'm Burnside. I called earlier," I told him, handing him my card.

"Sure," he replied, and pointed to the curb "Mind if I sit? Been a long day."

"Not a problem," I said, lowering myself down onto the curb to join them. "I'd like to talk to you about Rolf."

Montoya took a swig from his Gatorade. "Rolf. Yeah, real shame. Good guy. Had some problems, but don't we all."

I thought for a moment. "Did he have beef with anyone?" I asked.

"Nah. He got along with most people. A little quiet at times. He just moved here from Alaska, I think he was having some trouble fitting in. You know, L.A.'s not an easy place to live."

I sighed. I had heard it all before. L.A. was expensive, people could be nasty, it was a town full of phonies. All true, but if you found your niche and stayed around decent people, it could be a pleasant experience. L.A. was like anywhere else in that regard. You just had to find like-minded compatriots. It was also a place where almost anyone could come and get a fresh start. In that regard, it was like Alaska, but a little different as well. Some people moved to the great white north, specifically because they didn't know anyone, and no one knew them. Like in L.A., you could get that fresh start and begin a new life. But Alaska wasn't just a fresh start; it was the final frontier.

"Rolf have any bad habits?" I asked, watching him closely.

Montoya shrugged. "I don't know. Like what?"

"How about gambling?"

"No," he shook his head. "Rolf never mentioned that. And I'm sure you know about his cousin playing for the Rams. He was really proud of Walter. If he bet on any games, he didn't tell me. But I don't think he did. Guys who gamble like to talk about it. Especially when they win. Show how smart they are."

"What did Rolf like to do outside of work?"

Montoya hesitated and thought about this for a moment. "Well, he liked girls. But he wasn't the best looking guy, you know."

"He use some kind of service?" I asked carefully.

Montoya nodded slowly. "Yeah. And I feel bad. I'm the one who told him about it. I wish I never did. Rolf might be alive today."

I considered this. When a friend or loved one passes away before their time, people can take it upon themselves to absorb blame. If only they had done this or that differently, the person might still be alive today. It was survivor's guilt. In this case though, Felix Montoya might well be correct.

"I wouldn't blame yourself," I told him, trying to be benevolent. "Not everyone who pays for a girl ends up like Rolf. This was highly unusual."

"I guess," he said, not entirely wanting to lift the guilt from his shoulders.

"What was the name of this service?" I asked.

"It's called Loco Girls. Loco as in crazy. It's a website. You go on it, there's girls there, they live all over L.A. Most of them post pictures and phone numbers. You call them and talk for a few minutes about price and what they do. It's pretty simple. Not cheap, but I got the feeling Rolf wasn't hurting for cash. I think his cousin was helping him out."

"Then you've used this Loco Girls."

"Yeah. Can't say as I'm proud, but it is what it is. I never had an issue with any of these girls. They've always been pretty nice."

"Did Rolf talk to you about any of these girls? Maybe about a problem he was having?"

"No. But last week he was really quiet, I could tell something was bothering him. And Monday he didn't show up to work. I had to go over to Home Depot to grab a helper," he said, jerking a thumb to the large man sitting quietly next to him.

"When was the last time you spoke with Rolf?"

"Monday night. I asked if he was coming to work on Tuesday. He apologized and said he didn't think so. Had some personal stuff he had to do. Didn't sound like himself."

"Anything in particular?"

"He thanked me for taking him on. It was almost like he was quitting, but he didn't actually say the words. Almost like he knew he'd be leaving somehow. Like he knew something was going to happen."

*

Barney Sack looked distinctly overworked as he sat in his sterile office, giving direction to a pair of uniforms who stood rigidly in front of him. He noticed me but did his best to display no recognition. When he dismissed the pair, he watched them walk out the door before sighing and turning his eyes my way.

"Burnside. You should try calling first."

"I really should. But thanks for seeing me anyway."

"Uh-huh. When P.I.s drop by unexpectedly, they usually want something. So, what do you want?"

"I'd like to talk with Judy Atkin."

Sack snorted with the type of righteous arrogance that came part and parcel with being a boss. "Why would I do that? And why do you even want to see that skank? You brought her to us. Or is dementia now setting in with you?"

"I had a situation happen yesterday," I said.

"What's that?"

"Somebody planted a pipe bomb in my house. Got an elderly neighbor to let him in. He wore a disguise, but I'm pretty sure it was Lucas Jerikoff. You may recall he's part owner of that condo on 6th and Broadway."

"Right. Why'd he target you?"

"I told you I paid him a visit the other day. What I didn't exactly tell you is that it got a little rough. Hard to believe, but he took exception to something I said."

"Can't imagine how that could happen," Sack chuckled. "But Jerikoff didn't strike me as a tough customer."

"Don't have to be tough to blow up a house, especially

with my family inside. A lot more cowardly than tough, I'd say."

"And you think Judy Atkin will tell you where to find him," he said.

"I think I'm running out of leads. And I think people sometimes open up when you least expect them to."

Sack shook his head. "I don't normally let inmates visit with anyone besides their lawyer. Or family once in a while."

"I've got a bargaining chip for you," I said.

"Oh? What's that?"

"The murder weapon. At least for the Henry Knapp case. It's that old device called the Club. Something people used to slap onto their steering wheels to deter car thieves."

"I remember. All it did was scare off teenagers. You're saying Judy used a Club to kill Knapp."

"Someone did. I don't think it was Judy."

Sack snorted again. "Okay. We can run DNA evidence on it, I suppose. Where is it?"

"I don't know."

"Sheesh. You determined the murder weapon, you just don't have it?"

"Pretty much. If I come across it, I'll be happy to hand it over."

"Big of you. And I assume you're going to find the gun they used in taking out Rolf Anawak, too?"

"If I see it, you're my first call."

"I'd like to get this case wrapped up," he said. "But I don't know if Judy'll help you any. She's looking like she's ready to plea bargain this."

"Oh?" I said, feigning surprise.

"We've got some DNA evidence. Knapp's precious bodily fluids inside of her. Suspect says she was sexually assaulted. Can you believe that? A whore claiming she was raped?"

"Actually, yeah" I managed, recognizing that even prostitutes are human beings. Just because a woman agrees to provide sex for one client, it doesn't mean every male has suddenly been given a get-out-of-jail free card to have their way with her.

"Try finding a jury to buy into that one. Aw, what the hell, I'll send you through. I don't think you'll get much, but I do owe you for bringing her in. And for that measly tidbit of information on that Club. What color was it?"

"Blue," I said. "Bright blue."

"And how'd you learn about this?"

I thought of Stuart Kolodney and envisioned him being grilled by the police. "Thorough investigative work," I said.

Barney Sack rolled his eyes before reaching over, picking up the phone and barking a few commands into it. About thirty seconds later a young woman in a khaki uniform appeared at the door.

"Letty, take Mr. Burnside over to see Judy Atkin in holding. Put them in an observation room and watch them. Let me know if anything gets rough. I don't want Mr. Burnside leaving here with any bruises."

"Yes, sir," she answered, and made a quick motion with her eyes to follow her. I gave a wave of thanks to Barney

Sack, who had already turned away.

It was a good ten-minute walk to the jail area, and we trotted down a few flights of stairs and took an underground passage to get to the next building. Everything here seemed to be painted white: the walls, the ceiling, the banisters. Even the floor was a white linoleum, shiny as if a janitor had just applied some floor wax.

Officer Letty took me into a room with a large two-way mirror and told me to wait. There was a table and two gray-metal folding chairs. I sat down for a good twenty minutes before Judy Atkin was brought into the room. She wore an orange jail-issued jumpsuit with a white t-shirt underneath; her hands were bound to a belly-chain restraint. Leg irons were wrapped around her ankles. Her blonde hair was straggly and her big blue eyes looked tired. There was still a prettiness to her face, but it seemed to be eroding by the day.

"So we meet again," I said.

"You come here to gloat?" she asked, sitting down on one of the chairs.

"No. Just to better understand some things. Maybe get some closure."

"Well, you finally got what you wanted. I'll be going away for a long time. For something I didn't do."

I ignored the irony of her comment; ten years ago, I almost went away for a crime I didn't commit, thanks to her. "Heard you may be taking a plea," I said. "Why do the time when you didn't do the crime?"

Judy looked past me and seemed to be trying to put her thoughts into words. "I don't ... I don't think I really have a choice."

"Everyone has choices," I countered. "Why make this one?"

"I'll get twenty-five years for both homicides. The prosecutor said if I pled guilty to both, I'd get to serve them concurrently. With good behavior I might serve fifteen. I'll still have something of a life after I get out."

"And you'll have a criminal record," I pointed out. "Not that your career choices have been so good thus far."

"If you hadn't arrested me ten years ago, I would have been fine."

"No, you wouldn't. You were seventeen. If I didn't nab you some other cop would have. Or you would have eventually been picked up by a john with a few screws loose. You wouldn't be the first working girl to wind up dying alone and getting buried in a shallow grave."

"I've gotten by this far," she protested.

"Sure," I said, spreading my hands apart, palms up. "Look where it's gotten you."

"Okay, but what do you want? It's like, why do you even care about me?"

I thought about this, and I didn't respond right away. I felt sorry for Judy in the same way I felt sorry for a lot of people who grew up in a home where one parent wasn't there. Just like me. But I had the benefit of a loving mother, at least for eighteen years. Judy didn't even have that. I was still trying to figure out the answer as to why I really cared. But as is my custom, I always seemed to have more questions than answers.

"Why do you seem to *not* care about yourself?"

She frowned and looked a little perplexed. "I don't understand."

"You're going to plead guilty to two murders you didn't commit. And I'm sure you know who killed Henry Knapp. Why aren't you coming forward with this?"

"Like I said, I don't think I have much of a choice."

"And like I said, we all have choices," I said. "Sometimes they're just not good ones."

"Look," she said wearily, "if I keep my mouth shut and take the plea, I'll get out eventually. If I don't, I won't last twenty-four hours on the street."

Now it was my turn to look perplexed. "How's that? Because whoever did this will kill you if they find out?"

"Right."

"That makes no sense. If you hand over the murderer and testify against them, they'll be the one in prison for the next twenty-five years."

"It's complicated," she sighed and buried her face in her hands.

"Meaning what? That this person has a partner? Somebody that will commit another murder to shut you up?"

"Yes," she said, without removing her hands from her face.

I sucked in some air. I looked at the far wall. I turned and looked at the two-way mirror, which only showed my own reflection. I turned back to her.

"Your brother came to see me. He seems to think the same thing. Is Pete someone who might be able help you?"

Judy took her hands from her face and gave me an odd

look. "My brother?"

"Yes," I said. "Your brother came by my office this morning. Or stepbrother, I guess. Pete. He seems resigned to your going away, too."

Judy stared at me. "Pete?"

"That's right, Pete came by," I said. "Pete Atkin. Blond hair, goatee, from Des Moines? This ring a bell for you?"

"No," Judy said. "I don't have a brother. Or a stepbrother. I don't know anyone named Pete. In fact, I don't know what the hell you're talking about."

Fifteen

My talk with Judy Atkin created plenty of baffling questions, but had yielded precious few insights. Should a person who staunchly claims they did not commit a crime plead guilty to it? Is it more palatable to take a plea and serve a long prison sentence or risk the dangers freedom may bring? Could it be possible a jury would believe that a prostitute could be sexually assaulted? And if Pete Atkin wasn't Judy's step-brother, who in the world was he?

As I drove home, I pondered these questions, ones which made my long slog through traffic seem to go quicker. Maybe that was the trick to surviving the otherwise agonizing L.A. commute, to be thoroughly distracted with thoughts of an entirely unrelated topic, so that the endless mass of cars ahead of you became little more than scenery.

I walked into my house and received a surprise, although unlike yesterday's shocker, this was a surprise of a more pleasant kind. Marcus was sitting on the couch, trying to instruct a visitor on the rules for our game of Leaners, flinging cards against the far wall in the attempt to get them to land standing up. He was sitting in the middle of the couch, in between Gail and Honey Roper. He seemed, like any other red-blooded American male would, to be enjoying himself immensely.

"Daddy! Look who's here!" Marcus shouted.

"I can see. What a nice surprise."

Honey smiled, stood up, and gave me a kiss on the cheek. Not to be outdone, Gail stood up and gave me a slightly longer kiss on the mouth. Gail had never demonstrated any jealousy or concern about Honey, but she may have subconsciously been establishing territorial rights. I was happy to see them both, but I was mostly happy to be home.

"My three favorite people," I smiled and turned to Honey. "To what do we owe the pleasure of this visit?"

"I was in the neighborhood," she said, smoothing out her dark blonde hair. "Not far. A meeting at Silicon Beach."

"I hear that's what they're calling Venice now," Gail said.

"It is," Honey smiled.

"Well, I'm very pleased you thought of visiting us," I said.

"Daddy, can Honey stay for dinner?" Marcus asked.

I looked at Gail. "Fine by me."

"And by me," Gail said. "It's been a while."

"Sold," Honey said, and smiled down at Marcus. "That means you get to beat me a few more times at Leaners."

We took a poll and Gail decided I should go out and pick up something for dinner, preferably along the lines of salads for the ladies and burgers for the men. I had learned to not argue about such small matters, and mostly do what I was told. Happy wife, happy life.

After a quick scan through Yelp, we settled on The Counter on Ocean Park, just below Carl Hillebrand's office. I was now developing expertise in the gourmet burger market. I sat at the bar as my takeout order was being filled, downed a pint of Smog City IPA, a nice amber ale, and tried to reflect upon my day. I barely got past thinking of my call with Johnny Cleary when I heard my name called, and a large shopping bag full of food was awaiting me. I drove home wondering about Stuart Kolodney and about Judy's supposed step-brother, but all I really ended up with was a small headache and a growing thankfulness that, despite the problems I had experienced in my own life, things could be far worse. I was, after all, about to have dinner with two beautiful women and a marvelous child who seemed to utter mostly adorable things every day.

I arrived home and spread dinner across the kitchen table. While my cheeseburger was enhanced with grilled onions, tomato wedges, and a few dill pickle slices, Marcus understandably liked a plain hamburger on a bun and that was it. My one attempt, a few months earlier, at trying to sneak some lettuce and tomato on his burger was met with horror, outrage, and a refusal to even look at his meal, much less taste it. I had come to believe stubbornness is learned behavior, although I certainly can't imagine who he learned it from.

Marcus and I did agree on one thing: The Counter's

burgers were very good, in fact, remarkably good. They even bested my Plan Check burger, and I decided I had found my new local favorite, at least for one more day. The Counter actually formulated something better, and they didn't need to gussie it up with ketchup leather or a sunny-side-up egg. I'd still visit The Apple Pan, having practically grown up on their hickory burgers, but nostalgia and comfort food could only go so far.

Gail and Honey were happy with their salads, and after a quick cleanup, I took Marcus into the backyard and let him play fetch with Chewy, who would, after some prodding, go chase the ball after Marcus threw it. The adults sat down on the patio and watched them from a distance. Gail brought out two bottles of Blue Moon, one for me and one for Honey. She poured an iced tea for herself.

"Domestic life seems to agree with you," Honey commented, taking a sip of Blue Moon straight from the bottle.

"Today is a good day," I said, as Gail eyed me and slipped her hand into mine. Everything seemed remarkably calm and placid, but the idea that someone had entered our home with a pipe bomb yesterday still gave me the jitters.

"One day at a time," Honey smiled.

"Yup," I said, and decided to redirect the conversation to focus my mind on other things. "How did your evening go the other night with your father and that guy you're seeing, I think his name was Ethan?"

"Better than I feared," she said. "Ethan's an attorney, so Dad liked that. Something in common. My father went to law school mostly so he could understand contracts. Said it made him a better sports agent. He never actually practiced law."

Or obeyed many laws, I thought to myself. "Being a parent is a lifelong job," I mused.

"Well, you're off to a good start," Honey said. "Marcus is terrific. You should be proud."

"We are," Gail smiled.

"Speaking of parenting, how is your investigation going?"

I blinked for a moment and then realized she was talking about the Wynn family. Honey, with all of her beauty and charm, had this ungodly ability to move from subject to subject quicker than most people could keep up. I coughed and said I had made progress, but since I hadn't debriefed Gary yet, I should probably not comment. Honey smiled that glittering smile.

"All right," Honey said. "I know some things are confidential. If you're able to discuss it one day, I'd love to know the juicy details."

"Infidelity," I mused, taking a swig of Blue Moon myself. "I hate investigating it, but it seems to earn me a nice living. Figuring out if a spouse is cheating or not."

"Based on what I've been exposed to in life," Honey sighed, "the odds are pretty good they are. Marriages are tough to maintain."

"It's funny," Gail said. "When I was young, my grandmother told me she married my grandfather because he was a good man, he had a steady job, and he didn't drink. The main rule she had to follow back then was don't have sex with someone else before you got married. Today, so many people have had multiple relationships, breakups, cohabitations. Then they get married and the main rule changes to don't have sex with someone else *after* you get married."

"And a lot of people have trouble following that one," Honey remarked.

"Ah, yes," I said. "Growing up in Las Vegas and working in hotel management, I'm sure you've seen some things."

"More than I cared to," she replied.

"Understood," I said. "And I've got another investigation I'm working on now. You heard about those two murders in Santa Monica this week?"

"Sure, it's been all over the news. Including the one with Walter Anawak's cousin."

I peered at her. "You know about Walter?"

"Dad tried to sign him up this year. He went with another agent. Do you think he's involved in any of this?"

"Walter? No. But his cousin's boss told me the cousin liked to frequent an escort service. The pimp recorded a session and then tried to blackmail him. Apparently they thought he was Walter and figured they could get a nice payday. The cousin paid the money, but somehow things went bad."

"What was the other one about?" Honey asked. "Some security guard, or at least that's how the media described him."

"Yeah, he was brought in to protect this call girl. Tried

to force himself on her, and that went bad, too."

"A call girl does not have an easy life," Honey mused.

Gail and I both turned to look at her.

"Oh?" I said, trying to play dumb and probably doing a rather good job of it. "You know something about this?"

"It's not what you're thinking," Honey said, putting a hand up. "In any way, shape or form. I happened to know a girl in high school that got involved in that line of work. She didn't want to go to college, didn't know what she wanted to do with her life. And living in the shadow of the Strip, lots of tourists, lots of money, a million places to advertise, it all seemed so easy. And it was, at first. She was making thousands of dollars a week. In cash."

"And then something happened," I said, keeping one eye out for Marcus as he began to chase Chewy around the backyard. She had the ball and wouldn't give it back. So far, both seemed to be having fun.

"Something happened all right," Honey said. "A really nasty client. She got a bad feeling about him right away. But he had promised her a thousand dollars, so she went into his room anyhow. He got abusive. Threw the money in her face and then proceeded to, well, there's no polite way to put it. He threw her down and raped her."

"I hope she did a career change after that."

"She did for a while. But she missed the money, it was just too good. Money can be like a drug. When you're used to getting a lot of it, it's tough to give it up. She turned a blind eye to the risks. Last I heard she was working up in one of those brothels about an hour north of Vegas. People think prostitution is legal in Vegas, but it's not.

You have to drive to the middle of nowhere."

I turned to Gail to ask a question I had been pondering for a while. "Look, I understand the morality. But is it legally possible for a man to rape a prostitute?"

"Certainly, yes," Gail said, "but the practical aspects can vary from state to state. And community to community. But when a woman says no it means no. That's crystal clear, regardless of extenuating circumstances. It requires the police to make the arrest, which a lot are unwilling to do. Plus, it's very hard to convict on this. Finding a sympathetic jury would be a huge challenge anywhere."

"Understood. What if he pays her and she changes her mind?"

"We're getting into the legal weeds here. Technically, if he takes her against her will, it is a felony. But since both are breaking the law, it's unlikely she'd ever file charges, because she'd be admitting to having committed a crime."

I looked across the back lawn. Chewy finally dropped the ball and let Marcus run over to grab it. But when he tossed it to the other side of the yard, Chewy just stood there and looked at him. Marcus ran over and picked up the ball, ostensibly demonstrating how the game of fetch was intended to be played. Chewy sat down and began scratching her ears.

I turned to Honey. "Do you still keep in touch with your friend? Is she still in the business?"

"We drifted apart," she said. "It's been a few years, but I heard she's still earning this way. I'm not so sure I want to know anything more, I can't imagine she's in a good place.

The level of degradation she must be going through is heartbreaking to even think about. It doesn't matter how much money a girl takes in. She has to make a part of herself numb to get through the day."

"You know all this just through her?" Gail asked.

Honey shrugged. "My summer job working in one of the big hotels. I saw call girls hang out there all the time, usually in the bar. Once in a while I'd talk to them, I was curious. I'm something of a student of human nature. Most of the girls said the same thing. The abuse started at home, usually sexual, but sometimes the parents just made them feel worthless. They had to get out of the house, usually at a young age, and they had no other way to make money."

"It all starts in the home," I repeated.

"Yup," Honey said. "The good and the bad. In a few cases the parents wound up in jail when the girl was still a minor, and there were no relatives around to take care of her. There's supposed to be a system in place but it's not a good one. Some girls just wind up on the street."

I looked across at Marcus and Chewy and felt wistful. As I sat on our suburban patio, between two of the most beautiful women I had ever met, it occurred to me that we were casually discussing the dire impact of some of life's cruelties while our precocious three-year-old son was playing just yards away. I took pains to ensure that should he come within eavesdropping range, I would quickly steer the conversation away from a risqué adult theme to one he might better be able to handle. But I had little to worry about on that score. Marcus was far more interested in tempting Chewy to race him to grab the ball than he was in joining what was most likely, to him, a wholly uninteresting conversation.

I watched the two of them play and was suddenly immensely grateful for the gifts bestowed upon me. And I also began to feel sad that some people, ones like Judy Atkin, would never have the opportunities Marcus would have. Judy's unfortunate circumstances were dictating a life that was being spent in the shadows, surviving but not thriving, making what little she could out of a bad hand she had been dealt. Judy had hurt me, but she herself had been hurt to a far worse degree. I began to think about what, if anything, I could do. And then the phone rang. I answered it as I walked inside. It was Walter Anawak. The blackmailers had called him again. They told him to get the $50,000 in cash and be ready to drop it off.

Sixteen

I returned to my nice suburban patio, but my mind was no longer in the conversation. Honey and Gail continued to chat, their discussion drifting toward more benign first-world subjects such as traffic patterns, work-life balance, and whether organic food was worth the money. I pretended to listen, but mostly I thought about Walter. After finishing another round of Blue Moons, Honey said she probably needed to get home, as much as she was enjoying herself with us. Tomorrow was, after all, a work day. After she left, we put Marcus to sleep and Gail went to take a shower. I went over to my computer and found the website for Loco Girls. After a large pink X flashed on the screen, along with a box to check that somehow confirmed I was over eighteen years old, I was allowed entree into the site.

There were pages upon pages of images, nubile women in every repose you might consider, as well as quite a few you probably would not. Some were dressed in revealing lingerie, some in bikinis, and some in their birthday suits. Many had that come-hither look, the knowing glance, the pursed mouth, the hint of a naughty smile. The women were mostly in their twenties and thirties, and all were attractive, or at least sexy enough to generate some male interest. The majority had their faces hidden or slightly grayed out, a gesture to confidentiality, perhaps protecting against the off-chance an acquaintance from another part of their lives might recognize them. But a few did reveal their identities. And after combing through about a hundred images, I found the one I wanted.

She called herself Farrah, but there was no mistaking the blonde tresses and those big blue eyes. She hadn't bothered to mask her features, I guess after being in the business for a decade, any sense of shame or humiliation disappears. But there she was, Judy Atkin, in full naked glory, lounging seductively on a bed, one arm casually draped over her breasts, hips flaring, and leaving little to the imagination. Underneath the photo was a paragraph describing her as sexy, adventurous, willing to try anything, and always aiming to please. Some light bondage was acceptable. She provided an email address and a phone number. I rummaged through my desk and found a disposable phone I had purchased a while ago. The number was untraceable, and it allowed me to contact people without letting them know who I was. In this case, I wondered if I would get anyone on the line. I did.

"Hi," said the female voice on the other end of the line. She sounded cheerful and upbeat, but she obviously wasn't Judy.

"Hi yourself," I said. "Is this, uh, Farrah?"

"It is. What's your name?" she purred.

"John."

"Hi, John. What can I do for you?"

"Um ... I was going through this Loco Girls site and it says you'll do pretty much anything."

She laughed easily. "I'd say that's mostly true. What are you interested in?"

"Well ... let's just say I have some unusual desires."

"That's what I specialize in. Anything specific?"

"Is it okay if things get a little rough?" I asked.

"A little rough is okay," she said. "But are you willing to pay for it?"

"I'll pay whatever. IIow much do you charge?"

"Straight sex is six hundred dollars. If you want to get rough, it's a thousand. That's for a one hour session. Do you think that's enough time?"

"I don't know. What if I want two hours?"

"That would be two thousand," she said, and her voice softened and became a little seductive. "But I'll make it eighteen hundred. You sound like a great guy."

"Thanks. I think so, too. What time's good for you?"

"Tonight is busy, I'm taking a friend to the airport. But I'm free tomorrow. When would you like to come over?"

"Maybe around noon? That work?"

"Ooooh. Lunch at my place. I'm into it."

"Where are you located?" I asked.

"I'm in Hollywood," she said. "But why don't you call me tomorrow when you're ready to come over. I'll give you the address then."

"Sounds good," I said.

"And John?"

"Yes?"

"I can't wait to meet you."

"Likewise," I said, and hung up.

I went into the bedroom and laid down, and in a few minutes Gail came in and joined me. I took her through my workday scenario for tomorrow, explained the plan I had hatched, and told her not to worry. She said that was easier said than done. She also wished I had backup. This type of sting could always go wrong, you never knew what type of hornet's nest you could be walking into. I told her I'd be careful, but her words echoed a nagging concern, one that always shadowed me when I entered the realm of the unknown. She kissed me softly, and I kissed her back, admittedly, with a good deal more passion than either of us expected.

The next day was cool and cloudy, which I took as a good sign. In addition to strapping on my ankle holster, I'd be able to wear my .357 underneath a light jacket. This is why I liked the .357; in addition to being potent, it was easy to conceal under my armpit. I wasn't sure what tornado I might be heading into, but having multiple weapons at my disposal was a little reassuring. I also packed a special bag, a disguise I'd been saving for the appropriate occasion. This seemed like the right time.

Gail took Marcus in to preschool, I went to the office for a couple of hours and caught up on some paperwork. At 11:00 a.m. I opened up the disposable phone and called the phone number formerly utilized by Judy Atkin. The new Farrah reiterated she was eager to see me, and provided an address in Hollywood, along with a code for the intercom. This address was different from the apartment complex where I apprehended Judy. It was further east, close to Sunset and Western, not in the nicest part of town, but her line of work was not the nicest way to earn a living. I arrived a few minutes before noon and parked down the street from her building.

This apartment complex was like hundreds of others in the area. Three stories, nondescript, the façade looking old and tired. The exterior was a beige stucco with pink trim. The only sound in the neighborhood was a city garbage truck, heading toward me from the other side of the street. I reached into my bag and pulled out a black beard with the hint of some gray around the edges, a fairly good replica of what my own beard might look like if I allowed it to grow out. I applied a thin layer of glue and pressed it carefully onto my face, using a mirror app from my iPad to guide me. It took about two minutes to get the beard fully adjusted, but once in place, it looked natural, and I didn't think I'd be immediately recognized. I also pulled out a light blue baseball cap with the gold letters, UCLA, spelled out in cursive. I thought it was a nice touch.

Locking the Pathfinder, I walked to the apartment building and scanned through all the names near the intercom. None revealed an apartment number, only a code to type in. The code she gave me was 4-2-4, and I noticed that corresponded with the name O. Magid. I entered the code and a moment later I heard the sound of a phone ringing. Farrah answered, I said it was John, and she told me to come up to apartment 202 before buzzing me in.

The elevator was small and cramped and had seen better days. It rattled and groaned as it lifted me one flight up before abruptly jerking to a stop, the doors opening in a haphazard fashion. I walked down a musty interior hallway with uneven carpeting. I reached apartment 202 and rapped lightly on the door. It opened quickly, but with no one in immediate view. I crossed my arms over my chest, careful to gently place one hand on my .357 as I walked tepidly inside, my eyes darting here and there, mostly looking for whoever was situated behind the door. As I entered the apartment, I caught a glimpse of a tall girl in a skimpy tiger-striped bikini, long blonde hair cascading halfway down her back. The door closed, she smiled at me, and in an instant, everything became crystal clear.

"Hi there, John," she whispered as she moved forward to give me a hug, the type of embrace that extended a beat or two beyond the one you might give your first cousin. She let go first and stepped back, the smile still pasted on her lips.

"Farrah," I managed, searching her eyes, looking to see if she recognized me behind my beard in the same way I recognized her. We were two people in disguise, both trying to communicate we were someone else. I thought I saw a faint glimmer of familiarity in her look, as if she were struggling to place me; maybe she was just checking me out to see how rough that eighteen-hundred dollars might be to earn.

"Would you like a drink?" she asked, taking me by the hand and leading me to a cheap cloth sofa in the living room, where we both sat down, her eyes never leaving mine. A coffee table with curved legs and a walnut veneer sat nearby. There was a hallway off to the right with a few doors, all of them closed. The living room felt still and quiet, as if we were the only two people on earth.

"I'm good," I said.

"All right. So John. You told me you wanted things a little rough. Just what would you like to do?" she asked softly, moving her shoulders back to allow me an unobstructed view of her large breasts spilling out from her bikini top. Her outfit was tight, maybe a size too small, the same signature style she had employed when we had previously met. The blonde hair was a shiny color of yellow straw. At first I wondered if she had simply employed an unusual brand of hair coloring, but the texture was wrong. Seeing it up close, I recognized it as a wig. It was about as realistic as everything else about her.

"I'd just like to talk," I said.

She sighed and sat back in the sofa, and her mind practically screamed oh no, not one of *those* guys. "If you want," she shrugged and pointed to the coffee table. "But it will still cost you eighteen hundred. Why don't you put the money in the bowl. Then we can talk all you'd like."

I reached into my jacket, but instead of cash, my hand emerged with the .357 and pointed it at her bare belly. Her mouth dropped open and her eyes darted about the room.

"What is this?" she recoiled. "Just how rough were you planning to get?"

"We're not having sex, Candy. You're going to talk to me. And I'm not afraid to put a bullet or two in you. I could justify it as self-defense. And trust this, no one will care about a double murderer getting shot."

Candy stared at me, speechless, her eyes remarkably blinking away a couple of tears. The human side of her had finally kicked in.

"Shit. You're that detective guy. From the Saloon."

"Yeah," I said. "That detective guy."

"Just what do you want?" she whimpered.

"It took some doing," I answered a little wearily, poking the gun into her belly to remove any doubt she might have of lying to me further. "But I know quite a bit. Let me start by asking you something easy. What kind of a car do you drive?"

She stared at me in disbelief and began to shiver. "A black Ford Escape. Why?"

"Just putting the pieces together. But let's go back to that night at the condo at 6th and Broadway. You were there. With Judy and Henry Knapp and Rolf Anawak. And there were two other people in the unit at the time. In the back bedroom. Sadie and her john. Too many people, too many witnesses. It took a while for me to connect the dots."

"What dots?"

"The ones that point you out as the murderer."

"Huh? The police already arrested Judy for doing these two guys. She's going to plead guilty. How can you possibly say I did it?"

"Because there's no one else. At least no one who was there at the scene. No one who had a motive. Both Sadie and her client confirmed each other's story. I doubt they could have been in cahoots, the client's on tilt. And Rolf Anawak, as angry as he was, sure wasn't about to help Judy after she blackmailed him. But he had already left the scene. He wasn't there."

"Judy said she did it," Candy insisted.

"She's desperate. But it's the nature of the wound on Knapp's head. He was on top of her, he was raping her. Judy could have hit him over the head, but not with that blue Club. It left a very distinct wound on his skull."

Candy peered at me, her defenses seeming to shrink. "Doesn't prove anything," she managed.

"It will," I said and then tried a line on her. "Video camera footage at the building entrance showed you entering the building with something bright blue in your hands. And you were in a hurry."

She stared at me, mouth agape.

"Plus," I continued, "the police have Judy's cell phone. Want to bet she called you right around that time? Asked you to come in and help her? You were the only one who could have helped. There is just no one else."

Candy finally slumped in the sofa and the tears started streaming down. "I didn't mean to kill him. I really didn't. I didn't even think I hit him that hard."

"It sounds like you were almost a good Samaritan at that point," I said. "Stopping a sexual assault."

"I was just trying to get that pig off of Judy," Candy whimpered. "Yeah, I got a call from Judy, but she wasn't talking. I heard screams. I knew something had gone wrong. I needed something, so I grabbed the Club from my car. Yeah, I hit him over the head a couple of times, just to get him the hell off Judy. It worked."

I looked at her and shook my head. Many people experience a few of these seminal moments, when a decision, right or wrong, proper or improper, can change the course of their life. Or someone else's. Decisions at these crucial times can have either the most life-affirming, or at times, the most devastating consequences.

"And you left the premises after that."

"Yeah."

"But you went back to retrieve the Club."

"Judy did. I went and pulled the car around front."

"And so you both left Henry Knapp there to die."

"No! I didn't know he was going to die! How could I know that? And what was I supposed to do? Call the cops? You know what would they find. A bunch of working girls and a guy that got hit over the head with a blunt instrument. And a john in the back room. We'd have all been arrested, and they would have nailed me on assault with a deadly weapon."

I continued to shake my head. There were other options of course, but in the terror and panic of the moment, Candy and Judy chose to simply flee, take the easy path, and let everything else sort itself out. They could have called paramedics on the way out the door, maybe left the door open for a neighbor to see, but instead they did nothing except run to save their own skin. And Henry Knapp, who might not have been the world's most upstanding citizen, was left to bleed out, to die when he didn't have to die, to have his life end because a couple of whores chose to avoid a possible arrest on a nominal charge. He deserved more. Most people did.

"Then a few days later, you bring Rolf Anawak to the King's Head. The footage from the alley shows a person with long, blonde hair coming up behind him, pointing a gun at the back of his head and firing two shots. The cops thought it was Judy. But that wig you've got on tells me a different story. Who was with you? Lucas?"

She shook her head. "Lucas couldn't put two feet in front of himself."

"Okay," I said and pointed toward the hallway. Time to get all the players in the room. "Why don't you bring Owen out here. Like right now."

She gave me a weird look. "You know about Owen?"

"Uh-huh," I said. "This is Owen's place. That one didn't take much to figure out. His name is on the freaking directory downstairs. And don't try anything cute like tipping him off or you'll both get drilled in the head. I swear to you."

She took a deep breath. "Owen!" she finally called. "Get out here now! We have a problem!"

*

I rose and took a couple of steps away from Candy, going toward the front door, away from where anyone coming down the hall could see me. After a minute I heard a bedroom door open, and a few seconds later a man entered the room, his familiarity marked by the bleached blond hair and the blond goatee. Pete Atkin, or I should say, Owen Magid, froze when he saw me. He held a black pistol in his right hand. Fortunately for me it was pointed down at the floor. My .357 on the other hand, was pointed directly at his head.

"What the ... " he started, looking at Candy. "Hey, I thought you said you had a big-time client coming here."

"I'm big-time," I said, "I'm just not a client. Drop your weapon. Now!"

"Baby, what the hell is this?" Owen demanded, still staring directly at her.

"He knows, Owen," she said. "He knows. Pretty much everything."

Owen Magid stared incredulously at her for a moment. Then he looked over at me, and took greater notice of my gun, which was now directly aimed between his eyeballs.

"I'm giving you one last chance," I said loudly, my voice authoritative. "Put the weapon down. Right. Now. Or part of your head is going to be spattered against that wall."

"Okay, okay," he said, leaning over and gently placing the black handgun, which looked like a Glock 22 pistol, on the carpet.

"So much for you being Pete Atkin," I said, as I motioned for him to go sit on the couch. I retrieved his handgun and stuffed it in the back of my pants, wishing for a moment I could loosen my belt a notch.

Owen Magid began sizing up the situation and actually smiled, but it was the smile of a snake oil salesman.

"Yeah," he said. "I guess you figured out I'm not really Judy's step-brother."

"Something smelled fishy from the start. Let's just say you didn't strike me as being from Iowa."

"Well, now. You're pretty smart. But you're not really a cop. You're a businessman, right?"

"Private investigator."

"Same thing. Listen. I'm sure we can make a deal. How does $10,000 sound? I'm getting it tonight. You just take the cash and walk away."

I laughed in his face. "That's because you're planning to get a $50,000 payment from Walter Anawak. Better think again."

The smile vanished from his face. "You know about Walter?"

"I know more than you think I do. I know you're part owner of a call girl service. Your partner is an idiot, which probably doesn't make you too bright if you've gone into business with him."

Magid took this in. "Lucas provided the capital. He's more of a silent partner."

"You guys bought a condo together. Although it sounds like he put up the money and you ran the show. Makes sense. Lucas Jerikoff couldn't run a hot dog cart."

"Probably not. But look, what'll it take for you to go away?"

I thought about this. "How about my getting some answers," I said warily.

"That doesn't sound too hard," he said. "Go ahead."

"Let's start with how you and Judy became acquainted."

"Why do you care?" he asked.

"I like putting puzzles together. Everything needs to fit."

Magid eyeballed me, the look of a man knowing he had little to lose. "I've known Judy for a long time. She was a lost soul when I met her. Must have been ten years ago. I got her out of the streets, probably saved her life. I don't think she ever realized what I did for her. She wasn't very appreciative. But over time, things changed. She and Candy moved here a few months ago from Florida. We reconnected. Patched things up, as it were."

And then it was my turn to stare incredulously, for it had indeed been ten years since I had come across Owen Magid. He was not Owen Magid back then, and he certainly wasn't Pete Atkin. Rather, he was Tommy Lyman, a local pimp who had picked Judy up at a Greyhound Bus station downtown, gave her a few meals, and then put her to work on the streets. It was Lyman who had introduced her to prostitution and then bailed her out when I arrested her. It was Lyman who led Judy down the rabbit hole she could not emerge from, and ultimately setting things in motion so many years ago. It led to me trying to help Judy, which, in turn, resulted in my getting vilified. I was kicked off the LAPD for my role as the good Samaritan. Tommy Lyman got sent to prison for five years for pandering solicitation, and a host of other crimes.

"And just why would Judy make contact with you again?" I asked. "Being that you had, how should I put it, a complicated relationship?"

"I don't know," he said breezily. "Maybe she felt guilty about it."

"Guilty about sending you away, Tommy, about ten years ago?" I asked, thinking maybe, like before, Judy had nowhere else to turn.

He stared at me. "You remember me?"

"Of course I do, Tommy. It just took a while, people don't always look the same as they once did. Your hair's blonder and you have a goatee. And you two just picked up where you left off a decade ago. She started working for you again. Turning tricks in a brothel because it was easier than being a streetwalker."

"That's one way to put it," he laughed. "She was an escort. Just like Candy here. I was the rainmaker. I brought in the business, the girls followed through. We all made money. It all worked out. Victimless crime."

"Hardly. And how did you hook up with Lucas Jerikoff?"

Tommy Lyman smiled slightly, a little deceitfully. "He started off as a client. Had some money to invest, but didn't have a lot of know-how about the business world. I told him we could partner up. He fronts the cash, I set up the business."

"Then it was Jerikoff's money that bought that condo on 6th and Broadway."

"More like his parents' money. His dad was some kind of doctor guy, but he passed away a couple of years ago. Left Lucas some money that he didn't know what to do with. He tried being a day trader, but after losing almost a hundred grand in a week, he figured he wasn't cut out for the stock market."

"And everything was working out fine. Until you upped your game and entered the world of blackmail."

Lyman shrugged. "It's like that famous guy said. That's

where the money is."

I doubted that Tommy Lyman knew much about John Dillinger, although they were employed in the same general field of stealing other people's cash. "You just misjudged the mark for being a football player. You thought he had millions."

"Dude came up with twenty large," Lyman countered. "Worked out."

"Except then you had to go and kill him."

Lyman shook his head vehemently. "I didn't kill anyone."

I glanced at Candy and had an idea. "I guess he means you killed Anawak. And you better believe he'll testify against you to save himself."

Candy stared at me and then Lyman and then something very dark began to dawn on her. "You said this was foolproof, Owen. That no one would ever find out."

"That's the problem with foolproof schemes, Candy," I interjected. "They sometimes assume you'll be the fool. Tommy Lyman here got you to pull the trigger for him. It's all there on video footage, the long blonde hair, all that. Shooting out a light in the alley didn't change anything. You've been had. I'll bet you thought he was in love with you, too."

"Hey," Lyman started, his voice rising. "Don't listen to this asshole, baby. I'll never testify against you. And a wig doesn't mean shit. No way they can prove anything."

"We'll see about that," I said. "But Candy, this guy has nothing to gain by letting you walk. Because if you don't take the fall for killing Anawak, he does. That's a pretty easy move for him. What I don't get is why bother to kill him in the first place? You got twenty grand from him. You could have just walked away."

"We never got the cash," she said, her breathing starting to grow rapid. "And then Tommy put the video up on the internet. That fat Alaskan guy was furious. He called and said he wanted his money back, we hadn't lived up to our end of the bargain. He had been to the condo. He said he was going to hunt us down if we didn't give him back the money. We didn't have it."

I sighed. It was ridiculously naive of Rolf Anawak to assume that a digital recording could be kept secret forever. He had no guarantee. But I imagine he also knew that if he didn't pay the initial twenty grand, the video would surely have gone viral and have done irreparable damage to his cousin's career. If Rolf came up with the money, there was a chance the video might stay hidden from view. He had to trust a pair of blackmailers, which was a bad bet. Once someone like Tommy Lyman got his meat hooks into a mark, there would be no end to his demands for money. You paid or else. To him it was almost like an annuity.

"Then why send Judy in to be part of this?" I asked.

"She was on the video," Lyman said. "She was the only one Anawak had been with. She was involved up to her eyeballs. If Candy or me set up the meeting with him, he might not have believed it. Or shown up. He knew Judy."

"Plus, you told Judy you'd kill her if she didn't do it," I observed.

Lyman scrunched up his face and thought for a

moment. "I may have put it in different terms. That she owed me for all the time I spent in jail."

"I still don't get why she came back to you," I said. "After all these years."

Lyman stared at me. "The same reason dogs come back and sniff their own vomit. There's a certain familiarity, even though it's gross. Kind of like Judy's situation growing up. Getting raped by her father. You hate it, but you get comfortable with it. Becomes routine."

"You knew Judy pretty well," I said, and this was no surprise. Pimps have astounding judgment when it comes to human nature and how to exploit it. They get to know a girl, figure out her weak spot, and mine it for profit.

"I know all my girls well," he said, and placed a hand on Candy's bare thigh, which she quickly swatted away.

"Don't touch me," she hissed.

"Hey, baby, don't be like that. They got nothing. It's your word and my word. We stick together, we're fine. The cops can't prove nothing. We're in the clear."

"No, Tommy, you're the one in the clear," I pointed out to him. "Candy, on the other hand, will get twenty-five to life because she did the deeds. Isn't twenty-five years what they were offering Judy to plead guilty?"

"Look, baby," Tommy insisted, turning to Candy, "we had this all planned out."

"You had it all planned out," I broke in. "Get your revenge on Judy for sending you away ten years ago. Not to mention getting revenge on me for my role in it."

"You figured that out, huh?" he said nervously.

"I figured out a lot of things. You went to see her in jail

the other day, just to let Judy know what would happen to her if she didn't take the plea. She'd be dead within a day of her release. You told her the only option was to plead guilty."

"Look man," he said, his voice starting to rise and lose composure. "You better watch it. I'm not Lucas Jerikoff. You don't know who you're messing with."

I laughed and held out the .357. "I don't think *you* know who you're messing with," I said.

Lyman looked at the gun in my hand and slumped back onto the couch. I turned back to Candy.

"The one thing I don't get is why you sold out Judy. I thought she was your friend. You were ready to let her take the fall and do a long prison stretch, serving out your time. Why?"

Candy's eyes darted back and forth between Tommy and me, and her breathing escalated even further. It was as if she were trying to figure out who to believe and what to believe. It also looked like she might get sick. Her face was flush as she began to recognize what exactly was in front of her.

"It's ... because," she stammered.

"Go on," I said, leaning in.

"Because," she finally managed, "I told Tommy about what I did to Knapp. He said he'd protect me. But I had to do this one thing for him."

"Go and shoot Rolf Anawak," I said.

"Yeah. Tommy said Rolf was going to be a problem and needed to be taken out."

"And your boyfriend over here," I said, pointing the gun

angrily at Tommy Lyman, "was too much of a wuss to do it himself."

"Oh, I don't know! Everything was happening so fast. I was so stupid ... I thought we could ... we could all just get away with this."

"And then I picked up Judy, she got arrested and became the prime suspect in two murders. And this guy here made a convincing argument that it was either you or her that goes down for this."

Candy nodded and kept nodding. The reality was sinking in that she had been used and would continue to get used. That she was in a world of trouble with no exit, her trust placed in Tommy Lyman, a man who should never have been trusted, but who excelled in manipulation. She was like some of the girls who came to L.A., expecting a dream but finding a nightmare. Unlike them, her nightmare was just beginning.

It was at that point, that moment of clarity, when Candy reached the breaking point, when she had to let loose and explode, unleashing a horrific fury that had been simmering in her. Her breathing got extremely anxious. Her breasts heaved up and down unevenly, and she almost shuddered. Suddenly she screamed and jumped on top of Tommy Lyman, raking him viciously across the face with both hands. Her sharp nails dug clear red lines down his cheeks. She drew her right arm back, balled her hand into a small fist and began pounding him in the face.

Lyman, shocked at first by the temerity of her attack, fell back against the sofa for a moment before rearing back and smacking Candy hard across the face. She let out a yelp and tumbled off the sofa. Lyman rose and wiped his face with his left hand, seeing some blood trickling down his fingers.

"You stupid bitch," he said. "You stupid, fucking bitch."

Candy scrambled up, and for a brief moment they stared at each other, furious but almost frozen, unsure of what to do next, seemingly unaware that anyone else was watching. But Candy moved first, as she took a step back, positioned herself, and flung a long right leg viciously up into Tommy's groin. Lyman got a sick look on his face and doubled over in pain. He collapsed onto the carpet, both hands cupped around his testicles. Candy reared back and kicked him in the side of the face. I watched the fascinating scenario play out, and the sight of a girl in a bikini beating up a slime ball was not unappealing. But I also knew I was dealing with a culprit who had committed a pair of deadly acts, and she had little to lose.

And at that moment, Candy, comprehending the dire situation she was in, made a choice. Stay and go to jail; flee and have a slim chance at freedom. And while the spectacle of a bikini clad woman racing through the streets of Hollywood was not an everyday occasion, it was also something which would draw only modest attention, even with a middle-aged man in a fake beard trailing her, waving a gun and ordering her to stop. Most bystanders would assume this was just a scene being filmed for another TV pilot. The entire spectacle flashed before my eyes in an instant, the incredulity not beyond the realm of possibilities. Candy glanced at me briefly, sized up the situation quickly, and made a beeline for the door.

She had already unlocked the deadbolt and was working on the bottom lock when I reached her and grabbed her by the neck with my left hand. Pinning her against the door, I shouted at her to stop. She told me to go screw myself and with her right hand, reached toward my groin area. She clawed my left thigh by mistake, a mistake clearly made because her eyes were facing another direction. But rather than give her another chance, I stepped back, released the grip on her neck, and raised my right hand. The butt end of my.357 came thundering down on the side of her temple, and she let out a scream as she crumpled to the ground. She held the side of her head with both hands as I stepped back and surveyed what was in front on me.

Tommy Lyman was across the room, lying on the carpet, gripping his family jewels. Candy was also lying on the carpet, holding her head, as the blonde wig began to slip off. A pimp had just been beaten up by one of his hookers. The hooker, whose grander claim to fame was being a double murderer, had just been pistol whipped by a private investigator. The private investigator, while being employed by a football player who was being blackmailed, was also working to free a former teenage prostitute who had helped get him kicked off the police force.

As I continued to look down at the bizarre scene, I wondered how I ever managed to get myself into these situations. I had made one truly bad decision a decade ago, one that had propelled my life and career path to this calamitous moment. I was on this trajectory because of a sympathetic pang I felt for a little girl lost. I knew Judy's past had reminded me of my own sadness, but I also knew there was a good bit more to it. I sighed, pulled out my phone, and called Barney Sack, the one person I knew, who might actually find this scene amusing.

Seventeen

The jail cell probably held five people semi-comfortably. There were fifteen of us in there. I sat on the cement floor in the corner, hoping no one recognized me as a cop. The only thing worse than being a police officer in the prison world, is to be a child molester.

It took about an hour before a swarthy young man approached. He had a shaved head and tattoos up and down his thick arms. A pair of tattooed teardrops were next to his left eye. He had a barrel chest and acted like he was the boss of the cell.

"What you in for, man?" he asked, tapping my foot with his own.

There is a misinformed opinion that the best way to survive being locked up is to pick out a big guy and punch him out. The problem with that theory is that big guys who end up in jail don't usually allow this to happen. They're usually the ones throwing the final punches.

"Let's just say I met up with the wrong woman," I said.

"You hit her?" he asked, glaring at me.

"No," I said, well aware that people in here can go off at the strangest moments. "But that didn't stop her from setting the cops on me."

His gaze seemed to relax. "That's good. You should never hit a woman."

"What'd you do to get in here?" I asked.

He shrugged. "This dude slapped my sister around. Don't matter for what. When I found out, I went over to his apartment and stomped his ass but good," he said, and held up his hand showing swollen knuckles. "Gave him a beat down. Taught him a lesson."

"Bet he won't do that again."

"Good bet," he said. "Hey, you been in here before? I think I seen you."

"No," I said, "never been here."

"Mmm-hmm. I know I seen you. Don't worry. It'll come to me," he said, and strolled back across the cell.

I watched him as he walked away. As an LAPD beat cop for over a decade, my face was familiar to a lot of people in the 'hood. I hoped I'd make bail before he figured it out. Being in a cell with the same slime I had been locking up for years was not a good place to be. In fact, it was very, very dangerous. I thought of Judy and wondered just what on earth had I been thinking, when I invited her into my life.

*

The LAPD officers were the first ones on the scene, undoubtedly called by a neighbor hearing an unruly ruckus in apartment 202. Barney Sack and Detective Callaway strolled casually in about two hours later. They were ushered into the bedroom, where a uniformed LAPD officer was struggling to sort everything out. Sack flashed his deputy chief badge, thanked the officer for his help, and asked if he might take over for a few minutes. The officer did not hesitate in deciding that I was better off being someone else's problem.

"Ah, Burnside. We meet again," Sack said. He was dressed somewhat nattily today, in a white shirt, maroon club tie and a blue blazer. And yet no matter how hard he tried to look debonair, his outfit still smacked of being purchased off-the-rack at Target.

"I'd ordinarily joke that we'd have to stop meeting like this, " I said. "Except that today I really mean it."

"Yeah. What's with the beard?"

I reached up and began pulling my thinly veiled disguise off my face. The harsh separation of the glue was hurting my skin with every tug. "Just a mask I used so I could get in the door undetected. Part of the plan."

"Apparently it worked," he said. "Although judging by that scene out there, maybe not the way you mapped it out. The LAPD finds you with two people in need of paramedics, one in a bikini. Not to mention three handguns on you. That's quite an action packed day, and it's not even 2:00 yet."

"The day's still young. Never know what could happen next."

"Right, so help me out on this. How did you get from there to here?" he said, motioning his right arm in one direction, which I took to mean Santa Monica, and then pointing his left arm out to the living room.

"Mostly good detective work. Your staff should try it sometime." I said, looking at Callaway. "Nothing personal, of course."

"Move on to the details," Callaway snarled, and began rubbing his right fist with his left hand. "We can address your petty judgments later."

"Sure," I said. "Where should I start?"

"You choose," Sack said. "But hurry it up. We don't have all day."

"All right. Why don't we begin with Judy Atkin. She didn't commit any murders. If anything, she was the victim of sexual assault."

"A hooker?" Callaway cackled. "That's a good one."

"Yeah, well, even hookers can get raped. And speaking of that night, I'm glad you noticed that girl out there in the bikini. Name's Candy, you might want to speak with her. She entered the condo and popped Henry Knapp over the head to stop the sexual assault on Judy. That was her noble moment. Her ignoble moment was leaving him there to die like a dog."

"That was this bright blue Club you were telling me about yesterday. You find it yet?"

"No, but I've got a good idea of where it might be."

"Go on."

"It belongs to Candy. She drives a black Ford Escape. I'm not sure where it's parked exactly, but I'd say it's within a block of here. The Club should be attached to the steering wheel. It's bright blue."

Sack thought for a moment and then turned to Callaway. "Okay, why don't you go find that alleged murder weapon. Her car keys are probably around here somewhere."

Callaway glared at him. "Hey, boss, I'm not some gofer. I've got a gold shield. I'm a detective."

"Yeah, and I'm acting Chief of Police, so you just go do what I goddamn tell you to do, okay?"

Callaway, mouth curled, left the room without a word. I turned to Sack. "Acting Chief?"

"Just temporary. The Chief's in Washington at a conference."

"That explains your dapper outfit," I said.

"Yeah, yeah, I had a closed door meeting with the city council today."

"Got to look your best," I smiled. "I heard the last chief of police in Santa Monica got himself elected mayor of Inglewood. You never know where your career might lead."

"I'll be happy if mine leads me home safe every day," he said. "Go on. You say this Candy took out Henry Knapp. No guarantee the weapon is still in the car. Or that she didn't wipe all the DNA off it."

"Could be, but my thinking is she's not the sharpest tool in the shed."

"All right. Let's see what comes of that. What else? Who's the guy on the floor out there?" he asked, jerking a thumb toward the living room.

"Name's Tommy Lyman. You might know him as Owen Magid. He's Lucas Jerikoff's partner in crime, they run that escort service. They use the condo at 6th and Broadway as one of their places of business. Same as this one here."

"How'd you find them?"

"I came across Judy's online ad. Candy had apparently taken over her business, so we set up a date. Let's just say she was surprised when she figured out who I was."

"You were wearing a beard, and she was wearing a wig. Sounds like a bad movie. Go on. What else did you learn?"

"That Candy's the one who pulled the trigger on Rolf Anawak."

Sack nodded. "The blonde wig. The one who pulled the trigger had long blonde hair."

"Easy to conclude it was Judy," I said. "And I assume that was the idea. The whole thing was cooked up by Tommy Lyman. He and Judy have history and not a pleasant one. Lyman came up with the idea of Candy taking out Anawak."

"What was the point? They already had Anawak's money."

"The $20,000 he paid? It disappeared. Obviously into somebody's pocket, we just don't know whose. You might want to take a closer look at where your detectives go to for Christmas vacation."

"Let's cut out the smart-ass comments already. Tell me more about Rolf Anawak."

"You already know that video of Anawak was posted online. Rolf was ticked. He had just handed over $20,000 of his cousin's money for nothing. He wanted a meeting with them. Wanted the money back. Guess he didn't know the type of people he was dealing with. Blackmailers generally have a no refund policy."

"And why would Candy then go and shoot Anawak?"

"Lyman knew Candy took out Henry Knapp. Blackmailed her. Said she had to do this, too, or she'd be serving time for the killing."

Sack shook his head. "And she committed a second murder to avoid taking the rap for the first. Brilliant, just brilliant."

"Then when they discovered that Rolf Anawak wasn't the Anawak who played football for the Rams, they decided to go after the real football player. The guy with all the money."

"Walter Anawak?"

"Yeah. They wanted $50,000 this time."

"How come Walter didn't come to the police?"

I shrugged. "Look what happened to his cousin. Would you?"

Sack's mouth tightened. "I told you to knock off the wise cracks. I'm not going to tell you again. So Walter came to you for help."

"He did."

"And he wanted some vigilante justice. Work over who did it?"

"Um ... well, that might have been his original intent, but I talked him down from that. You have to understand he was pretty furious about what they did to his cousin. Not to mention getting swindled out of $20,000 because they videotaped Rolf in a compromising position and used it as blackmail."

Sack's phone rang. He answered and listened for a minute before thanking the person and hanging up.

"That was Callaway. He found the car. The blue Club was there after all. We'll get it tested, but Callaway said he thought he saw a little dried blood still on it. Can't believe that skank didn't toss the thing right away. Who keeps a murder weapon in their car?"

"I don't know," I said. "A guilty conscience is a funny thing. Maybe it was someone who wanted to get caught."

*

The police were done with me a few hours later, and through the assistance of Barney Sack, I even managed to get the LAPD to return my two handguns. The one I took off of Tommy Lyman would go to the lab for testing, but there was every indication this was the gun used in the murder of Rolf Anawak.

My phone rang as I walked toward my Pathfinder. It was Gary Wynn. He had just returned from his business trip and wanted me to come to his house that evening to debrief him. My preference at this point was to go home and take a shower and hug my family. But Gary Wynn was insistent and demonstrated the persuasive abilities that had undoubtedly sent him flying up the corporate ladder. It had to be tonight. I shuddered at the prospect of dealing with Friday night traffic but eventually concluded it was best to get this distasteful event over with, and maybe, just maybe, enjoy a weekend off.

Gary Wynn lived in Toluca Lake, on a narrow street

that also housed a reality TV star. A gaggle of photographers were camped outside a three story mansion a few houses down from where Wynn lived. I inched my way past them, taking care not to run over anyone's shoes, although crushing the toes of some paparazzi would not be the worst thing in the world. In L.A. they were an annoying fact of life, and because tabloids paid good money for celebrity photos, the paparazzi would always be a fixture here, albeit at the same level as a nest of cockroaches. At one time I wondered how they knew a star would be coming or leaving home, but a certain sports agent, Cliff Roper, provided that answer. Some celebrities would often text a few paparazzi and tip them off. So much for being bothered by the media. Celebrities needed the paparazzi almost as much as they needed the celebrities.

The home Gary Wynn lived in was not as spectacular as the celebrity mansion down the street, but it was unquestionably nice. Two stories, tastefully designed, with ivy climbing partway up the front walls, and a working fountain in the middle of a circular driveway. Stylish wrought-iron gates surrounded the property, and they did not give off the feeling the fencing was imprisoning anyone, nor keeping anyone out. They simply looked ornate.

I rang the doorbell, which sounded a long series of chimes. Gary Wynn answered the door with a drink in his left hand. It was clear, bubbly, loaded with ice, and had a wedge of lime nestled at the bottom. With his right hand he waved me in and patted me on the back.

"Glad you could come on short notice," he said. "I've had the craziest week, London on Monday and Tuesday, and then called to New York. Thank goodness for first-class travel, I managed to get some sleep on the way home. But I'm still feeling the jet lag. Want a cocktail?"

"Just water," I said and then added, knowing where I was, "but with a wedge of lime, if it's not too much trouble."

"No trouble at all," he said as he led me through the foyer, which had a fifty-foot ceiling and a sparkling crystal chandelier hanging down from it. We made our way into a magnificent open kitchen, trimmed in blue granite and exquisitely tiled soft orange walls. We came upon a housekeeper wearing a frilly black dress.

"Rosa, could you get our friend Burnside a glass of ice water with lime, *por favor?*" he directed. She smiled and said yes, of course, in perfect English.

"I have my son and daughter-in-law coming here. I'm wondering how you think we should break this to them."

Rosa handed me the glass and I struggled to make sure it didn't slip from my grasp. "Break it to them?"

"Yes, of course. That's why I brought you in. I can't tell them. It has to come from an objective third party. That's why I hired you."

"Mr. Wynn," I started, "I don't think you understand the circumstances here."

"Which are?"

"I didn't find your daughter-in-law having an affair. If anything, it's your son who's been cheating."

Gary Wynn stared at me. "That's absurd. He's

completely in love with his wife. That's just impossible. It's Madison I was concerned about, this is why I hired you. And what were you doing following Trevor? I didn't ask you to do that."

"It, um, got a little complicated. They both have BMWs, so I put GPS devices on each car. When I discovered one of the vehicles was at a hotel in Burbank, I assumed it was the wife. I went over there to investigate, and it turns out it was the husband who was there."

"Absurd!" he shouted. "I can't believe it."

"Can't believe what, Dad?" came a male voice, and a husky, good-looking man in his twenties entered the kitchen. To her credit, Rosa quietly departed.

"Trevor, I didn't think you were here yet," he said.

"Came in through the garage," he said, and reached for a bottle of Grey Goose vodka before he noticed me. "Hey, I'm Trevor."

"Burnside," I said and shook his hand.

"You look familiar."

"I get that a lot. More than you might think."

"No, I've seen you somewhere recently. Are you an actor?"

"Not exactly," I said, but silently acknowledging a lot of my job involved role playing, pretending I was someone else, and lying through my teeth.

"Hello, everyone," came a high-pitched voice. A tall woman with red hair entered the kitchen. "Looks like the party's in here."

I waited a moment for her take in the curious scene, as she pieced together what was in front of her. I tried to use

246

that moment to do the same, but none of the pieces snapped together. Trevor Wynn bringing his girlfriend to his father's house was the last thing I expected. But today had been loaded with a cornucopia of surprises. This was yet one more in a string of astounding revelations. Finally, after giving Gary Wynn a kiss on the cheek, she noticed me and her jaw dropped.

"You!" she exclaimed.

"I think you're supposed to say that gee, I look familiar somehow."

"What the hell is he doing here, Dad?" she demanded.

Gary Wynn looked at her. I looked at Gary Wynn. "Dad?" I repeated.

"Yes," he said, sounding a little confused. "This is my daughter Shawna. Shawna, this is Burnside."

"Daughter as in ... daughter?" I said stupidly. "Not daughter-in-law?"

"No," Gary said. "Shawna's my daughter. She's down here from Seattle this week on business. I was unfortunately traveling, too. Why? What's going on?"

"Trevor, this is the guy I was telling you about from the other night. At the hotel," Shawna snapped, heatedly.

"Stop," Gary said. "Someone please explain what the heck is happening here."

"Maybe this Burnside character can do that, Dad," Shawna said, the steam practically coming out of her ears.

Gary Wynn looked at me, suddenly appearing very helpless. He motioned for me to go ahead, although it was the gesture of a man who looked like he was sinking into the abyss and had no idea how best to pull himself out.

"I'm a licensed private investigator," I said. "And like I told your father a few minutes ago, I was at the hotel in Burbank. I thought Madison was there. Turns out it was Trevor. And Shawna. I honestly can't say if there was anything illicit going on. At least I sure as hell hope not."

"You're damn right there wasn't anything illicit going on," Shawna snarled. "A brother was visiting his sister. That's hardly illicit. But why were you there? And why did you ask me if I were Mrs. Wynn?"

I looked at Gary Wynn. "You better take that one. I'm only paid to do so much."

"Shawna, this has nothing to do with you. It was a mix-up, is all. Look, one of my hotel managers saw Madison down at our hotel in Anaheim last week. She was with another man. I was afraid she was having an affair. I brought in this Burnside to look into it is all."

"How did you think to find me in that hotel in Burbank?" Trevor asked bewilderedly.

"GPS devices. I wasn't sure which was your wife's car. Turns out you must have taken hers that day. I thought she was the one at the hotel. Sorry about that."

"It was you who called us from the lobby?" Trevor asked.

"Yes."

"That's why you asked for Madison. To see if she was there."

"Yes," I said.

Trevor turned to Gary Wynn. "Holy crap, Dad. This is really beneath you. I can't believe you would hire a ... a detective to spy on us."

"I'm ... I'm really sorry. You have to understand, I was concerned. The manager in Anaheim didn't think it was a business meeting. Madison and this guy were drinking and laughing and having a good time. He wasn't sure what was going on. I'm sorry to have to tell you that."

"I know she was in Anaheim," Trevor said. "And I know who she was with. Dad, you couldn't have just asked me?"

"Look son, it's not a subject I felt I could broach with you. Not without substantiation. I didn't want to get you upset over something unless there was proof."

At that point, another attractive woman walked in. I was beginning to feel like I was a bit player in some production within the theater of the absurd.

"Hi, this is quite a scene. What did I miss?"

"Oh, Madison, we were just discussing your affair with Kenny," Trevor said and then turned to me. "Kenny Medalie has been my best friend since kindergarten. He was in Anaheim with his wife and kids on a vacation."

"My what?" Madison frowned.

"Yes. Dad thought you were having an affair because some idiot saw you and Kenny at the Disneyland Hotel having too good a time in the restaurant."

"That's crazy," Madison said. "Even if I wanted to, which I certainly don't, how was I going to have an affair with Kenny? With his wife and kids upstairs?"

Gary Wynn began getting very red in the face. "I ... I didn't know all the specifics."

Madison continued. "Kenny's wife and kids were wiped out after three full days at Disneyland. Kenny wasn't. We had dinner. And wine. And yes, we enjoyed talking to each other. He's Trevor's friend, and mine, too, now. Is that so terrible?"

"No," Gary Wynn managed.

"You don't seem to know your son very well," Madison said. "Or me. And you sure don't seem to trust me."

"Dad," Trevor broke in, "you spent your whole life chasing your career. You have kids you don't even know. I hope you're happy with all this."

And with that, the three adult kids walked out, emitting sighs of exasperation and disgust. Gary Wynn was left staring at the floor, his face drawn, his spirit crushed. I was still learning how to be a parent, but all I seemed to be encountering were demonstrable lessons on what not to do.

Eighteen

My life as a private investigator has been dotted with periods of adrenaline-induced excitement, tests of physical and emotional strength, and a few near-death experiences. For the most part however, it has been a job with long patches of waiting. The drudgery of sitting, either observing what might be a cheating spouse, or what might be someone just going through the paces of ordinary life. Or that equally interminable period where I sit in my office and wait for something to happen, be it a client entering, a journalist calling for details on a case, or a law enforcement official swaggering in and demanding information.

It had been almost two weeks since Candy Pence and Tommy Lyman were arraigned in district court and charged with murder, conspiracy, and blackmail. During that time, I spoke with esteemed members of both the LAPD and the Santa Monica PD, beat reporters for the *Los Angeles Times* and the *Daily News*, and a certain alcoholic British filmmaker who was eager for any details I could provide on my most recent case. I cooperated fully with the police, marginally with the journalists, and told my brief King's Head drinking buddy to go jump in a lake.

It was close to noon and I was mostly focused on what to have for lunch. My office was in a high rise near the intersection of Sepulveda and Santa Monica Boulevard, and when in doubt, I would normally just go down to the strip mall across the street for something quick. There was a Fatburger, a decent Chinese place, a pizzeria, and a sushi bar. There was even a hot wings outlet, which I occasionally subjected myself to when Gail came over for a quick lunch. The things you do for love.

Before I could settle on what to eat though, my office door opened, and a very large figure threw a shadow over my desk. He said hello and apologized for not calling first. I invited Walter Anawak to sit down.

"I've been meaning to come see you," he said. "Things have been hectic."

"Understandable. Football takes up most of your life."

"Yeah. Although the past few weeks have been especially challenging. The police called me last week. Told me about what happened. Or at least a very general overview. Looks like they arrested the wrong girl. The video from behind that English pub was misleading. Hard to tell one blonde from another, I guess."

I smiled a sad smile. "Welcome to L.A."

"So, I understand I have you to thank for closing out this case. And for bringing these two people to justice."

"It's what I do," I said. "Or what I get paid to do, more accurately."

"Sure. But the police would only give me vague details.

What really happened?"

I leaned back in my chair. "I was pretty sure they had the wrong girl. I knew Judy Atkin. She was many things, most of them bad, but she wasn't a murderer. Something smelled very wrong about this. You heard about the murder in the condo after Rolf had paid the money and left."

"Yeah. What I thought had been for Rolf's gambling debts turned out to be hush money to try and keep that video under wraps. He was just trying to protect me. And himself, I guess."

"That's the most likely scenario," I said. "Rolf handed over the $20,000, but the money never made its way to the guys doing the blackmailing. So they posted the video online. Rolf got really angry at them, and said he would hunt them down for taking the money, and not keeping their end of the bargain."

"That's why Rolf went to the King's Head that night."

"Apparently the video went online after he paid the money. He called Judy and began making threats. She told her pimp, and he said he'd handle it. This was how they handled it."

"And then they called me to try and extort more money," Anawak said.

"And that's why they upped the price to $50,000, they were ticked, too. They showed you where to find the video on that internet site. If you didn't pay, it would go viral."

"I don't understand something," he said. "Where'd the $20,000 go then? The money I gave to Rolf. The money I thought would pay off his gambling debts."

I shrugged. "We may never know. When this Henry Knapp was killed, there was a lot of panic. In the heat of the moment, when they needed to flee the premises quickly, the girls may have left it behind. There were a couple of other people in the unit, it's possible one of them grabbed it."

"Or one of the cops took it?" Anawak asked. "Maybe the first ones on the scene?"

I recoiled slightly. This was possible but very unlikely. The idea of police stealing money was not unique, but those types of crooked cops were the exception. And the odds that the first cops on the scene would be dirty, and canny enough to see a pile of cash and go hide it, seemed unlikely.

"I would bet against that theory. That's not what most cops are about."

Anawak let out a breath. "Maybe I've watched too many TV shows."

"Look, you probably won't get your $20,000 back. That's the bad news. The good news is you're getting paid a ridiculous amount of money. You'll make more in a few years than most people will in a lifetime. To play a game. In that sense you're very lucky. Just be careful about who your friends are. I've seen young players blow through millions in a short period. Be careful."

"I'm learning all about that," he said. "But I'm curious. How did you locate these horrible people who went after Rolf?"

I waved my hand. "I had a hunch. I learned the name of the escort service Rolf had used. I looked them up online and saw Judy's profile was still up. I tried to make contact, curious if anyone would respond. They did."

"Oh, yeah?"

"Turns out it was Candy. She wore a blonde wig to match the way Judy looked in the online photo. The same wig she had on when she was in the alley behind the King's Head. She was waiting for her pimp to get Rolf to come into the alley and talk."

"Then how'd you find the pimp?"

"Little bit of luck, little bit of cunning. I mentioned to Candy that I liked it rough. When you tell that to a call girl, they get a little nervous. It's more money but it's more risk. They want some muscle around in case things get out of hand. Some clients have been known to beat call girls badly. Her pimp was in the apartment. In another room."

Anawak nodded, impressed. "Clever."

"Lucky, too. Guys like that usually carry weapons. The one he had on him was a Glock. It was loaded with .40 caliber bullets, the same ones that were used on Rolf. The gun had been fired recently. Everything added up."

"But, wasn't it your word against theirs? I'm sure they denied it."

"Of course," I said. "But I managed to pit them against each other. Convinced Candy that her pimp, name's Tommy Lyman, would pin the whole thing on her. Wasn't that hard to convince her, Tommy's a slime from way back."

"The police told me they were pleading guilty."

"Yes. By the time the cops got them to the station, they had turned on each other. Each one swore it was the other's idea, everything from the videotaping to blackmail to murder. They thought at first they could both pin the whole thing on Judy, and they practically did. They also convinced Judy if she tried to finger one of them, they'd kill her right away. Had her scared to death. She was ready to accept twenty-five years in jail, because at least she might walk out of there alive one day."

"Wow," Anawak said. "That is an amazing story. But I still have the problem of that video. It's still online. Someone's bound to access it."

I thought for a moment. "Let me see what I can do."

"Cool. That would be great," he said, sounding relieved. "Thank you. For everything. This has been a really tough period, I haven't been thinking straight for weeks. I needed closure here. It still hurts, but it feels like things are going to get better."

"They will. I'm sorry about the way this worked out for Rolf. He made a mistake but he paid a huge price. He didn't deserve what happened to him."

"No, and I feel terrible. If I hadn't suggested he come down here to L.A. and live with me, he'd ... he'd still be alive." Anawak brushed away a few tears.

"Don't be too hard on yourself. You didn't do anything wrong. In fact, everything you've done has been righteous. You gave your cousin a place to live, gave him money to pay what you thought were his gambling debts when he asked you. You didn't pay blackmailers when they threatened you."

"And I hired you," he said smiling a little.

I smiled back. "I was nicely compensated. Thank you

for that."

Anawak shrugged. "I can afford it. Honestly, I have more money than I know what to do with. I just wish I could find a decent girl in L.A. The only ones I meet have dollar signs in their eyes. Once they figure out I'm a football player, they're overly enthused. It's pretty obvious they're after just one thing."

"There are good women around here," I said. "And they're worth waiting for. I found one, but it took me a while. Don't settle. If you remember nothing else from this conversation, remember that."

"I will," Anawak said as he stood up and shook my hand. He turned to leave, but stopped for a moment.

"Something wrong?" I asked.

"Oh, not at all," he said and reached into his pocket. The thick hand emerged with a large manila envelope. "Quentin asked me to give this to you. He said he thinks you'll like it."

With that, Walter Anawak left my office. I stared at the envelope for a minute before opening it. Inside were four tickets to the game on Sunday between the Rams and the Bears. I noted the section, it was right smack on the 50-yard line. I also found a note inside from Q. He told me to enjoy the game, and also admonished me to please not sell these on the internet.

*

Maybe it was all the talk about the case, and the sad and tragic ending for Rolf Anawak, but I was no longer hungry. I thought about Gary Wynn and his ill-fated efforts to make up for lost time with his son, only to create a chasm that further divided them. I looked down again at the tickets Quentin sent and felt a little better. And then my phone rang. I glanced at the number and did a fast Google search on the 813 area code. It was from the Tampa area.

"Burnside," I said tentatively. I waited a long moment before I heard a response.

"Um, hi. It's me."

"Judy?"

"Yes."

"Where are you?"

"Um, I'd rather not say."

"All right."

"Listen. I just wanted to talk for a minute. You must have heard the police let me go. They dropped the charges."

"Congratulations," I said dryly.

"I sense you're unhappy about that."

"You didn't kill anyone, so you shouldn't have to serve time for murder. But you participated in a blackmail scheme. Maybe it wasn't your idea, maybe you were coerced. I doubt we'll ever know for sure. But given what you do for a living, I sure don't trust you."

"You're being a little rough on me, don't you think?"

"Hard to say. I don't condone what you do for a living. I know you don't have a lot of options, but plenty of other people have it tough. And they get by without breaking the law."

"I'm trying to get out of the life. It's difficult. I don't know how to do anything else. I wish I did."

"You can learn."

"Yeah."

"So why are you calling?" I asked.

She paused. "To thank you, I guess. The police told me what happened. You didn't have to help me, you didn't owe me anything. I still don't understand. Why'd you do it?"

I leaned back in my chair. I had been dedicating a lot of onerous thought to this very question for the past week. My own background of losing a parent early on in my life had certainly come into play. But my life turned out differently, I was lucky in certain respects, and when my mother died of cancer when I graduated from high school, USC became my adopted family. Judy did not have anything like that to fall back on. And understanding my involvement with her took some soul searching.

The closest I came to figuring this out was from a passage in a John Steinbeck book. He was traveling in the Mojave desert and had come upon a pair of coyotes. He knew they might attack and kill his dog. He raised his rifle to shoot the predators and had one of them right in his sights. But he stopped and put the gun down, choosing to let them live, as nature perhaps intended. And in so doing, he had saved their lives in a way, and when you save a life, you take responsibility for that life. You change the natural course of events, so if that person or animal goes on to have a miserable existence, then maybe it would have been kinder to let them meet their final fate quickly. By sparing them, you now bore a burden for their future.

Steinbeck couldn't help the coyotes much after that, although he did make a token effort by leaving them some food. In Judy's case, I got her off the streets and away from Tommy Lyman ten years ago. Had she stayed with him, being a streetwalker on the mean streets of L.A., it was possible she'd have wound up dead at an early age. Maybe at the hands of some deranged john, maybe Tommy would have seen her as expendable at some point, maybe she would have descended into drugs or homelessness. There is no end to the tragic possibilities once somebody goes down that path of selling their body for money.

A decade ago, I pulled Judy out of the life, I put Tommy away in prison, and then was excoriated for my efforts. But Judy managed to survive. Whether it was a life worth living was dubious. But she was still alive, which meant she still had a chance. I managed to put Tommy Lyman away again, as well as Candy, his new partner in crime, and they'd most likely be out of circulation for many years. Was it worth it to help Judy? I didn't know, and I probably wouldn't know for a long time. But I did bear that responsibility, and as such, I felt I owed her something.

"Let's just say," I told her, "that I know you got dealt a bad hand in life. I've tried to show you that not everything is bleak and not everyone is bad. I don't know that I've succeeded at it. Probably I haven't. But your story isn't finished. You've got time. There is still hope. You're only

27. If the police haven't told you to stick around town, you should probably leave L.A.; it's not for you. I'd tell you to stop turning tricks, but I've told you that before, and look where it's led."

"I know," she said. "I don't exactly have a plan. When Tommy and Candy pled guilty, it meant I wouldn't have to testify against them, no need to stick around. But you're right. L.A. isn't for me. I'll try for a fresh start somewhere else."

I thought of something. "How did you hook up with Tommy Lyman again? Why did you go back to him?"

Judy sighed. "I was living in Tampa with Candy. Things weren't going well. We moved out here because we thought L.A. might be different. At least I knew what it was. And Tommy had an escort service, he was making a lot of money, and he wasn't putting girls out on the street any longer."

"Sometimes the street can be safer," I pointed out. "You choose whose car you get into. You can walk away. With an escort service, that's not so easy. Especially when Tommy arranges for you to get a client."

"No such thing as a safe place. Yeah, I can always walk away from a john on the street, but he can always follow me. At least when I worked on the inside, there was someone nearby. In case I needed help."

"Like Candy. When she hit Knapp over the head."

"Yeah."

"What happened with you and Candy? I thought you two were friends."

"I dunno. I brought her into the life and it's a crappy

life. But there's money in it if you're smart. I imagine she saw how much money she could get. Maybe that blinded her. She was ready to send me up the river. Crazy what money can do to a person."

"Speaking of money," I said. "Fresh starts usually take some. I hope you saved a bit from the work you did here."

There was another long pause. "Money isn't an issue for me right now."

"Oh?" I said, and my mind started whirring. "Not an issue?"

"No, I'll be okay for a while."

I began to think back to my conversation with Walter Anawak. "Don't tell me you did it," I finally said.

"Did what?"

"Took the $20,000 that Walter Anawak's cousin paid for the video."

There was another long pause. "You're right," she said. "I suppose I shouldn't tell you."

Nineteen

The Los Angeles Coliseum was built almost one hundred years ago, and it is showing its age. Numerous paint jobs have covered up some of the blemishes, but the uneven walls, crumbling cement, and groaning chairs were painful signs of disrepair. The seats themselves were more narrow and confined than most newer arenas, and they were clearly not equipped to handle the more stout and chunky football fans of today.

We arrived a good hour before kickoff, Gail, Marcus and myself, along with a special guest, Albert Rocca. I figured I'd owed him something, and a 50-yard-line ticket to a pro football game covered that type of debt. And once Marcus had learned of the tickets, he insisted we take him, and he promised he would be able to last the full game. Given that a three-year-old's ambition does not always match his ability to go long stretches without a nap, Gail and I agreed she would take him outside if he started to fade. And if he lost interest in the game, the Science Center was right next door to the Coliseum, and that would surely be entertaining enough to grab his attention.

It was football weather today, but unlike the cool, blue-gray afternoons in the upper Midwest, football weather in Los Angeles meant sunny skies and 70 degrees, typical for early November out here. We did get a few chilly afternoons, but those were normally reserved for what passed for winter in southern California. The two teams were on the field now, engaged in warm-ups, languidly doing their stretching. I used my guest pass to take Marcus onto the field and introduce him to a few players on the Rams. Quentin Ware and Walter Anawak seemed very happy to meet him, gave big high fives and hugs, and called him Little Burnside. Marcus was in awe of just how enormous Walter was; I confirmed he was a big man, even when compared to the standard of other offensive linemen.

I waved to Johnny Cleary, who was involved in a deep conversation with one of the game officials. There are some coaches who are light and breezy and relaxed before a game, but Johnny was not one of them. He gave me a quick wave and went back to his discussion. His assistant coaches on the Bears were nearby and acting just as intense as he was, and they provided a stern reminder of the life I had led. Gail had taken Marcus to a few USC games last year, but I was normally too busy with pregame preparations to spend much time with him; it was one of the reasons I had quit coaching and didn't look back. Going to the NFL was a non-starter for me.

The Bears returned to their locker room but the Rams players remained on the field. The Rams had left for Anaheim and then on to St. Louis many years ago, so I never viewed them as our local team. For me, USC was always L.A.'s heart and soul, and I recalled countless memories of extraordinary games in the Coliseum, some of which I had played in. Even now that the Coliseum is showing its age, I still get goose bumps when they light the cauldron atop the peristyle end of the Coliseum right before the fourth quarter of USC games. The orange flame of the Olympic torch danced to the strength of the wind, and added to the drama and urgency of the moment.

The Rams' return to Los Angeles was met with a collective yawn by most Angelenos. The team was building a sparkling new stadium in Inglewood, and once that opened, the city would probably embrace the team again. But for now, the reception was blasé. About 50,000 fans would file into the Coliseum today, and in some cities that would be close to a sellout. At the Coliseum, this just meant that almost one-half of the seats would be empty.

As the teams got ready for kickoff, I leaned over and asked Albert Rocca if he minded talking shop for a moment. He took a sip from his beer, laughed, and said no problem. I provided the tickets, the very least he said he could do was pretend to cooperate.

"Walter Anawak's cousin. That video of him and Judy is still up on the internet. Walter's concerned someone may use it against him, his cousin bears a close resemblance. Know anyone who can get it pulled down?"

Rocca nodded. "I know a few agents at the Federal Building. Shouldn't take long. Send me the URL and I'll take care of it."

"Thanks. And can you give me an update on Lucas

Jerikoff?"

"Yeah," Rocca said. "We got a search warrant and went through his house. Or garage, as the case may be. No definitive proof he built the pipe bomb, but he did have some old batteries lying around. Your security camera picked up his image, but we couldn't formally match it. No fingerprints on the bomb."

"I know you need a lot of evidence to go forward with an arrest here."

"We do. But I had a conversation with that Detective Callaway. Looks like those hookers are back in business, so the SMPD is setting up a sting pretty soon. They'll see if we can get Jerikoff on a soliciting charge, but I wouldn't hold my breath."

I shook my head. "That's disappointing. I was hoping the long arm of the law would reach out and grab him."

"We're watching him, don't worry. I passed his name along to vice, along with the apartment buildings those girls were working out of in Hollywood. We'll get him. Just a matter of time. And hey, Burnside."

"Yeah."

"Don't go off the reservation here. Let us handle this one."

I told him I'd think about it, then turned back to the field to watch the kickoff.

The game was a see-saw battle, and it was fairly close for most of the way. Amazingly, Marcus did not seem to get tired and actually looked quite enthralled, maybe not always with the game itself, but with the crowd, the players, the colors, and the pageantry. He asked where the band was, and I informed him that marching bands typically just played at college football games. He nodded but didn't seem to understand why that was. In a way, neither did I. After explaining the basics of the game, I told him there were a few rules that probably wouldn't make sense, and a few trick plays that would likely come as a surprise. I had no idea how prophetic those words would prove to be.

The Rams led most of the way, but with two minutes to go in the game, the Bears scored a touchdown on a long punt return, taking the lead 21-17. The Rams received the kickoff and the crowd began to get animated. At this stage of the game, sports fans in Los Angeles typically start to pack up and leave, as beating traffic often trumps watching the game to the bitter end. Not today. People stood up, began to make a lot of noise, and I needed to hoist Marcus onto my shoulders so he could see the action. The Rams passing game started to click, and they were deftly moving down the field on short passes. Marcus was getting visibly engaged too, although to be fair, he was probably excited because everyone around us was getting excited. I was sure he didn't understand most of the nuances of the game. But he did seem to be enjoying it.

"Are you becoming a Rams fan?" I asked, needing to yell.

"Yeah! They're going to win!" he exclaimed.

Albert Rocca took a sip of beer and shook his head. "I think your son's right," he shouted over the din of the crowd. "The Bears are going into that damn pre-vent defense. Guaranteed to let the other team win the game."

I shook my head "It's the best defense they can use," I argued, trying to use my status as a former coach, albeit to minimal avail. Everyone who attended a game was a football expert.

"Why?" Rocca asked. "The other team always flies down the field. Look at that! Their safeties are playing twenty yards off the ball."

"It's called the Tampa Two defense."

"Is that because Tampa usually stinks and loses their games at the end?"

I smiled. "No. Some coach from Tampa came up with it. It's meant to keep the other team from beating them with a big play. Bend but don't break. The defense will tighten once the Rams get close to the goal line. It's supposed to be risk-averse."

Rocca shook his head. "Seems pretty risky to me."

And indeed, the Rams drove methodically down the field and got to the 10-yard line. There were just 20 seconds left in the game, although that was enough time to score a touchdown and win. But on the next three pass plays, the ball fell incomplete and it was now 4th down. There were 3 seconds left on the clock, time for one more play. I looked over at Johnny Cleary, who was bent over, hands on his knees, watching intently. And then it happened.

The Rams quarterback dropped back to pass, didn't see a receiver open so he began to scramble out of the pocket. Finally, at the last second before he stepped out of bounds, he fired the football across the goal line. There was a Rams receiver open at the back of the end zone, but the ball never reached him; a Bear safety jumped in front of him and intercepted the pass. He began to celebrate immediately.

There is a rule in football which says a play isn't over until the referee blows his whistle. And a referee won't blow his whistle unless the player with the ball gets tackled. Or runs out of bounds. Or goes down on one knee. Once in a great while, a clever player will take advantage of that rule. And today one did.

The Bears safety who made the interception was excited and wanted to show off. He started to dance, holding the ball over his head. He turned to the crowd and preened, showing off and taking a bow. What he didn't seem to realize was that the play had not been blown dead, and the ball was still live. His Bears teammates did not seem to realize this, and neither did most of the Rams. But a referee standing ten yards away knew this. And so did Walter Anawak.

It is very difficult for a 340 pound giant to sneak up on someone; his physical stature makes him striking and obvious. But since the Bears safety thought the game was over, he didn't pay attention to Walter running up behind him, swinging his right arm upward and punching the ball out of the Bear player's hand. No one else did either and when the pigskin soared high above the Coliseum turf, only Walter Anawak followed the ball's trajectory. And then Walter, all 340 pounds, gathered himself and leaped off the ground, arms outstretched as he gathered in the football. He secured it against his chest and dropped to one knee, both arms wrapped tightly around the football.

The referee nearby waited a full three seconds before raising both arms directly over his head. It was the signal for a Rams touchdown.

The next few minutes was a mixture of confusion and pandemonium on the field and in the stands. The coaches of both teams raced onto the field to understand what had just happened. After much discussion among the officials, and a review of the videotape, the head referee turned on his mike and made an announcement to the crowd.

"The ball was intercepted in the end zone by the Bears. The play was not blown dead. The defender had the ball legally stripped from him, it is ruled a fumble, and the Rams recovered in the end zone for a touchdown. There is no time left on the clock. Game over."

And with that, the Coliseum exploded into cheers, the Rams players jumping on Walter Anawak, hugging him and slapping his helmet. He had won the game using an agile mind and a surprisingly agile body. He didn't hold up the football, but rather, kept it tucked under his arm. Walter Anawak had been enduring an enormous amount of pain these past few weeks. But I could see the healing process had finally begun. And another person was feeling good, too.

"They won!" Marcus exclaimed, his voice ringing with joy. "The Rams won! I told you they would!"

Indeed he had.

The End

About The Author

David Chill is a USA Today bestselling author. He was born and raised in New York City and educated in the public schools. After receiving his undergraduate degree from SUNY-Oswego, he moved to Los Angeles where he earned a Masters degree from the University of Southern California. David Chill is the author of nine mystery novels: *Post Pattern, Fade Route, Bubble Screen, Safety Valve, Corner Blitz, Nickel Package, Double Pass, Tampa Two,* and *Flea Flicker*, all featuring Burnside, a private investigator and former LAPD officer and college football star. David Chill is also the author of *Curse Of The Afflicted*, a political suspense novel which chronicles the journey of a political pollster diagnosed with cancer.

Post Pattern was awarded a prize in the St. Martin's Press contest for New Mystery Writers. The Burnside series has received much critical acclaim, and all of his novels have spent time on the Amazon.com best seller lists. David Chill currently lives in Los Angeles with his wife and son. If you would like to contact David Chill directly, please email him at the following: davidchill3214@gmail.com

If you enjoyed Tampa Two, then be sure to read the next novel in David Chill's Burnside series....

Flea Flicker

Here is a sample chapter of this terrific mystery...

FLEA FLICKER PREVIEW

A wayward drunk can cause a lot of harm, but he normally inflicts most of it upon himself. This was largely true in the case of Tyler Briggs, although being accused of cold-blooded murder was an unusual way to wrap up a weekend.

Tyler Briggs was an unemployed former football coach with a nasty drinking problem. And a womanizing problem. So, when an upstanding citizen like this fails to arrive home one night, it's normally not a cause for alarm, except perhaps for the man's long-suffering wife. The police will pacify her by checking the drunk tanks, the local ERs, and then the county morgue. If none of these prove fruitful, the cops will just shrug and say she has to wait 24 hours before filing a missing persons report. Some wives rail at the narrow-minded rules. Some just shrug and go along. And then there are the ones, be they peeved or petrified, that get the innate sense that something is very wrong. That's when they talk to someone like me.

I normally don't make house calls, but this was an exception. Hannah Briggs worked in the City Attorney's office with my wife, Gail. When her husband Tyler had moved to Los Angeles to take over the Chargers' head coaching job last year, he reached out and asked if I knew where a beautiful attorney might find gainful employment here. He figured I might know something about this, and he was right. My wife was an attorney, and she was also beautiful. I personally didn't think Hannah held a candle to Gail, but I admittedly looked at the world through a different lens.

Tyler and Hannah Briggs lived in a spacious five-bedroom house along the Silver Strand in Marina del Rey. A century ago this area was mostly wetlands, not far from the Pacific Ocean, largely uninhabitable and mostly populated by an occasional duck hunter and his prey. That changed dramatically in the 1930s with the discovery of crude oil beneath the terrain, and for decades it featured an ungodly skyline of oil wells. Once the black gold was pumped from the ground, though, the oil men left and the real estate people swooped in. What they inherited was an ugly mess, but any property close to the ocean had value. Lots of value. After the cleanup, Marina del Rey was born, home to everyone from yacht owners to flight attendants. And within the Marina was the Silver Strand, a narrow strip of gorgeous homes, and for the most part, gorgeous people.

Today was overcast, and there was even some fog rolling in. It was typical of L.A. weather in December, a phenomenon that happened like clockwork. I waited a minute before ringing the doorbell, taking time to step back and admire the home and admire the neighborhood. The house was the type of elegant structure you might see featured in architectural magazines, owned by people who earned or inherited fortunes. In the case of Tyler Briggs, it was actually a combination of the two. Born into a coaching family, his father had been an NFL head coach for years and had raked in the money. Even before the NFL coaching boom had begun generously paying head coaches upwards of $10 million a year, they were still very well-compensated.

Other young men in Tyler's situation had drifted into becoming trust fund babies, enjoying the fruits of their fathers' labor. But Sid Briggs was old school, and he wasn't keen on his offspring becoming an idle layabout. He pushed Tyler into playing football, but he wasn't able to go far; his talent earned him a college scholarship, and a seat on the Miami Hurricanes bench for four years. Tyler did take an interest in coaching though, and soon found himself rising quickly through the ranks. Too quickly perhaps.

The front door opened and a tall blonde with platinum hair and high cheekbones opened the door. She was attractive, but her face was taut, her comely looks impacted by a harsh weariness. Her brown eyes sagged, and her pink mouth was drawn. But she was still quite fetching. Some women look good no matter what storm they might be weathering.

"Mr. Burnside," she managed, her voice lightly brushed with a melodic southern twang.

"That's me."

She opened the door and motioned me inside. She was wearing a pink sweater and faded blue jeans, slashed appropriately at the knees. Her legs were like long sticks, seemingly going on forever until they nestled into a new pair of pink and white Nikes.

The Briggs's home was impressive. The foyer opened up into an expansive, sunken living room. A pair of blue velvet couches faced each other, and an assortment of toys, games and stuffed animals were sprinkled haphazardly across the floor. A working fireplace crackled in the corner. I stepped over a colorful little toy piano and found a seat on one of the couches. Hannah Briggs sat down on the other side of the couch after discreetly scooping up a few errant Cheerios in her hand and dumping them onto the corner of a walnut end table.

"Thank you for coming on a Saturday," she started. "I didn't know who to call. Then I thought of Gail. And you."

I shrugged. "It's okay, this is what I do for a living. I only take weekends off when there's no work."

She looked around the room and sighed. "I apologize for the mess. With a toddler, our home is in a constant state of chaos."

I waved a dismissive hand. "No worries. I have a little one at home, too."

"How old?" she asked.

"He'll be five in a couple of weeks. Born on New Year's Day. We're planning on taking him to the Rose Parade in Pasadena. Maybe to the Rose Bowl game, too. If I can score a few tickets, that is."

"Yes," she said absently. "I've been to the Orange Bowl game a few times. That's where we're from. South Florida. Although it seems like a lifetime ago."

"You've only been in L.A. for a couple of years."

"A tough couple of years," she sighed. "You know about Tyler's situation. The Chargers brought him out here and then fired him after one season. He's had it rough."

In some ways that was true. Tyler Briggs had been the boy wonder of football coaching, and as such, he had been cursed with achieving success at a too-early age. When he took over the New York Jets five years ago, he became, at age 29, the youngest head coach in the history of the NFL. Following three years of progressively worsening results, the Jets fired him. The Chargers, thinking he might regain the magic he once had, quickly brought Tyler in upon moving to L.A. from San Diego, then just as quickly fired him when the team had a spectacularly awful season. No one hired him this year, and rumors were rampant that no one would, at least not anytime soon. In shooting up the coaching ranks quickly, he had alienated more than a few people with his attitude. Arrogance probably helped propel his career, as team owners often equated that with future success. My experience had been the two were not connected.

"So Gail told me a little about your situation," I started. "Tyler didn't come home last night. Ever happen before?"

"No, never," she said, shaking her head briskly. "I mean, Ty would go out drinking plenty of times. Too many. But I'm used to that. I just go to sleep and when I wake up, there he is, always next to me."

"Except for this morning."

"Yes," she said, her face becoming even more drawn. "I went to the police, but they couldn't help much. He wasn't in the system, at least we know *that*. They said I'd need to wait a day before I could file a missing persons report. I knew that too, but, well, it doesn't hurt to ask."

"And that's what led you to me," I mused. I knew the routine. The police would look the name up in the system, but beyond that, they were much too busy to do any investigation. The reality was that people who didn't come home one night often came home the next day, and usually with a lame excuse, a sheepish expression, and the enduring scent of alcohol and infidelity oozing out of them. But my 13 years with the LAPD also taught me something else. If they didn't come home the next day, the chances that they'd never come home increased exponentially.

"You have a unique background," she said. "You're a private investigator who's been in the football world. Not too many people like that around here."

"I'm indeed unique," I agreed, not bothering to stray further down that path. Potential clients don't like to know their new hire had once been kicked off the police force and endured more public humiliation than any decent person deserved. The fact that I hadn't broken any laws was immaterial. My reputation as a disgraced former cop would overshadow and stain the fact that I was a darned good investigator.

"I need you to find Tyler. Bring him home. Wherever he wound up. I'm hoping he just realized he drank a little too much and slept in his car."

"Always a possibility," I acknowledged. "I'll need a few things. Recent photo, type of car he drives, license plate number, bars he frequents. That sort of thing. Whatever might be relevant. Names of people who might know something about this. What he was wearing last time you saw him. Anything would help. No detail too small at this stage. And I need to tell you my rate is a thousand dollars a day. I'll prorate it by the hour so it doesn't pile up too quickly."

Hannah looked down at the gray-and-blue speckled Berber carpet. "All right. Money's obviously not an object for us. You know, Tyler often frequents some of the bars along Venice and Washington. He likes a place called the Alibi Room. He took me there once, they serve this bizarre plate of Korean tacos. There's a few other places. Babe's, the Harborside Grill, The Mar Vista."

"Those are very different types of bars," I mused. "I don't see a pattern."

"Are you familiar with alcoholics, Mr. Burnside?"

"Somewhat," I said, recalling that my past careers as a police officer and football coach both had more than their share of heavy drinkers.

"Well then you know they are not always particular about where they drink. In Tyler's case, he wasn't particular about where he ate these days, either. Sometimes he ends up at one of those greasy spoons like Tito's Tacos, Johnnie's Pastrami, or that awful Tom's Burgers. Sometimes it's a donut shop, depending on what time of the night it is and how many beers he's had."

I took this in. All of those greasy spoons were well-known; all had been local landmarks for many decades. But a few were familiar simply because these were the places I frequented as a teenager growing up in Culver City. They were also the places I stopped going to when I became an adult with an occasional interest in eating healthy. The things that tasted great at age 17 no longer tasted so special.

"Let's step back a little," I said. "Did Tyler always have a problem with alcohol?"

Hannah frowned for a moment. "Drinking's been part of his life since high school. That's where we met. Sophomore year. He was the quarterback, the captain of the football team, the big man on campus everyone looked up to. I was this nerdy, awkward girl no one noticed."

I looked at her. "That's a stretch."

She shook her head. "I was always tall, and I had a weight problem. The summer before my sophomore year, I lost the weight and suddenly became popular. Funny how that works."

"High school kids aren't known for their depth of character," I commented.

"Yes, that's for sure. I let my hair grow, too, and well, the ugly duckling turned into a swan. People noticed. Tyler noticed."

"You've been together ever since?"

"Pretty much," she replied. "He got a football scholarship to Miami. I got a financial aid package and cobbled it together with student loans. I actually turned down a scholarship offer to Duke to be with him."

"Duke's a great school."

"Yeah. But love makes you do strange things. I figured if I let Tyler go, I'd never get him back."

I thought back to that old chestnut. If you love someone, set them free. If they return to you, they're yours. If they don't, they never were. It's an easy bromide to recite, a tough one to follow. After Gail and I had been together for a year, she was accepted into law school at Berkeley, and was even offered a full scholarship. She was torn about going, upset about the three years we'd be apart, but I convinced her she shouldn't pass up the opportunity. I wasn't actively trying to set her free or provide a test for us; I just wanted her to take advantage of something good. If I held her back by not being supportive, she might have resented me for it. Maybe not overtly, but I knew there would be disappointment. I also figured our bond was strong enough to survive three years of separation.

"Okay," I said. "So, how did Miami work out for you guys?"

"Better for me than for Tyler," she admitted. "I made the dean's list every year, he couldn't get past third string on the football team. Miami recruited lots of good quarterbacks. By his senior year he was ready to quit the sport. He was also drinking a lot, but you know, it was college. Everybody was drinking. Then his dad suggested coaching, not surprising since his dad's been a coach since like, forever. Tyler gave it a shot. Took to it well. The following year they gave him a graduate assistant's role, and he moved up to QB coach the next year. Then he got really lucky."

"How so?"

"Miami's offensive coordinator got a job in the NFL. Larry Tenant. He got hired as an OC with Jacksonville, and he brought Tyler along as his QB coach. I don't think they even interviewed anyone else. I swear, that profession is so insular, it's almost inbred. After a couple of years, Larry moved up to head coach at Jacksonville and he promoted Tyler to take over his old job. So Tyler became the offensive coordinator. Ty was all of 26 years old. That was a blessing and a curse."

"I can imagine. Pretty hard for someone that young to command respect from players who might be five or ten years older. Guys who had to work like a dog for everything they got."

"Yes. And that's when the drinking started getting out of hand."

I thought back to my own days as a former football coach at USC. I was only in the coaching ranks for three years, but the pressure to win was enormous. Most coaches are driven to succeed, but at some point they need something to take the edge off. The smart ones find a physical outlet, be it lifting weights, running, something that can create positive energy when blowing off steam. The others usually turned to alcohol. Drinking was an easy lure. You didn't have to do much beyond open a bottle or a can. It could quickly relax you.

"He seek out any help?"

"The usual. AA. But he couldn't stick with it. And by that point, I had my own career to think about. I was a straight-A student throughout school, and here I am, sitting in a big house in Jacksonville, with not much to do. When he became the Jets' head coach and we moved to New York, I applied to law school. Tyler did his thing, I did mine. It worked out fine. For a while."

"Then the Chargers made him their head coach last year," I said. "He just kept hitting the jackpot."

Hannah Briggs drew in a breath and thought twice about what she was about to say. She smoothed her blonde hair back, and at that moment an adorable toddler with the same light blonde hair as her mother skipped into the room. She wore pink and light blue as well. She was followed by a heavy-set nanny who smiled apologetically.

"*Madison. Ven aqui!*"

"It's all right, Tia," said Hannah, and scooped the little girl in her arms.

"I want Da Da," the little girl said with a small pout.

"We're working on that, hon," Hannah replied, rocking the girl in her arms as she turned back to me."You may recall I had a job offer lined up with the U.S. Attorney's office in New York. Southern district. It was a big deal."

"And you had to pass because of Tyler's job offer here."

"And because I was suddenly expecting. The funny thing was, if we didn't have Madison, I might have just stayed in New York," she said a little wistfully.

I nodded. This was not unusual, either. Women sometimes put off their own career ambitions in deference to their husbands. They get paid back with a big house, stylish clothes, and a lot of empty nights. Then, just as the woman's questioning if it's worth it, a baby comes along.

Sometimes it's a blessing, in that they turn their attention to the child. Sometimes they resent both the husband and the child. As they say, kids change everything.

"Okay. Anyone on the Charger staff that Tyler stayed close to? Or really anybody who might know something?"

"Not many. Oh, there's Anthony Riddleman, he's been friends with Tyler since Miami. He's actually still with the Chargers, coaches the quarterbacks. Most of the coaches fanned out around the country, got jobs with other teams. Funny how they can just up and move, and keep doing what they're doing. I've moved three times in six years, and I'm just over it."

I understood. Coaches were like soldiers of fortune, always moving around, their loyalty intense to the team employing them, and then becoming equally loyal to the next team that hires them. It was a life which required adapting quickly while still maintaining ties within the coaching fraternity. Getting fired was an occupational hazard, and not always the coach's fault. But if he handled it well, there would normally be another gig around the corner. One door closes, another opens.

"All right. I'm not sure how long this case will take. Could be an hour or two, could be a couple of days. It's hard to say," I told her, thinking if I didn't find her husband today, I might be looking for weeks or months.

"The important thing is you find him."

I watched Madison climb across Hannah's lap onto the couch, reaching for a little stuffed blue octopus. I didn't want to ask this in front of her daughter, but sensed I wouldn't have an opportunity to ask again. "And might there be anyone who was on any not-so-so friendly terms with Tyler?"

Hannah Briggs drew in a breath. She looked down at her daughter playing with the toy, oblivious to what we were discussing. She turned her big brown eyes back to me. "Yes. In fact, there might be a few of them."

To purchase the full copy of Flea Flicker, or any other David Chill novel, please visit Amazon.com

Tampa Two

Tampa Two

www.ingramcontent.com/pod-product-compliance
Lightning Source LLC
Chambersburg PA
CBHW020559260626
47157CB00003B/781